MORE PRAISE for *ONE SIMPLE THING*

"A twisting, twisted tale full of well-developed characters and dense setting, *One Simple Thing* is a story that will hold you in its grip until the satisfying end."
—JESSICA BARKSDALE INCLÁN, author of *The Burning Hour* and *When We Almost Drowned*

"This tense, layered story brings us into the world of hardscrabble folks who are fighting and often failing to get by. Opening on a boy's heart-wrenching journey through the implosion of his family, *One Simple Thing* flowers into a captivating crime mystery. While tempting to compare Warren Read to classic crime writers, he also vividly chronicles lives lived on the margins, like writers such as Larry Brown or Willy Vlautin."
—THOMAS KOHNSTAMM, author of *Lake City*

"Disguised as a tense crime story set in the sparse landscape of the American West, Warren Read's *One Simple Thing* is really a probing evocation of loneliness and the ways it skews the search for meaningful relationships. Read writes dialogue as if it were an industrial diamond, sharp and faceted and capable of cutting through granite. Rodney and Otis are as original a set of partners-in-crime as you'll find in American fiction, and Nadine is trying so hard not to be disappointed in men that she latches onto despair and convinces herself it is hope."
—KENT MEYERS, author of *Twisted Tree* and *The Work of Wolves*

One Simple Thing

WARREN READ

New York, NY

Printed in the United States of America.
First Edition

No part of this book may be used or reproduced in any manner without written permission of the publisher. Please direct inquires to:

Ig Publishing
Box 2547
New York, NY 10163

www.igpub.com

ISBN: 978-1-63246-119-3

For Barbara, and the road to simplicity.

PART ONE

Albany County, Wyoming
1976

"April, month of dust and lies."
—Naguib Mahfouz, *Adrift on the Nile*

1

"Would you look at her?" Rodney's father hovered in the kitchen doorway, jutting his chin to the boy's mother. "If she ain't the Queen of Farm Supply, then I don't know what."

Her laugh was almost a whisper. She kept her back to her husband and lifted the ladle from the pot, letting the liquid drip like a red waterfall. "Is that meant to be a compliment?" she asked. "Am I supposed to be flattered?"

Rodney's gut drew in and he steeled himself for another round—another round of the usual moves and strategies, rules confusing and ever-shifting as his parents navigated the vast space between them, each one perfectly finding the other's buttons along the way. Rodney sat in the center of it all at the square Formica table, his finger rubbing the chipped edge of his plate as he watched the whole thing unfold. They were stationed opposite one another like gunfighters, his father in the kitchen doorway, gripping the casing over his head while his mother crowded the stove, lost in the rising steam of a simmering saucepan.

"If it feels like a compliment," his father said. "Run with it." He looked to his son and gave him a little wink.

There was a momentary pause, a stalemate, maybe.

"Today was a perfect one," Rodney tossed in.

"A perfect what?" asked his father.

"Sunset," his mother said, grabbing a tea towel and lifting the pot from the stove, walking it over to the table. "Nearly every day, Gil. If you paid attention."

Some two hours before all of this Rodney sat on his bicycle as always, pausing for the light to hit Kruger's feed store. It was something he'd had to time right, but it was worth waiting for. Because when it finally happened, over half the storefront lit up like a bonfire and Rodney felt the rush bloom from his knees to his shoulders. It was only the late afternoon sun, but there was a kind of magic in the way it hovered just below the western tree line, its rays breaking through the topmost branches to land squarely on the paned glass in a white blaze. At the loading bay, a big flatbed truck pulled in and was backing up to the feed store platform, taps on the horn giving a warning. Two Mexican workers, whose names Rodney had not yet learned, appeared from nowhere to stand on the dock and wave the rig in with their thick, bare, arms and gloved hands, all yips and hollers and echoing whoops.

Rodney stuffed the last of a Hershey bar into his mouth and tossed the wrapper onto the ground, coasting on his bicycle along the rutted road to the corner, to the lone traffic light that blinked yellow over Charlotte Street. The wrinkled cloth banner sagged beneath the cable that ran from post to post, stars and stripes pocked all over like it was a disease. *Hope Celebrates the Bicentennial, 1776-1976*: a lazy suggestion for cars to pause, he guessed, to consider for a few seconds all the lives that might be trapped in this thumbprint of a town. He straddled the bar and worked the handlebars, zeroing in on the feed store, the sun's glare and the rusted, corrugated front. At the busiest time of day, a person might need to wait out three or four cars before crossing Charlotte safely. For most passing drivers, though, both the light and the town were nothing more than an inconvenient tax on their brake pads as they traveled the 230 toward Laramie.

He pedaled across the street and over the gravel lot to the south side of the building, where he locked his bike to the downspout before walking back around to the front door and going inside. Behind the main counter, his mother sat on her high stool, a hand-written nameplate pinned to her blouse, thumbing a spiral notebook that was splayed out in front of her.

"Staring at the sun?" She did not look up from the pages.

"Just for a second."

"You're late."

"Hardly."

"Hardly's enough. It's also enough that I stuck my neck out to get you this job. I'd appreciate it if you didn't make me look like an ass to my boss." She got up then and walked to the end of the counter where she snatched the push broom from the corner. "Be thorough," she said, swinging the broom over the register.

It was a lousy five bucks to sweep up the entire warehouse floor from corner to corner—nowhere near a fair deal, but what could he say? Twelve-year-olds desperate for pocket money didn't get the luxury of whining or negotiating, not in an armpit place like Hope, Wyoming. Hope: a town, Rodney decided, that was not only poorly named, but proof that even God needed a place to dump all the shit he didn't get right. With the broom, he moved past the wall of windows toward the side doorway, where the echo of voices knocked around out in the loading bay like cow bells.

And as he got to the doorway, there in the space that led from the open loading dock to the warehouse behind, he saw it.

On the opposite side of Charlotte, parked beside the high chain link of the 76 station, was the midnight blue Impala, its black top catching the very last of the day's sun in a single stripe over the door. A white-shirted elbow poked out of the open driver's side window like a flag.

"It's him." His mother had come from behind the counter to stand beside Rodney, her shoulder almost touching his. She stared out the open bay in the direction of the gas station. "Tell me this isn't the first time you've noticed it."

"I never saw him sitting over there," Rodney said, and that was true. There were drive-bys now and then, but those had always been by chance. He guessed, anyway.

"Now you have. Just ignore him. Get your work done and go on home and don't say anything about it."

Rodney leaned back from the doorway. "What's he doing there?"

"God knows why your father does what he does half the time." A man in a fat, red beard appeared from the rear of the store, a discovery of rubber boots and rain gear cradled in his arms. Rodney's mother straightened up and quickly returned to the register, a smile stretched tight over her face as if someone had pulled a string from her back. "Looks like someone's hoping for a change in the weather," she said.

"Praying for it, Rosie," the man said. He dropped the gear onto the counter and scratched at his chin, his fingers disappearing into the orange tangle of fur. "I'd give my last born kid to be able to use these." Rodney's mother gave a worried laugh, and the man added, "You ain't seen my last born."

"Oh, Norris, I believe I have," she said. "All the same, a day of rain would sure be a blessing."

"From those pretty lips to God's ears."

Rodney's mother punched her fingers at the register, smile radiating a stripe of pink gums over her teeth. She was, it seemed to Rodney, a woman who managed to look best when she tried the least, when she let her thin, dark hair fall loose from whatever ponytail or bun she had forced it into. Here she was now, stationed behind the counter of another dusty county feed store in another farm town, passing chatter back and forth between herself and all the hayseed townspeople who wandered in. It was a skill of hers that he both admired and feared, the way she could settle into the space behind a shop counter, rattle off customer names and wrap her hands around a world that only recently had been alien to them.

The red-bearded man gathered up the pile of rubber and canvas, and Rodney's mother said, "Good luck" and looked back out the open doorway toward the gas station. She gave a gravelly sigh and murmured something that Rodney could not make out. Something about his father, probably.

Certainly, the way she talked *about* him was different than the way she talked *to* him. When the three of them were together, she often acted like she was a guest who had been invited at the last minute. His father might be rattling on about Cambodia and the Republicans, or the latest boxing match playing on TV, the merits of Ali vs. Frazier, and she'd hang back from it all, ever the observer. She might go as far as interjecting a laugh or a shake of her head, but more often than not she'd just look away and pretend to busy herself in the kitchen, maybe thumb through the mail or the day's newspaper, talking to herself in mumbled, broken chatter that Rodney would strain to pick up, thinking perhaps she might actually want to be heard.

Housemaid.
Past due.
Invisible.

Rodney moved from one end of the warehouse to the other, past the hay bales and rolls of chain link, stacks of re-bar and split rails, and mattress-like sacks of grain, the broom handle thumbed to his chest, a haze of dust blooming around him. The guys near the dock had loaded the last pallet of alfalfa pellets into the truck and were horsing around at the forklift, laughing and taking turns punching one another on the arm, and Rodney considered the notion that he could ever be in one place long enough to make a friend like that, or for that matter, that there could ever have been a time when his parents might have been that friendly with one another. Even more, that they could have been so in love that there was no other option than to be with one another. Was it possible? More likely it had been nothing more than one unplanned incident after another. A night of liquor and dancing, in the sweaty basement of a local grange hall. A drive back to somebody's apartment, or maybe not even that far. This and that, fast-forwarding to the three of them packed into their little house on Smith Street in God's Dump, Wyoming.

Neither his father nor his mother had ever shared with Rodney the seeds of what would eventually grow into the thing that lived in their living room each night, or crowded around the kitchen table, or hovered on opposite sides of Charlotte Street. And that was fine by Rodney. Because when all was said and done it didn't really matter how it all started, only that it all seemed to be ending in the way that it was.

Rodney finished up and went back into the store and returned the broom to his mother, who tucked it back into the space at the end of the counter before opening the register and plucking out a five-dollar bill. As he reached to take it, she pulled it back.

"Come here," she said.

"I'm here."

She moved closer to the counter. "Come here," she repeated, and waved him in with a nod of her chin. He stood against the counter and she reached out and pressed her hands to his cheeks, her skin like a heat pad. "I don't want you to worry about it," she said, her eyes moving over his face as she talked. "It's just your dad being your dad."

"I won't," he said. "I know." He pulled against her hold, though not with any real effort.

She kissed him on the forehead and let him go, and he went out to reclaim his bicycle from the downspout, then walked it around to the front of the loading dock where the whole bay sat empty now, except for the two Mexicans who were sitting on the edge sharing a cigarette and swinging their legs beneath them. Rodney straddled the bar and listened to them for a bit, though he could not make any sense of what tumbled out with all that smoke.

The Impala was gone. Rodney rumbled his bike over the graveled shoulder of Charlotte Street, and broke off down Pine, past CJ's Grocery and the Soak 'n' Suds Laundromat that only ever seemed to have the same three people in it, cutting across the highway and into the little tree-lined streets with old-people names like Victor and Clay and Alfred, crisscrossing his way to the strip of little sun-blistered bungalows that hugged the murky drainage creek. The layout of the streets and houses and shops in this place were as familiar to him as any place he'd ever lived. Rackett, Nebraska; Eddy, Colorado, and now Hope, Wyoming—all cut from the same dirty dishcloth. A downtown grid of shops probably hanging on by a handful of coins, a cluttered general store among them. A few rusted silos on the horizon. An old roadhouse somewhere on the outskirts where they could play loud music and not bother the church folks.

When Rodney was nine, they settled for about six months in Pueblo, Colorado, and it was a nice place, with crosswalks and a river running right through. It had a downtown that was big enough that a person could walk from one end to the other every day for a week and still not see the same person twice. Best of all, in the middle was a store that carried only comic books, comics Rodney had never heard of; he would stand in that place for hours after school until the owner, a quiet man who smoked skinny cigars and wore his shirts buttoned all the way to the neck, would flicker the lights to warn of closing time.

As always, though, something happened and they moved on. In his twelve years of life, Rodney and his parents seemed to change homes like some people change from one boring pair of shoes to another, never varying the size or style. For a long while Rodney imagined there must be something they were all running from, and that there would come a day when a policeman would be standing on their porch with a piece of paper in his hand, and they would be taken to his waiting car for one final trip together. It was, at times, an exciting thought. To be able to hear the story at last, the details of the bank robberies or some elaborate jewelry heist while the siren lights flashed over their heads for all to see. But that faded away before long. Because the truth, Rodney decided, was that his father was not running away from anything, but rather running *toward* something—something that always managed to be just a little bit faster than old Gil Culver.

That evening, the gunfighters resumed their positions in the kitchen, Rodney's mother at the stove, his father opposite him at the table now, legs stretched out so that his feet pressed against his son's. Rodney had mentioned the sunset, and his mother seconded it. A momentary diversion. An electric charge seemed to travel over him, though, working its way from his skin down into his muscles.

"I sure as hell can't do this much longer," his father suddenly announced, rubbing his fists over his eyes.

"Do what, Gil?" Rodney's mother said this with a heavy sigh, she the Queen of Farm Supply, dropping mounds of spaghetti noodles on their plates, steam billowing from the pot and clouding her face.

"Do what?" he repeated. "Keep trying to peddle sprinklers in the middle of a goddamned drought, that's what."

"It's what you chose," she replied. "Moved us five hundred miles for it."

He sucked in a quick breath and held onto it, as if he was deciding what he ought to do now that he had it behind his lips. He turned to Rodney. "How's that job of yours?"

"Fine."

"Just fine?" He cocked his head. "A job ought to be more than just 'fine,'" he said, as if he was living the example. "You spending or saving?"

"Saving," Rodney lied. It was hard walking past the grocery without stopping in for a little something, a Coke, or a box of sour chews. Plus you never knew when a good comic book issue would show up. Five dollars didn't stretch far.

"What's on the horizon? What are you saving for?"

Rodney shrugged his shoulders. "A bike. I guess."

"You have a bike," he said.

"I want a ten-speed."

"What do you need a ten-speed for? Everything from here to the next twenty square miles around us is flat as a board. Don't throw yourself into a money pit that you won't be able to climb out of."

Rodney said nothing, instead glancing up at his mother as she poured the watery red sauce over their plates. She held the saucepan in one hand and worked the sauce with the other like a server in a cafeteria line, keeping her eyes on the ladle the entire time.

"I've been by the feed store, Rose," his father said suddenly.

For a quick moment—a blink—she looked to Rodney. "You think I don't know that?" she said. Her tone was not curt, but rather matter-of-fact. As if he had told her he made his own coffee that morning.

They were all together in their tartan-papered kitchen with its buzzing overhead lamp, and the marbled Formica dining table shoved against the window. The plates of noodles and boiled broccoli, and dry white toast crowded the table, pushing out like they were moving to the edges of the world. And it didn't seem possible that there could be any space left for the three of them, with their clumsy arms reaching out for water glasses and paper napkins, all of it lost in the veil of steam.

"Those guys on the loading dock," his father went on. "They act like shirtsleeves are optional."

"In this heat, I suppose they are," his mother said, sitting down in her chair. She took up her fork and began turning it in a circle on her plate.

"It's showboating," he said. "That's what it is."

"What do you suggest I do about it?" Her eyelids drooped, already bored with both him and the conversation. "I don't spend my lunch breaks smoking cigarettes and ogling muscles on the loading dock if that's what you're worried about."

"I never said that," he said, folding his bread and biting it in half.

"You insinuated it." She stabbed at her food so that the tines clinked against the plate. Rodney's father gave no response this time, instead glancing at his son, cheeks flushed.

"I don't know what kind of place that Charlie Kruger is running there," he said.

"Charlie Kruger is a good man," his mother snapped. "He runs a good business."

"Not a very professional one, from what I can see."

Rodney watched as this game unfolded, as his mother continued to move the food from one side of the plate to the other. She was navigating this carefully, her forehead pressed down into her eyebrows, the lines reaching from the edges of her nose to the corners of her mouth. Something, and someone, always had to give.

His father stood from his chair and took his plate with the remaining food uneaten, carrying it to the counter where he let it drop into the sink. The response he would not give with his own words. Every footstep mattered. Out the front door and down the steps, the rattle of glass on the front door threatening to break into a million pieces with the slam behind him.

They remained there at the table, Rodney and his mother, eating what was left of the dinner she had made for them. With the exception of the noise of steel scraping ceramic and the creak of his mother's body shifting in the seat of the old spindle chair, they sat in silence. Only once did his mother lean in toward him.

"I know what you're thinking," she said.

"I'm not thinking anything," Rodney said through a mouthful of broccoli.

"Really?" She took a drink of water and set the glass down so that it hardly made a sound. "I hope to God there's something going on in that head of yours," she said. "Otherwise you'd be more like him than I ever imagined."

2

The woman leaned beside the cash register and dialed through the pages with those cherry red nails of hers, pausing here and there to judge, her mouth curling more with each turn.

"This is disgusting," she said, still flipping through the comic book. She smacked her lips and held her hand to her chest, her eyelashes flickering behind her moon glasses. Rodney knew the panels she was looking at. Some were better than others. Finally, she slapped the magazine down onto the counter. "I am not letting you buy this trash."

Rodney reached for the magazine but she slid it away from him, sucking in air as if he'd pulled a switchblade on her. "I said no," she practically shouted.

"There's no age limit," he said. "You can look."

"I already did." She grabbed the comic and shoved the cover toward him, clipping her finger over the top corner. "You can read, can't you?"

Recommended for Mature Readers.

"I'm mature," he said.

"Says you."

He told her again it was only a comic book, but she just

shook her head at him. "There's nothing comical about that thing. There's plenty of other ones back there that you can get. Popeye. Donald Duck. What's that kid—the rich kid?"

"Those are cartoons," he said. "Plus, you read through 'em in five minutes. It's a waste of money."

An old woman moved in behind him, clutching a wire basket filled with soup cans. She leaned forward, craning her turtle neck to get a look at what could be creating such a fuss.

"*Twisted Tales*," he said over his shoulder. "It's a comic book."

"It's smut," the cashier said. She held it up so the woman could see just how bad it was. The man's head floating in the water, bloody and raw. The screaming woman crumpled against the rock wall, a good deal of her private parts pushing out of her dress where they could. The way the magazine shook in the cashier's hands made it look a lot worse than it was.

"Oh my," the old woman whispered.

"The guy that usually works here," Rodney said, "with the tattoos. He lets me buy them." This was true, and by saying so he probably killed any chance of the guy ever doing it again.

She glanced back at the soup woman and shook her head, as if Rodney was the tenth kid to pull this on her today. "Go and pick out a different one. Or not. I don't have time to be your mother."

"Then don't," Rodney said, and the old woman said *Oh my* again, as he turned and moved quickly past her.

There was nothing to choose from, not for him. *Archie*, *Spiderman*. Disney stuff. He grabbed last month's *Superboy* from the rack and tucked it under his arm, not even giving it the courtesy of a look-through. There were two other copies of *Twisted Tales* on the rack, and he thumbed at the edge, at the No. 4 right there next to the title. What did she know about how mature he was? He might only be twelve, but he had seen things in his life.

He pedaled his bicycle from the grocery straight to the feed store, weaving in and out of parked cars and hopping up sidewalk curbs, dropping from his seat to dig the heels of his tennis shoes into the ground as the rear tire fishtailed on the loose-packed gravel of the alleyway opening to Charlotte Street. There were two long-bed pickup trucks backed to Kruger's loading dock and about a half-dozen men hoisting bales of hay down into the back-ends. They were in their T-shirts, their woolen hats and lined denim jackets with sheepskin collars tossed aside probably hours ago, long before the early summer sun had poked up over Rattlesnake Hills. It was nearly touching the tops of the Medicine Bow peaks now; the sheet of store windows facing the street reflected a sky that was almost bronze.

Rodney stopped and straddled the bike, emptying the last few pieces of candy into his mouth, sweet and gummy, just north of stale. He chewed and chewed until it felt like he'd been punched in the jaw—and then he gave it a couple more chews for good measure before sliding the copy of *Twisted Tales* from inside the front of his jeans, the paper damp with sweat. He flipped through it quickly, at the man falling down the well and the woman screaming over his mangled body, her dress hanging off her in shreds. The amphibious creature coming at her, with bold words like *Chunk*, *Sluck* and *Plat*, all drippy and melting down the pages just as they should. He closed it and tucked it inside the *Superboy* rag and folded it onto itself, then stuffed them both into his back pocket.

It was quiet in the store, and his mother was not where she was supposed to be, in the space behind the front counter. In fact, there was no one behind that counter at all. Anyone could just reach into the register and take whatever they wanted, Rodney thought. He waited there, not really thinking of stealing anything, but leaning his body over the countertop, hoisting himself onto the glass to look behind at the stacks of boxes, and clipboards that hung from nails, the simmering pot of black coffee, jeweled beads of sweat against the glass bulb. From somewhere near the back of the store there came a tumble of voices, low and clipped.

He slid from the counter and followed the noise, down the center aisle past the shelves of horse tack and rubber boots and sheepskin-lined jackets, to where the whispers grew louder. It wasn't until he rounded the corner at the end that he saw three of them there, huddled against the wall. His mother faced him but stood looking down at her shaking hands. A man Rodney recognized as Charlie Kruger was at her side and he kept a hand resting on her shoulder, his curled, silver mustache poking from his profile. Patchy cheeks flushed pink against a stiff collar, too snug, his white hair clipped short and tight, like a patch of frosty grass sitting there on top of his head.

Between them and Rodney stood a woman with her back to him, a globe of blonde curls and frizz ticking as she shook her head from side to side. Rodney forced a sniffle and it was then that his mother finally looked up at him. Her eyes were raw, the lids red and angry.

She said, "What are you doing here?" and when Rodney cocked his head at her she quickly answered, "Oh God," and wiped at her eyes. "Right," she said. "Of course."

Mister Kruger glanced at Rodney briefly, the pouches beneath heavy and reddened, then turned back to her. "What do you want to do here, Rose?" he asked.

The blonde woman said, "You want me to call the cops?"

Rodney's mother shook her head. "It's fine," she said. Her hand went to Mister Kruger's, her knuckles white as she squeezed. "I'll deal with it."

Rodney asked what she was talking about and then she put her hands to her eyes, and said, "Just stop," as if he had done something. She turned and pushed past them all and began walking the aisle to the front of the store, her pace clipped and intentional. "When you're done sweeping I want you to wait up here for me," she said to Rodney, shaking her arms at her sides as if coming in from a thunderstorm. "Don't go anywhere until I say so."

There was a moment when he thought he would refuse, that he would just stand there and stare at her until she told him what had made her so upset. But then she turned from him and found a stack of papers and started flipping through them, pausing now and then to wipe at her eyes.

He had seen his mother in situations that had caught her off guard or rattled her cage to the point of anger. A lying refrigerator repairman, a roadside flat tire in the middle of a storm. And there was his father. But in all these, no matter how far she had been pushed, he could not remember ever having seen her cry. It was something he could not make sense of, and he wondered if his being there to see it only made the whole thing that much worse.

He pushed the broom through that warehouse like it was a race, the dust thick and choking, corners and perimeter lousy, but he didn't care. And when it was all good enough he dropped the broom against the wall and slipped from the edge of the loading dock to his bicycle, climbing aboard and letting his weight move him over the rutted parking lot to the main drag. He opened up and sailed down Charlotte until he got to Cedar, then he cut across the short route, side-cutting streets by sticking to the alleyways and vacant lots before finally coming out onto his own block. Half the driveways up and down the street were occupied with cars, including his own father's blue Impala, backed up tight to the garage. And as Rodney got closer, he could see on the passenger side of the windshield a golf ball-sized sunburst, the fissures in the glass webbing outward to crackle over the driver's view. He gave the pedal a final pump and coasted up onto the sidewalk, dismounting on the last fifty feet or so and dropping his bicycle on the lawn like a bad experience.

The house was silent and choked with shadow. Rodney could see that his father was in the living room, seated backward in one of the dining room chairs, his legs spread and planted on either side of the seat back. His chin rested on the top rail, and his fingers curled around the spindles, one hand wrapped in white gauze. A quarter-sized patch of red seeped through over the knuckles.

There was two pieces of luggage at his feet—a mismatched pair that Rodney had never seen before. His father did not look up, but simply stared at the television as a program flickered silently over the screen: two men with pistols drawn, each of them hugging the outside of a warehouse building.

"Why do you have those?" Rodney motioned to the suitcases. His father looked at them as if they had suddenly appeared. As if he'd just awakened to see them sitting next to his shoes. "Where are you going?" Rodney asked.

"I don't know," his father said. "Missoula, I guess. For a while."

"For work?" There had been times when he did this, for a day or two. Those had been one-bag trips.

"We're not divorcing," his father said. His voice was coarse, as if the mere idea was unheard of. Insulting. "Your mother and me. We're not getting a divorce." He closed his eyes and drew in a deep breath.

Rodney's eyes stung and his throat felt like a marble had jammed itself down there. His father's shoes were scuffed and gouged from the edges all the way up over the toes.

"Were you at the store?" Rodney asked, and the sound of his own voice—the severe, callous edge—was not him.

His father leaned over and slid a suitcase to his knee. He fiddled with the handle, flipping it from one side to the other, not looking up at his son. "You must think I'm a goddamned monster," he said.

Rodney said, "I'm not thinking anything."

"I can't do this anymore," his father said. "Your mother—" he stopped, cleared his throat. "Goddamn it," he said. "Your father's turning into someone he doesn't even recognize anymore."

Rodney went to him then, stood between the television set and his father. "I don't know what that means," he said. His father was scaring him. This was different than times before, when he might just drive around for a few hours or, at worst, grab his coat and disappear until morning.

His father coughed, almost the beginning of a cry, perhaps, into the circle of blood at his knuckles. "She's making me crazy," he said, looking up at Rodney now, brows raised into a field of ridges. "I just can't do it anymore."

Rodney turned and looked back out the window, at the street that ran east, back toward the feed store. "Did she tell you to leave?" he asked.

"She didn't tell me anything," he snapped. He stood from his chair then and took up the suitcases, and lingered there in the middle of the room. A scarecrow in the field, aching for some sort of reaction to his presence. His eyes bored into his son and Rodney knew it and he felt it, and it was all he could do to keep from looking up, from matching his father's stare. He kept his head still as a fencepost, his jaw pulsing in and out, while the people on the screen threw silent shouts at one another so that their necks strained, and their eyes bulged from their sockets.

"I want to go with you," Rodney said, and there were all kinds of crybaby in those words and it embarrassed him. It embarrassed him that he should be coming apart like this, and it embarrassed him that his father should have to hear it. If there was ever a chance he might bring Rodney with him, it was dead now.

His father reached over and put his hand on Rodney's shoulder.

"Walk with me," he said. And then he gave the boy a tug on his sleeve that lifted one of Rodney's feet from the floor.

Outside, Rodney could see that there were bedclothes folded on the rear seat of the Impala. His father dropped the bags inside, sliding them against the blankets, then leaned against the closed door, hands shoved down into his trouser pockets. His keys tumbled in there.

"You're not coming back," Rodney said.

"The hell I'm not."

"You're just lying to me, so I won't cry." Rodney felt the tears pushing at him hard, but he would win this one. He ground his teeth and dug his fingernails into his palms.

His father said, "You're twelve now, right?"

"Yes, sir."

"You've got a long way to go till you can wear these shoes," he said, nodding toward his feet. "When that happens maybe then you'll understand things better."

Rodney shrugged. What could he say to that?

"Or maybe you never will," his father said. "Till then I don't want you judging your old man, cause you don't know what you don't know." His father reached over and scratched his son's head with his fingers, like he might scratch the belly of some dog.

He told Rodney he would call when he got to where he was going and then he climbed into the car and fired it up, and backed slowly out of the driveway, his elbow in a V over the seat back, head craned to one side, not facing his son. At the street he tapped the horn twice and drove off down Smith Avenue, the streetlamps rolling white circles over the hood, then sliding across the roof and down the trunk as he went.

It was well past dark by the time Rodney's mother finally came home. She wore her purse on her shoulder like it was a punishment, the front doorknob a lifeline beneath her hand. Rodney lay stretched out on the sofa, hands folded on his chest as if in prayer. The television flickered, an old movie that he had lost track of a half hour earlier but continued to watch.

"You didn't do what I told you," she said.

"I forgot," he lied.

She closed the door behind her. "Did you talk to him?"

"Yeah."

She paused, nodded her head. "Is there anything you want to ask me?"

"No."

His mother nodded again and went into the kitchen. Rodney watched her in the alcove as she moved some plates and glasses around, turning the dial on the oven before opening the door and waving her hand around inside. She moved from sink to refrigerator to cabinetry as if she had come from a daylong war and had no fight left in her. Every movement was coupled with a hand on the counter, a hip resting against anything that would help support her weight. She reached up and pulled a clip from her head and let her hair fall around her shoulders, dragging her hand through it twice to sweep it all it back over her head. At one point she turned and her eyes found his, and she gave him a little smile. As if he had caught her in the act.

The movie flipped to a commercial with a man shouting over a huge parking lot of cars, and Rodney stretched on the sofa so that his toes pointed sharp, and sat up, rubbing his eyes with his fists. He looked out into the kitchen again. Now his mother was sitting at the small table with a mug in front of her, stirring it in circles with a spoon.

Outside the wind began to kick up, the branches of the large holly bush scraping at the window glass like fingers. He was probably all the way to Casper by now, Rodney thought. And in that same thought he felt his heart hum as flat as the expanse between them. Shouldn't he be feeling more? Anything? If it was one of his comic books there would be screaming and tears, and beads of sweat like tiny glass rivulets running down his face. The sky would be crowded with black fists, and something horrible would be waiting on the next page. Yet here he was, in front of the television, feeling next to nothing.

Maybe, he wondered, his father was someplace giving a backward glance at Hope, perhaps imagining his son and wife lounging there in the living room, the two of them pretending at normalcy. As if they expected any moment he would come in the door and say he was sorry and that it was all a mistake, that he had never meant any of it. That when he did so they would all laugh, and agree it had all been a misunderstanding, and there was nothing on the next page other than the words, *The End*, written in big, curled letters.

3

Rodney sat on the edge of the feed store loading dock, watching the highway and counting cars as they passed under the faded bicentennial banner on their way to somewhere else. It was not a big number. The other workers had gone home and the noise of closing doors let him know that his mother would be out any minute. She had told him to wait for her when he was finished sweeping. She had plans for the two of them.

They walked together down Charlotte into town, taking the four blocks at a good clip, past the post office and library, and Dino's Smoke Shoppe, where a straw hat-wearing woman closed the door behind her and waved at his mother, and called out her name.

"That's Dino's wife, Sadie," his mother said, waving back at her. "She runs the place."

"Why does she run it?" he asked. "Is her husband dead or something?"

They walked a little farther and she leaned into him. "He's a drunk," she said. "If he's not down at The Hitching Post then I imagine he's at home in bed, just waiting for his liver to give in." She tapped him on the shoulder. "It's no secret, really, but all the same don't go spreading it to your friends."

"I won't."

"It's a sad thing, and Sadie doesn't deserve the gossip."

"I said I won't," he repeated. "Besides, I don't have any friends to tell anyway."

She faltered in her walk then, only for a brief step, and her face fell into a snapshot of worry, of borderline pity that rolled Rodney's stomach from one side to the other. He didn't want her to feel sorry for him. His lack of friends was his choice, not the result of some kind of phantom social plague stirred up by the kids at his school. Not this time.

"Anyway," she said. "I thought we'd eat out tonight. Have a little date for ourselves."

She turned off the sidewalk and up to the front door of the Iron Rail Diner, where she pushed through and led him to a booth near the back, adjacent the kitchen, separated by quilted, aluminum saloon doors. It was chaos in there, men shouting back and forth, cussing at one another now and then, metal knocking against metal, the hiss of meat being slapped onto a hot griddle.

This was something because, as a rule, his mother did not care to eat out, not even when Rodney's father had been home and working steady. It was ridiculous, she insisted. Unnecessary. Why pay an arm and a leg for someone else to cook meat that you could get for fifty cents at the supermarket? But she'd been working more, it seemed, since Rodney's father had left. Coming in some nights after he had gone to bed, trying to be quiet but failing. Rules that had once been steady were peeling away like the paint on their little house. And now, here they were at the Iron Rail.

Rodney slid into the seat opposite, and his mother did not pick up the menu that lay in front of her but instead nodded her chin at the waitress, who came straight up to them and put her fingers on the edge of the table. Her nails were long and glassy pink, and the two women smiled at one another. "So this is him," the waitress said.

"In the flesh," his mother said.

"Handsome boy." She smiled, waxy lipstick bleeding into tiny cracks at the edges of her lips. She wagged a pen at him. "I'll bet you get all the girls chasing you through the schoolyard."

His mother beamed at Rodney and, for the first time since they'd left Kruger's, he saw how she had painted herself up, that she'd run a cherry red over her lips and done something with her eyes—brushed a smudge of green over them and darkened the lashes so they looked like the tips of tiny paintbrushes. She nudged his foot with her toe. "Don't just sit there like a mute," she said. "Say something."

Rodney said, "Nobody's chasing me at school."

"Well, that's a shame," the waitress said, tapping her pen on her pad. "Give it time."

He'd barely had the chance to look through the menu before his mother declared that it would be a burger and fries for him, and a salad for herself. The whole exchange was quick and businesslike, the waitress snatching up the menus with those fingernails and the lowest of whispers. *You got it, hon.*

His mother turned herself so her back nudged the wall, facing the door to the kitchen. She smiled at Rodney and reached across the table to wipe at something on his cheek with her fingers and when he pulled away she just rolled her eyes at him and turned back toward the kitchen. Something was there, distracting her. It was as if there was some big story unfolding behind those aluminum doors, a scene that she should be a part of.

"Are you too old for crayons?" she asked him.

"I don't want to color," he said. He'd seen the pages on his way in. Bunnies and flowers and little kid stuff. He wasn't going to be caught dead with that nonsense. Instead, he dumped all of the sugar packets onto the table. They were inventors or some such thing, the Wright Brothers, Eli Whitney. People like that.

His mother reached into her purse and slid out a cigarette and tapped it on her arm. In his life he'd probably seen her smoke a dozen times. It was never something she seemed to enjoy, but rather something she *needed*—a way to smooth out moments of stress, maybe punctuate the tail end of one of her battles with his father.

She smiled at him. "Hungry?"

"A little."

"I hope a hamburger was fine."

He guessed it would have to be, since she'd taken it upon herself to order it. "It's fine," he said.

"I just assumed." She reached back into her purse, the unlit cigarette a tiny flagpole still held in the fingers of her free hand. She dug around in there like she was a scavenger, and her forehead shrunk into itself with the growing frenzy of her search. After a minute or so she gave up, throwing the cigarette back into her purse and shoving the whole bag aside.

There was kick of a desk bell and someone yelled, "Order up!" and the waitress appeared again with plates in her arms and another wink at Rodney.

"Thank God," his mother said to her. "I'm starving."

"Hope this will do," she said, sliding the sleepy pile of lettuce in front of his mother almost apologetically.

Rodney pulled the vegetables from his burger and layered the meat in ketchup. He had barely taken his first bite when one of the aluminum doors punched open, knocking against the wall. A man who was mostly arms and sideburns waltzed through, like some actor making his first appearance on stage. His spider hands worked eagerly at the grease-smeared apron wrapped around his waist, and there was a kind of paper towel cap over his head, pulled almost down to eyes a color of green that Rodney didn't think he'd ever seen in a person before. It was like they'd been painted on his face along with those sideburns of his that dripped like black ink from his ears to his jawline.

"So?" he said. "How is it?" And when Rodney didn't answer quickly enough he added, "That burger you're eating there. I cooked it."

There was the sharp stab of his mother's toe against his shin. Rodney shot a look at her. The hamburger tumbled dry and unyielding in his mouth.

"The name's Otis," the man said, reaching his hand across the table. "Otis Dell." He held it there like he was a statue, and only when Rodney's mother said, "Oh for goodness sake, shake his hand," did Rodney take it, damp and cold as it was. Otis stared at the boy, sugar-cube teeth pushing through pink lips almost woman-like, a grin of expectancy, or worry, perhaps. As if his job—or something, anyway—depended on Rodney's approval. "Well?" he asked.

"Well what?" Rodney said.

"Rodney," his mother whispered—another kick to his shin. "How's the hamburger?"

"It's fine," said Rodney. God. All this over a lousy burger

His mother dragged her fork through the salad, the leaves limp and soaked in clumpy, pallid dressing. She stared dreamily at her plate, now and then glancing up at Otis.

"As for me," she said, "I've had better in the world of salads." She lifted a dripping fork to her mouth. "But I suppose it'll do." She gave Rodney a wink and it seemed that she might be trying to pull a fast one with this Otis fellow, but doing a lousy job of it, what with the thin smile that she was giving away so easily. The whole thing pulled on his stomach, too, the way the two of them looked at each other, their gaze welded together as if connected by some hidden joke. A flush of pink bloomed from his mother's collar to her chin.

Otis said, "Guess you'll have to come back then and give me another chance to get it right."

"I guess I will," she answered.

They were both quiet then, Rodney's mother eating lettuce in tiny bites, like some rabbit-human, this man Otis standing over her with his dingy white T-shirt and filthy apron and that sugar grin stretching ever wider across his unshaven face. And while he knew it would send his mother in a whirlwind if she saw him do it, Rodney rolled his eyes.

"You trying to get a look at your brains back there?" Otis was looking at him now, his lids narrowed and still.

The burger turned in his mouth as if it was made of rubber, and Rodney held his eyes firm on Otis as if looking away might end his life. They stood like that for some time, minutes it seemed, until his mother whispered, *Oh dear—Rodney,* and someone thankfully hollered out from the kitchen.

"Dell!"

Otis said, "That's my cue." He tipped his head at Rose and gave a measured wink to Rodney before turning and punching the doors on his way through, the metal ricocheting off the kitchen walls as they swung.

"That wasn't your finest moment," she said.

In the quiet that followed, Rodney forced himself another bite, picking at the edges of the burger, doing all he could to avoid looking up at her. He took his time, scanning the walls and other tables as he chewed. There were paintings of freight trains and dense forests and mountain ranges, all jagged peaks and patchy snow pack. He counted four different clocks, all made from glossy chunks of wood, each with a colored sticker with what looked like a price, if a customer wanted one for his very own. A couple tables over a toddler in a high chair ate scrambled eggs straight from the tray.

His mother shifted in her seat, and the water in his glass danced in ripples from the center to the edges. "Did you hear me?" she asked.

"Yes," he finally said.

"You were pretty rude," she said. "It wouldn't have killed you to be nice. He was nice to you." And when Rodney simply shrugged and went back to his burger, she moved her plate to the center of the table, tapping it against his.

"I don't know why it matters," he said. "He's just some guy, right?"

She put her hand to her forehead. "What? You can't be polite unless it's someone important?"

Rodney laid his burger on his plate and pushed it away from him, sliding it in her direction. There was something in all of this that tasted foul. The dinner, the waitress, and the way she seemed to know him already. *So this is him*, she'd said. And this cook. Otis. Everyone in this whole place seemed to be in on this date except him.

"Sometimes I feel like I don't even know you anymore," she said. This person who was, herself, turning more and more alien each day. Like something in the pages of one of his comics.

"I'm just Rodney," he said, picking at the bread on his plate. "That's it."

"Okay, Just Rodney. You should pay attention to first impressions," she warned, leaning in. "Because you never know when you will meet people a second time."

4

In the two months since Rodney's father had gone away it seemed that, along with his blue Impala, he had taken with him the last days of spring. The distraction of school was gone as well, and Rodney's days had melted into an endless routine of pedaling his bicycle from one end of Hope to the other, yellow grass and concrete to yellow grass and concrete, over and over, back and forth. The high point of his day was when it was time for him to sweep out the warehouse. There, at least the dust moved around him, and he could see some sort of change occurring in his world from one minute to the next.

And yet.

It was clear to Rodney that his mother was discovering change of her own, and that the shift in her world seemed to be suiting her just fine. Hers had become a world of longer nights now, of makeup and shoes with heels, and frozen dinners left for her son in foil trays. There were the late-evening voices echoing outside in the street, the bell-like laughter between her and a girlfriend or two, finishing up gossip or whatnot, the noise of her shoes like drumbeats as she marched up the front steps. There were nights of dancing and pool, she told him (when she told him), and though he occasionally caught the glimpse of close silhouettes in the dull light of a parked car's interior lamp, Rodney never said a thing about it to her. He wanted desperately to believe that men and women could be allowed to spend time with one another as children did, and nothing else. Laugh, and tell stories. Enjoy one another's company but at the end of the day, return home to their families where they belonged. More than anything he had to believe this, but as time went on it was harder and harder to fool himself that any such thing could be possible.

"You're old enough to stay home alone sometimes, right?" she asked, taking the broom from him and setting it behind her. She counted out a stack of ones from the till, putting five of them on the counter for him. There had been no reason to think she worried about him being home by himself, not in the last couple of years. He'd stayed home alone plenty of times.

"Why? So you can go out more often?"

She pulled back from him. "Listen, you. I work hard around here," she said, waving a hand like she was casting a spell over the empty store. "I deserve a little time to myself now and then, you know?" She closed her eyes, her lips pushed together in a rosebud. "I don't mean that as a judgment against you. You'll always come first. You know that, don't you?"

The words felt as vacant and dead as the space around them. He fought back the stone in his throat. "When dad comes back—"

"Oh, Rodney don't," she said. "Don't keep trying to force yourself into a life based on your father's timeline. I don't have the foggiest idea what his plans are and neither do you. It's okay to look for something else, when what you hoped for isn't there anymore." She leaned into him. "Does that make sense at all?"

It did, at least as it related to her, and what she wanted. So, he thought, that's how it was going to be. They would just move on—as if Rodney's father had been nothing more than a character in a scene, who'd simply walked off midsentence and disappeared from the story completely.

Rodney finished up his second can of ravioli and, as his mother had told him to do, cleaned up his mess, drying the dish and putting it back into the cupboard—the same dish that he used every night, now.

The late movie on television had grown complicated and he could not follow it anymore. Between the convoluted plot of stolen diamonds and too many double-crosses, and his drifting in and out of sleep, he finally turned it off and put himself to bed. Lying down so he could see the window, he watched for the wash of headlights against the drapes, and the inevitable sound of outside chatter.

The nonsense of the movie continued to play in his head, though, his mind stubbornly trying to untangle the bad from the worse, who had stolen from whom. And then his eyelids weighed heavy and thoughts of diamonds dissolved into flying, soaring over yellow fields and the stripe of a blue car racing over a black roadway.

And as quickly as he'd drifted he was jarred awake by the rumble of a muscle engine, and the slamming of doors. Quiet at first, and then the familiar tones of his mother, with a man's voice layered in. Another pause and then his mother's high giggling, and the clicking of heels up onto the front porch. The low light of the hallway spilled in through the wedge opening of his bedroom door, a habit he could not seem to break, keeping the door cracked. It was a guide to help orient himself when he opened his eyes in darkness, in those moments when he woke up and could not tell where he was. He had always liked this part, when he could look past his parents' door to the kitchen alcove, at the flickering blue light against the wall coming from the television and know that his mother was there, still awake, curled up on the sofa watching Johnny Carson before she went off to bed all by herself.

It was the man's voice again, louder, weaving in and out of his mother's, just outside the front door. Rodney lay silent, blankets pulled to his chin now and he stared at the ceiling, at the putty texture, with eyes so easily tricked that they began to form clouds and constellations, shapes that turned and drifted until a simple blink of the eyelids reset the entire scene, back to the beginning.

The front door rattled and creaked and the conversation tumbled into the house with the knock of shoes on hardwood. His mother laughed again.

"Stop it." Her voice. "You'll wake up the whole neighborhood."

It was quiet for a moment, and then there was a low hum, and a shuffle of some kind, a jacket maybe, sliding off and into a chair, or onto the floor.

"Slow down, cowboy." His mother, almost a drawl.

"I will when it counts." The man again, and then nothing. Nothing but the noise of breathing. A quick shadow fell across the floor and he heard his mother's bedroom door click shut.

Rodney did not sleep yet, though there were no sounds happening that should keep him awake. He strained to listen for something—for anything—that might help him craft a believable story, a "safe" explanation for what could be happening in that room. A late movie playing out on the tiny black and white

RCA she kept perched on the dresser. Two people, seated on opposite sides of the room, telling stories, the mother going on about her son who was in the very next room and a husband who might just walk in the front door at any moment.

In the stubborn silence Rodney seemed to drop off at last, though it was hard to tell if it was truly sleep, and whether the span of time had stretched itself over fifteen minutes or two hours. A flood of light spilled in from the hallway with the creak of the door.

"You awake over there?" A man's voice.

The figure took up the open doorway, nearly a full silhouette, though Rodney could see that the man was draped in a bathrobe, and the robe was tied loose at his waist, the hair on his stomach sprayed thick like moss from the white waistband of briefs that showed just above the knot. In one hand he held a milk bottle and he tapped it against his leg, shifting his weight from one foot to the other. The light filled in around one side and Rodney recognized the robe as the one his father had always worn.

"What do you want?" Rodney said.

"I don't want nothing," the man said. "Just saying *hey*."

"I got school tomorrow," the boy answered.

"In summer?"

Rodney's eyes adjusted some to the low light, and it was then that he was able to finally make out the man's face. It was the cook from the Iron Rail, with the hair thick and shiny and black, all of it swept back over his head as if it had been combed or raked back with fingernails until it finally just gave up and fell down into its place. And those sideburns, dripping down from the whole mop, from the top of the ears to the hard jawline.

"Hey man, how old are you?" he said. His lips pushed from his mouth like he was holding something in there. "You old enough to drive a car?"

Rodney said, "I can't drive. I'm only twelve."

"Jesus. You look a lot older than that." He tipped the milk bottle to his lips and swallowed a mouthful, the white washing around the glass as he brought it back down to his side. He wiped a sleeve over his mouth, the sleeve of Rodney's father's bathrobe. "I figured you'd already be trying to sneak girls in through the window."

There was the sound of a door behind him, and Rodney's mother's voice, low and soft. Otis looked over his shoulder and scratched at his naked stomach, fingers raking at the black fur. A monkey.

"We shall talk another time," he said. Then he stepped off and closed the door behind him and a breath of moonlight seeped in through the window, and for a moment Rodney thought there was someone else in there with him, a figure standing at the far side of the bedroom. His jacket, maybe, draped over the corner of his closet door. There came the low hum of voices again on the other side of the door and he turned his back to them, taking hold of his pillow and carefully wrapping it over his ears like a hood.

5

Rodney came into the kitchen to find his mother sitting at the small table, still in her bathrobe, hunched over her coffee, a cigarette smoldering between her fingers. Her hair was pulled back from her face with a fat, plastic clip and the skin below her eyes was thick and reddened, as if she had been sitting up all night.

He tugged at the refrigerator door and stared at the bottle there on the shelf. There was Otis Dell in that milk for sure, and all over the glass, where his mouth had wrapped itself around the rim. Everything in that space had been touched, Rodney was certain—things opened and prodded through, a stranger's fingers picking at their bread and cheese, moving things willy-nilly from one place to another.

"You want some breakfast?" his mother asked.

"We need more milk."

"I thought we had some," she said. She shifted in her chair to look part-ways over her shoulder.

Rodney swung the door closed and went to the cupboards, opening and closing them one by one in search of something he could take with him. There were cans of soup and sauce, and boxes of crackers and dry casserole mixes, as there had always been.

"Is he still here?" he asked.

His mother shook her head *no*.

He opened a box of soda crackers and took a sleeve from it. "So is he your boyfriend, now?"

"Oh, Rodney. Don't do this."

"You said before it was okay to look for something, right? I'm just wondering if that's what you were talking about when you said it. You had to have known him a long time if—"

"You want to know if I've been carrying on with Otis for a while," she said, rubbing her fingers over her eyes. "You want to know if maybe your father had good reason to be sitting there in his car spying on me."

He wanted to answer that, tell her *yes* or even *maybe*. But nothing would come.

"Things can happen fast, Rodney. I can't explain it so you'll understand. I'm not perfect."

"No one's perfect. Dad's not perfect."

"I'm not a bad mother, or a bad wife." She took a drag off her cigarette and held it in for a moment. Rodney said nothing, and she watched him from her chair, her eyes ticking over his face, before finally blowing out the smoke in a blue tumble.

"I don't like him," Rodney said. "There's something about him that's not good."

"I wasn't aware someone died and made you judge of everyone." She closed her eyes and put her head in her hand. "Let me tell you something that might serve you well someday. A woman's life doesn't stop the second her husband decides to pick up and run off to God knows where," she said.

"Missoula."

"Whatever. I'm entitled to have friends."

"He's in Missoula," Rodney repeated.

"So you say." She tamped her cigarette in the ashtray, hard. "Let's not fight about this," she said, fingering a new cigarette from the pack but not lighting it up. "He's a nice guy, Otis. But he's not worth all of this heartburn."

Rodney took an apple from the bowl in front of her. "I'm going to a friend's," he said.

She looked at him then, a teepee of lines on her forehead, and she didn't need to say a single word for Rodney to hear what was on her mind. *Friend.* When had he ever mentioned a single friend since they'd come to Hope? Never—not even a name.

She nodded, her forehead smoothing over, and said, "That's good." Then she pushed off from the table and got up, brushing a hand over his back as she walked out of the kitchen, the smell of her bathrobe trailing as she left, through the living room and down the hall to her bedroom.

6

On the backside of Hope, in a small space between CJ's Grocery and the Drive On Inn there was a little burger stand called Val's, and on the side of the building they had a covered, outdoor area that was closed up with a metal cage at night. In that cage was a row of video arcade games, and on most days after school, and on the weekends, Rodney could put himself with other kids his age, mostly boys but not always, packed around the machines, knocking fists against the metal sides and feeding those machines a week's worth of quarters in a single afternoon. He spent a good amount of time and pocket money there himself, when he could. It was easy to blend in with the bodies that crowded that place, to pretend he wasn't alone, not having to worry about saying or doing the wrong thing.

On this day, Rodney put his bike out front where he could keep an eye on it, because he knew that a simple padlock wouldn't keep people from messing with it as they had before, pulling his chain off or loosening the bolts on his wheels or emptying the tires. He positioned himself near the Night Driver machine though he wasn't playing it, or even planning on playing it, really. Sometimes, he decided, it was better to watch everyone else at their consoles, to see the way they drummed on the buttons and swore at the screens, amped up like addicts, many of them *this* close to crying. Even with the all racket and chaos, Val's was something of a calming place for Rodney, the kind of space he could enter into and be invisible for a while. Invisible in plain view.

"Gimme room, dumbshit." Two boys crowded the Sea Wolf screen, all block shoulders and cracking voices. High schoolers, Rodney figured. He didn't know them, but he'd seen them most every time he came to Val's. They wore their hair in spikes and jeans with holes torn in the knees, and they smoked joints in the small space behind the cages, joints that they called *Jesus' Candy*. And even though everyone knew what was what, nobody ever said anything about it.

"You're wasting your quarter," the taller one said. There was the *ping* of the fake sonar, and a static explosion, and he slammed his hand against the console.

The shorter one dug his hands into his pockets and said, "I'm empty." And when he looked past Rodney, out into the street maybe, he straightened up and said, "Oh baby, look who rolled up."

It had been a week since Otis Dell had been by the house and Rodney had not seen or heard from the man since, which was fine by him. His mother hadn't mentioned his name, and Rodney had not brought it up again, not since that morning in the kitchen. Lately, it had almost been as if he had never existed. Except here he was.

Otis kept on the street side of his car, and Rodney did not get the sense that anyone around him was concerned that he might do anything more than what he was already doing.

He walked around casually to the front end of the car and rested his hand on the hood. He was wearing blue jeans and a baseball T-shirt this time, with chunky combat boots, but there were still those sideburns running down his face like smears of shoe polish. Rodney stayed well behind the others, holding himself safely in the shadows.

This all went on for a while, Otis walking from one side of his car to the other, stopping to lean on the fender. Now and then someone would walk past, falter in their step and look back over their shoulder at him. At one point, Otis called out something, and one of those passersby stopped in his tracks and circled on back to him. This was an older fellow, older than Rodney's father maybe, and while he stood there with Otis he kept his hands tucked down in the pockets of his camouflage jacket.

They talked for just a minute or so, and then the man looked back up at Val's for a split second before moving a hand from his pocket right into Otis's, straight into the front jeans pocket it looked like. And with that, Otis gave the guy a slap on the shoulder and climbed back into his car and left without another word to anyone, but not before gunning the engine a good three or four times and laying a stripe of rubber all down the concrete. Someone said, "That dude is crazy."

People went back to their games. Rodney counted out the quarters in his pocket and when he looked up, he noticed a couple of girls leaning over a pinball machine in play, staring at him. They were girls he knew from school, though not very well. The stout one, named Donna, glared at Rodney, raising an ugly crook in her lip. Barely a week after he'd showed up in class she had tried to talk him into letting her copy his geography map. There had been sweet talk, and an effort to play herself as some social queen, someone he'd want to be friends with. He'd refused though and, as a result, wound up as more or less dead to her and everyone else. Which was fine by him.

"Your mom works at Kruger's." The other girl—he thought her name might be Kate, or Katrina, maybe—screeched over the racket of the pinball machine.

"So what," Rodney said. "Like I don't know that."

She leaned in to her friend, her black hair ratted out like crow's feathers, and yelled something into her ear that Rodney couldn't make out. She looked back to him. "I seen your mom and Otis Dell around town. My apartment is right across the street from Swain's Tavern. They like to go there an awful lot."

"So what?" he said again.

"So what?" she mimicked, folding her arms over her chest and throwing a smirk at him. "And yet you stand there, acting like you don't even know him."

"I don't know him," he said.

Katrina said, "Wait till he starts beating on her. My mom works with a lady who went with him for a while, last fall. She mouthed off to Otis this one time—the lady did, not my mom. Anyway, he backhanded her right across the face."

Rodney said, "They just barely met. He hasn't done anything yet."

"*Yet*," she echoed, her mouth pinched tight. A beak.

"Anyways, he wouldn't dare," he added.

"Or else what?" she said, looking him up and down. "You'll kick his ass? Yeah, right." Donna reached across the pinball glass and swatted at her.

There were options that drifted into his mind, things he could do to Otis—the kinds of things the people in his comics did (but seldom got away with). All the same, he could not imagine his mother letting anyone so much as lift a hand to her, much less strike her.

Katrina shook her head. "Don't bother calling the cops,"

she said. "My mom said that if the cops could do anything with Otis he would have been in jail a long time ago." She nodded to her friend and the two of them left the machine, whipping their hair like horse tails as they pushed through the crowd and disappeared out the back of the arcade.

7

He remembered the fishing lure with its kaleidoscopic shimmer and its angry triple hook, all peeking out from the sand. The water brushed over it easily and maybe it was that rhythm and the gentle nudge that let him see the lure before he might carelessly let his bare foot sink right down over those barbs. He dug the thing from the sand and held it over his head and called to his father. He was six then, and boy had he found a treasure.

His parents were some distance away, back at the picnic table, that weathered, splintered thing built of cedar logs and chained to a rugged maple, the tree bark scarred with hearts and letters, and three-pronged peace signs. Rodney's mother sat on the bench closest, cigarette fuming from her fingers, right leg over her left knee, sunglasses hiding her gaze. She might be looking at him. There was no way to know.

His father stood squarely behind her, and he was talking with one hand moving in loops while the other held a brown bottle by the neck. On and on he went, no notice of Rodney and his wonderful discovery, saying something important, worthy of sharing and yet Rodney's mother looked to be a world away from it all. She brought the cigarette to her mouth and held it in her lips, chasing some insect from her orbit with her free hand. Then his father put the bottle down and placed his hands on his mother's shoulders, moving them back and forth. She tightened up at first, her forehead breaking into lines as if he was hurting her. And then there was a grin, her teeth, as his father leaned in and whispered something to her, and her laughter and smile seemed to open her whole face.

There were other people there at the lake, people they did not know who shared the beach and the grass and the mood. A man strolled toward Rodney, his long shadow curling over neglected sandcastles and discarded towels. "That's a nice spinner you got there," he said, stopping at the water's edge. He cupped a hand over his forehead, his stomach chalky white and spilling out the bottom of his T-shirt. A sack of flour peeking over his waistband.

"I found it," Rodney said. "Right here."

"You're lucky you didn't step on it," he said.

"I'm careful," Rodney said, and then he pointed at the shade of the maple tree. "That's my mom and dad over there."

The man looked over to the table, at the scene that was persisting, the blue feather of smoke and the tumbling hands and the beer bottle dancing from one side to the other. He laughed softly and Rodney imagined that the man had heard something he'd missed, a joke maybe. And then the man clapped Rodney on the shoulder and told him to watch for more hooks, and he continued to make his way down the beach, his eyes tracking the picnic table as he went.

Rodney carried that hook in his hand all the way back from the lake. No one asked him what was there in that clenched fist, not when his mother helped him with his seatbelt, not when he tapped it against the side window, loud enough to be heard over the thrum of the engine. Not for the entire ride home.

8

In time, Rodney had grown used to Otis like he would a fresh scar, some ugly mark that might have come from a collision with a low branch while navigating his bicycle on an overgrown trail. The heavy crawl of his voice late at night, the crude outline of his body lumbering between Rodney's mother's room and the bathroom. Otis's slumped figure waiting at the kitchen table most every morning now, drinking coffee with Rodney's mother, her hand over her mouth, giggling at some joke that was not for her son to hear.

On a whim she had cut her hair short, and colored it a shade of brown that was not her own and she said nothing to Rodney about it, but she liked to flick her fingers through the sides as if baiting him to bring it up. Pushing him to say something—anything—which he would not.

"He's a little younger," she'd said, as if it was Rodney who had brought up the wide gap in their ages. "Things like that shouldn't matter," she went on, picking at her bangs. "People are people."

What else would they be? he wanted to say. *Rocks? Squirrels?*

"People are people," he repeated, and she smiled at him and

said, *Yes they are*, as if they had come to some kind of agreement at last.

It wasn't much longer until Otis's green Bonneville claimed the driveway as its home, and a greasy path was worn between the car's trunk and the garage—Otis moving armloads of power tools and stereo equipment and small appliances, microwave ovens and blenders, and toaster ovens, some still in boxes with price tags attached.

"There's deals to be had," he'd say to Rodney, waving him from the sofa or porch, or his bedroom, to walk him through the growing inventory, maybe enlist his help in carrying more crap into the garage, into storage. Otis would not say where he happened to find these treasures, other than vague references to rummage sales and swap meets. There were outlets for this sort of venture, he explained—pawn shops and auctions where if you knew what you were doing, you could double your money and come away twice the man you were going in.

Otis waded deeper into their lives, and the subject of Rodney's father came up less and less in that house. He had phoned twice since that first month of being gone, and though Rodney caught himself watching the wall phone for hours most nights, there hadn't been a single call in two weeks. It was as if the man didn't give the slightest shit about his family, about Rodney. In time, Rodney simply gave up mentioning him to his mother at all. The labored sighs, the shrug of her shoulders, sometimes simply ignoring him altogether like he wasn't even there. It was almost as if he had never been real to begin with.

And so it had to be. There was, now, this strange new world of his mother and the slick Otis Dell and what a pair they made, and this was a world in which she smiled warmly and shut her eyes as Otis touched her hair or stood behind her with his arms layered over her stomach, things Rodney's father almost never did, not that he'd seen, anyway. Otis tried toward Rodney as well in his own way, the kind of sad gestures that the mother's new man will do, things that hinted of friendship: asking for the names they might both know, trotting him around town in that loud car of his, to the grocery store, or on generic errands where Rodney waited in the car by himself while Otis disappeared into trailers or strip mall offices, or into the cab of an eighteen-wheeler parked at the truck stop just outside of Hope.

Rodney's mother stood in the doorway to his bedroom. She was wearing the bathrobe she'd always worn, even before, in the days when he curled up with her on the sofa when he was little. It was a powder blue thing, long to the floor, with little white butterflies stitched on the front. It was not velvet, but it had felt like it.

"Look at you. The little student."

Rodney lay under the low light of his desk lamp, in bed, an oversized book perched on his chest, something about Presidents. Hidden inside was an old *House of Mystery* issue, one he was rereading for the third or fourth time. A woman had just turned herself into a giant spider and was about to eat her unfortunate new husband. He closed the book.

"I was just going to bed," he said.

She closed the door behind her and went to him, taking a seat on the edge of the bed. "You need a haircut," she said, running her fingers over his head.

"Not yet."

"You're getting so big." Her eyes roamed his face, and over

that hair of his that she wouldn't leave alone. "Some days I feel like I don't even know you anymore."

He didn't know what to say to that. If she didn't know him, whose fault was that? He wasn't the one sneaking off someplace, staying out all night. He wasn't the one changing the game.

"Do you remember that lake we went to?" he asked. "Where I found the fishing lure?"

She looked at him as if he had drawn out something from one of his comics, some odd story that she couldn't begin to imagine, not in a million years. Her eyes searching his, her brow collapsed into layers under that short, chopped hair of hers. Moments like this, his mother was not his mother at all. She could be anyone, just another shopper in line, holding a basket of soup at CJ's Grocery. Maybe, when all was said and done, that's what she wanted—to start over.

"I'm sure I would if I thought for a while about it," she said finally. And then she kissed him on the forehead, told him she'd see him in the morning.

"Maybe he'll come back," he said, just as she was opening the door.

She stopped, looked back at him over her shoulder. "I don't think so."

He might, Rodney thought. Why was she so quick to say otherwise? "What if he does?" he said. "What happens if he just shows up and wants to move back in? What about Otis then?"

"That's a lot of *what ifs*. We could make a list of what ifs to last from here to next month. Sometimes, honey, a person has no choice but to just go on."

"You mean give up."

She pushed her lips together, that brow of hers folding again. "Don't confuse acceptance with giving up." And with that, she gave him a feeble smile, clicked off the light and slipped out of his room.

Rodney broke from a heavy sleep with a sudden jolt. In that moment it seemed as if there had been a kind of sharp push from below, and he sat up quick and felt down into his covers, starting at his waist and moving to his feet. There was nothing there. He slid from his bed and walked to his door, where he could see the light from the television washing out into the kitchen alcove. He crept out into the hallway, to the edge of the wall where he could see Otis sitting on the sofa watching something on the television, his arms stretched over his head in that way police will want you to do before they snap a handcuff on your wrist. He stayed like this for some time, the television flickering blue and gray in the darkened living room, the rolling credits of the late movie just starting up. Rodney couldn't make out what it was. The numbers on the clock radio read 11:39.

Otis leaned forward to get up, and Rodney shuffled back to his room, to the safety of his bed. Through the open door he watched Otis lumber to the bedroom that he and Rodney's mother now shared equally, and he stood next to the door, his head dipped toward the floor. She had turned in long before; the line along the bottom of the door had gone to dark a good hour or so earlier. Otis touched the wood with the palm of his hand, then he backed away and went into the kitchen, and Rodney caught the flash of a lighter, the roll of cigarette smoke tumbling into the hall.

The floorboards in that house creaked no matter where you walked, but there was something about the darkness that amplified everything. Otis moved on past Rose's room to stop at

Rodney's door, and he pushed it open all the way. A runway of light from the hall lamp widened onto the bed.

Rodney remained quiet and still with eyelids open to slivers. Otis continued to stare at him, at the bedspread that was pulled neatly up to Rodney's chin. The scene was a curious one, the way Otis held onto that door and leaned into the room, his head drifting from side to side like a drunk man.

"Hey," he said.

"Hey what?" Rodney screwed his face and looked up into the glare, cupping a hand over his eyes. He stretched under his blankets, putting on the show of having been pulled from a deep sleep.

"I seen you the other day," he said. "At Val's." When Rodney didn't say anything he added, "I bet you thought you were hiding pretty good. Casper the ghost."

"I wasn't hiding."

He laughed softly and looked back over his shoulder, toward Rodney's parents' bedroom. "I imagine your feed store money don't last long in a place like that," he said.

"No."

"Well get dressed, then," Otis said. "I got a job for you."

Rodney sat up on his elbow. "Yeah, right."

"God damn it, I'm not screwing with you, kid." Otis kept his voice low, and closed the door a sliver more. "Use the back door and meet me at the car. And don't wake up your mom."

By the time Rodney got out to the Bonneville, Otis was already in the driver's seat, drumming his fingers on the steering wheel and staring at the back door to the house. He waited until Rodney was in his seat before starting up the engine. The air blasted stale and humid from the dashboard, blooming a haze of fog over the windshield. Otis pulled from the curb and drove on down the road anyway, hunching over the wheel and wiping clean a space in front of him as he drove, before finally opening up the accelerator and pushing on down Smith Street. It was late, and there were no lights on in any houses, not a single one.

It was a good distance before the windshield finally started to clear up, and in that time neither of them spoke—not even when Otis raced a yellow and missed it by a mile. Rodney sat with his head against the window, not looking at him. They were about a mile and a half off the highway, onto Airport Road, when he finally turned to him.

"Otis," he said. "What are we doing?"

Otis sighed, and ran his fingers through his mop hair, like this whole thing was an inconvenience for him, exclusively. "There's this guy," he said. "He took out a loan from somebody and he ain't paid up. I'm just bringing in the collateral."

Rodney did not know what collateral was, but he understood plenty about unpaid loans and the bad things that could come with that.

"Who does he owe money to?"

"None of your business, that's who," he said, short and hard.

It was after midnight on a July Wednesday, and they were coasting up to a closed, fenced-off storage yard, when Otis suddenly turned off the headlamps. He hit the brakes just before the chain link, shut down the engine and turned to Rodney.

"I want you to just sit here in the car," he said, his voice pushed down to barely a whisper. "Keep your eye on that road behind you. If you see any headlights coming down, you give a little tap on the horn." He sniffed, and wiped his wrist over his nose. "Notice I said *tap*. Don't lay on it."

Otis took a pair of bolt cutters from the back seat and went on over to the chain-link fence and scaled it like it was nothing, dropping to the ground on the opposite side and breaking into a jog, over to the long row of paneled doors closest. He moved quick, quicker than one would have imagined he could, letting the flashlight sweep over the storage containers from one side to the other before disappearing around the corner.

Rodney sat there dumb and did exactly as he was told, shifting himself to see out the rearview. He kept his eyes squarely on that mirror, making sure not to fiddle with anything inside the car, to give Otis any reason to accuse him of messing with his stuff, one tic away from leaning on that horn each time he saw or heard even a hint of movement or noise. The distant yap of a dog. The rush of a passing semi-truck, somewhere on the other side of the trees, near the highway. The blur of Otis drifting in and out of view, among the shadows of the storage huts. And after what seemed like hours he finally showed up at the fence, an armload of boxes and bags falling all around him. A long, leather sheath, one of those Japanese swords with straps and carvings up and down the handle, was strapped to his side.

He waved Rodney out and climbed up that fence with one hand holding at the top and dropped what he could down to Rodney. The heavier things were tricky, and Rodney hovered near the fence with his hands upstretched like he was catching a baby from a burning building. There was a shoebox-sized wooden case, half-filled with gold and silver coins, and a collection of old magazines, mostly comic books kept in a bulging cardboard box, each magazine secured in its own plastic bag. A few of the thicker magazines had pictures of women on the front, almost completely naked, hands laced over breasts, legs raised just enough to cover what was sure to be on full display inside.

"Don't dig through it," Otis said. He climbed up and over

once more and landed hard next to Rodney. "Move it," he snapped, and kicked the box of magazines into Rodney's shins.

Otis kept to the side roads most of the way back, taking streets parallel to the highway when the route allowed for it. Rodney fingered through the magazines, stealing glances at Otis here and there.

"There's a lot of comics here," he said.

"People pay good money for the right ones. That's why they keep 'em in plastic." He looked over at Rodney and grinned. "But I guess you know that."

"What do you mean?"

Otis echoed him, repeating the words in a droning, nasal tone. Mocking. "I been in your room," he said. "I've seen your little collection of books."

There was what felt like a knife in Rodney's gut then, a sense of sharp sickness at the whole thing. That Otis had been in his bedroom, when Rodney hadn't been home to see it. His dirty hands digging through dresser drawers and the shelves of his closet, and in boxes he'd closed up and stacked away long ago. He wanted to throw up. He wanted to smash something against Otis's face, and tell him what nasty scum he was and then—he didn't know what.

"That's my room," he said, his throat clenched like it was choked. "It's my stuff."

"Relax," Otis said, swiping his hand over Rodney's hair. "You're hiding a hell of a lot less than I did when I was your age." He nodded to the box. "Check 'em out."

Rodney shook his head, sliding his hands under his legs. Otis just laughed at him then and slid a comic book out of the box, tossing it into Rodney's lap. Reluctantly, Rodney picked it up. It was an issue of *Soldier Comics*, brown-helmeted men crouched under a stream of warplanes overhead, explosions lighting up the distance.

"It's old," he said. "Pretty rare I think."

"Oh shit. Probably the most expensive one in there, then," Otis said. "Put it back."

They drove the rest of the way without talking much more, or at least not about what they'd just done. Otis said that it felt like they were due for rain anytime now, and Rodney mentioned plans with some friends that he thought he had in the morning, though there were neither plans nor friends. What happened at the storage yard or the things that sat between them on the bench seat remained unspoken, at least until they were almost to Garden Street.

"I don't like doing this, Otis," Rodney finally said. His voice measured a tremor, as if they were driving over gravel, and it bothered him that Otis might think he was scared at that moment.

"You're not doing a whole hell of a lot, kid. Riding along."

Rodney shook his head. "It feels like I did something wrong. Something I could get in trouble for."

"Shit. You don't know what you don't know."

Rodney looked over at him, at the downturned grin and the dark eyes that bore straight ahead, through the collage of spattered insects.

"You're just a dumbass kid," Otis said. He chewed on his lip and looked to Rodney, a throwaway glance. "Helping me with something that had to be done. As long as you keep your mouth shut about it, nobody will know a damned thing."

He turned down Smith then and hit the lights, taking the last two blocks with only the streetlamps to guide. Right at the end, just before reaching their house, he killed the engine and let the tires scrape up against the curb. Leaning to one side, he pushed the box of magazines into Rodney's thigh. "Take a few," he said. "Your choice." When Rodney did not move, Otis reached in and pulled a half-dozen out, a thick, glossy one among them. "There's probably fifty bucks here, maybe more." Still, Rodney remained where he was, gazing over the prize in Otis's hand. "Take 'em, god damn it," he said, dropping the batch in Rodney's lap. "It's an investment. Payment for your help."

Rodney reached down and fingered the plastic spines, one by one. There was money in there. He knew it, probably better than Otis did. More than fifty bucks for sure.

"Leave 'em in those sleeves," Otis said.

"I know that."

"And by the time you're my age they'll be worth a fortune."

Rodney knew this too, but still—he didn't answer. He wanted the silence, to make Otis simmer maybe. If he wanted Rodney to get pulled into his mess, he was going to have to wait for it.

Otis finally said, "Jesus Christ," and he pulled his wallet from his pocket and drew out a twenty and tossed it onto Rodney's lap. "There," he said. "Do we have a deal now?

Rodney took the bill and nodded.

Otis added, "Be best if you went in the same way you came out. If your mom asks, tell her I needed a hand pulling a buddy's car out of the ditch."

"What's his name?"

"Who?" Otis screwed his face at Rodney.

"The guy. She'll probably ask."

"Jesus, I don't know." He rubbed his chin and stared out the window, a little curl growing at the edge of his mouth. He peered at Rodney, as if the two of them were playing some kind of game.

"Lester Fanning," he said. He clapped his hands together. "If she asks, you tell her this crazy old sonofabitch Lester went and drove his Studebaker straight into the ditch."

"Lester."

Otis began to laugh then, a wheezing, sickly sound that caught up in his throat. "Tell her he was crying when we got there," he coughed. "Like a little baby."

Rodney wanted to say that he didn't want any more details, that he already knew he would never remember the name of the guy or his truck. But he nodded at Otis anyway and left him in the driveway there, slipping in through the back door and into his room, closing the door behind him to let the room fall into near complete darkness. He slid the magazines under his top mattress, all the filth of anticipation and hunger, and yearning, over the wonders that surely lay in those pages. He fished his flashlight from his desk drawer and sat on the bed. Pulling the twenty from his pocket he dropped it into his lap like a soiled bandage, and with it the smell of Otis filled room, the sourness of his sweat and stale cigarettes and sweet cologne. Outside in the hallway the old floorboards groaned, and with a snap the stripe of light beneath his door disappeared.

PART TWO

Stevens County, Washington State
1976

"April is the cruelest month, breeding
lilacs out of the dead land, mixing
memory and desire, stirring
dull roots with spring rain."

—TS Eliot, *The Waste Land*

9

Nadine LaSalle kept herself a few paces behind her man as she walked with him from the front porch down the slope to the old well. He didn't push her to hustle up or anything like that, the ground being so uneven and steep, and peppered with baseball-sized rocks half-buried in the dirt. She carried the week's trash in a paper bag clutched to her chest while, just ahead of her, the tin bucket knocked against his leg as he lumbered along, a black storm of flies swirling around the glistening slop inside.

"I don't see why we can't use the fur," she said.

"We ain't using the fur."

"Seems like a waste to me." Her voice came in punches from the unsteady path. "We ought to be using the fur."

"I don't need the hassle," he said. "Tanning's a pain in the ass."

There were four rabbits in the bucket, four minus the meat and bones which were presently simmering on the stovetop in a pot of broth over a low pine wood fire. She could learn to tan hide if she had a book to show her how, or if there was someone who could walk her through it once. She had learned to do a lot since she met Lester Fanning. Since the day he spotted her outstretched thumb and pulled over, inviting her into the warmth of his old Ford's cab.

"It's complicated," she'd said to him then.

"I hate complicated," he said back to her. "What do you think of 'simple'?"

"I'd say 'simple' sounds like a nice, juicy slice of heaven."

Three hundred miles and a thousand acres of forest later, and here's where she was.

They came down the last part of the ridge to where the black hole of the old well looked up at them from its spot in the midst of young alders. She stopped at the triangle rock like always, tossing the bag in a high arc so that it dropped easily into the mouth. Lester walked right up to the edge and stared down. He looked back over his shoulder at Nadine and winked.

"Make a wish, baby."

"I want an electric stove," she said. "And a dryer."

He tipped the bucket upside-down and the stew of innards and matted fur, red on mottled gray, fell silently into the hole. "You ain't supposed to say it out loud," he said. "Now it won't come true."

Lester turned and walked past her back up the hill to the house. To the house with its wood-fired stove and tin can candles, and the wringer washer, a house that might have been modern fifty years earlier. A tiny hut that you had to go out the back door and walk through a gauntlet of dusty old cars with rims sunk into the dirt, all under a hundred feet of low-hanging ponderosa needles, just to take a take a piss. Thirty years old with everything either behind or ahead of her stinking like rot, Nadine had wanted simple. And with Lester Fanning, lucky or not, she got simple.

He powered ahead up the hill with the bucket swinging

like a crank, pushing him farther and farther away from her. The incline was tough on her legs. Nadine was not a petite woman, though she was slimmer now than she had been before all of this. Everything about her body was just as it should be, she decided. And anyway, Lester liked a woman with some extra meat on her. "It gets cold up there in the winter," he told her that day. The decision to go ahead with it had been sealed at the Hardy Pine Diner only a couple hours after he'd picked her up, somewhere between the short stack of pancakes and her fourth cup of coffee. "A little extra insulation will do us both good."

He was older than her by a good fifteen years, but his eyes held the surprise and eagerness of a boy, and it was that combination that stirred a mixture of comfort and excitement in her, like she could curl up in those blue pools and sleep for months. They kept her that way the entire time in the diner, as she poured the past decade of her life over the table between them, the men who had showed up and then run off or pushed her away with nasty habits or the hard revelation of a closed fist. She talked on and on, her hands clasped together and tucked between her knees, denim taut and strained. And somewhere in there, she couldn't remember when, he said, "I got no mercy for any man who dares to raise his hand to a woman." He reached across the table and she slid one hand from her lap and let him hold it in his. It warmed her like a velvet scarf, and when she found her voice catching he said, "I got a place a little out of the way that you could stay if you want. No expectations."

He was up on the porch by the time she soldiered up over the ridge. The sun was hovering over the tips of the hemlocks now, limp like the cowlicks of little boys' hair. She was sweating already but that was nothing new. It would only get hotter as the day went on, and the constancy of the woodstove would make it all that much more ridiculous. He had the Hills Brothers can on his lap, and he drew out dollar bills one at a time.

"I'm heading into town for a couple hours," he said, licking his thumb. His hair was not fit for town, swept back over his head like some fifties guitar player, oily and streaked yellow among shocks of gray. "Anything we need that I don't already know about?"

She wiped her arm across her forehead, slick. He'd fill up the gas cans for the generator; that was typical. They were well-stocked with chicken feed and toilet paper, and most all the usual amenities for the rest of the month.

"Nothing comes to mind," she said. "If there's a new *Enquirer* out I'd like that."

He laughed. "I got a shelf full of books in there and you won't crack a single one. You'd rather read that trash."

"I can't concentrate on a whole book," she said.

"That shit is empty calories, Nadine. You're better than that."

"Jesus Christ, Lester. It's cheap entertainment," she said. "We got no TV up here. The radio doesn't pick up but a half dozen stations and it's not like I've got some lonely housewife next door I can walk over and meet at the fence for lemonade."

He set down the can and walked down to her, where she stood at the base of the porch steps, and cupped his hand behind her neck, his palm callus-riddled, the scratch of fingernails bitten to serrated edges. Still, the touch was warm and forgiving.

"You've got me, baby," he said. "Ain't I entertaining enough?"

She reached up and held his wrist and he tightened his hold. Those blue eyes squinted against the sun, lines like hens' feet stretching from the edges.

"In your company, who could ever be bored?" she said. She leaned forward then, and he kissed her, his sandy face scratching at her lips, the smell of coffee and wood smoke almost, but not quite, erasing the tang of his hair.

Nadine went on into the house and then to the kitchen and lifted the lid from the simmering pot and stirred the contents around some. She picked up the black, round plate and tossed another chunk of alder into the firebox. It was already hot as hell in that kitchen. She went to the window and propped it open with a stick of kindling and undid the buttons of her shirt to let the halfhearted breeze find her damp skin.

In the ten-plus months she had been with Lester, Nadine had grown to love the roundness of her own hips, and the way her breasts pushed against her arms when she leaned over to lace her boots or worked her hands through a mound of dough on the flour-dusted countertop. She no longer gave a minute's notice to the texture and fullness of her hair but appreciated the ease with which the whole chestnut mane could be tied back in a rubber band and forgotten, her skin like a baby's, free of the greasy cosmetics she had spent so much time trying to apply just so, all in accordance with other people's expectations. Here in the hills she didn't even have to look into that little round shaving mirror if she didn't want to, clouded and scratched as it was, not even for the occasional guest who happened by. She knew nearly every trail and grove and meadow on the hundred or so acres around them, and while she longed for some of the conveniences she had always taken for granted, there was a security in not worrying about when the next thing would give out, or catch on fire. Or leave her hurting.

Outside under the big cottonwood, Lester was mucking around at the back of his Buick, the trunk lid standing straight up like a topsail. Boxes moved from his arms to the open space, sliding back and out of sight. They were the things he dealt in, tools and connectors and circuits. Stuff she likely could have helped him with if she'd had the slightest inclination, and if Lester hadn't warned her in no uncertain terms to stay out of the shed for fear of her messing it all up and tossing the next month's income down the old well. Truth was, she was more than happy to oblige. What she didn't know about the shadows in Lester's life could keep her free.

He shut the lid and gave the car a bounce, then climbed in and fired it up, a plume of blue smoke farting out the backend. As he rolled off down the drive, Nadine undid the rest of her shirt and let it fall open. She took one of his beers from the icebox and went on out to the porch, sinking down in the rocker where she took a good swill from the bottle and scanned the edges of the forest for any rabbits that might have avoided the traps this time.

10

Louis Youngman stepped through the living room in bare feet, the floorboards creaking under him like a bear's growl, so much louder in the dim light of dawn than at any other time of day. There was a racket still lingering in his jaws and teeth, as if he'd been pummeled about the face in his sleep. He ran a finger through this mouth, half expecting to find it covered in blood when he brought it out.

The grind of his brother's snoring seeped in from the opposite wall, rhythmic and intrusive. He did not want to share this time with Vinnie. There was so little of it for himself anymore, these moments of quiet solitude. Outside in the driveway, the streetlights washed his cruiser in a gentle coat of ashy blue. The sky was only now beginning to break. A single pickup truck passed by with barely a hum.

On the ridge of the sofa was his uniform, exactly where he'd laid it the night before, the star barely winking where the five-thirty sun caught hold of the tines. There were wrinkles in that shirt that he ought to have ironed out, but then wrinkles and creases, and dust, seemed to be the way of Louis's world. Some days, he felt like it was all he could do to swing those stubborn legs of his out of bed and walk across that cold oak floor to see what the previous night had left for him.

"Lou." Vinnie's voice, dropping like a dead branch.

Louis froze, his bare feet still waking up. Tiny needles. "Go back to sleep," he called out. He went on by his brother's bedroom, then past the dining room table that hadn't been used for anything other than bills and paperwork in years, and the framed photos he hardly noticed anymore. There were, instead, the scattering of handwritten signs taped up as constant guideposts for Vinnie—directions to close the door and stay inside, to leave the plugs and outlets alone. Phone numbers to call and reminders that no one other than Delores Jackson was allowed inside the house while Louis was gone.

The bulb over the mirror was lousy and fluttered like a moth, but it cast enough light for Louis to shave without the risk of cutting an artery. He leaned in and opened his mouth wide, and ran his finger in there again, looking over his teeth. They were one of the few sturdy things in him left, he thought. And as he stood there, gaping like some trout left on the creek bed, the dream came back to him.

He had been drinking beers with Vinnie at a roadhouse, some place that probably existed in the world somewhere but nothing that sparked a memory for Louis in any real way. Vinnie had reached over to take the bottle from Louis's hand. "It's busted, Lou," he said, his walrus-mustache working over his lip. And sure enough, the thing was jagged halfway down the neck. Louis fished a finger into his mouth and began removing spires of glass, blood washing over his hand as he drew them out.

"That ain't a good look on you," Vinnie said to him.

"It sure isn't," Louis answered. He ran his tongue around the inside of his mouth, and the molars broke loose like pebbles from a mud bank. Vinnie's eyes gawked at him in horror, and it was then that Louis woke up, wrapped in an ache like he'd been socked in the jaw, his teeth ringing from back to front.

There were times when this happened more often than others, these dreams where, at some point, his mouth came apart in pieces. Dr. Syd told him it was all connected to his teeth, from the sleep grinding, and the unreasonable stress he wasn't bearing up well enough under.

"What the hell are you doing?"

Louis started, knocking his hip against the sink edge.

His brother stood there in the bathroom doorway, yellowed long johns sagging from stumpy hips, shock of white hair sticking out all over like a dandelion head.

"Jesus, Vinnie," he said. "You look like you just hatched out of an egg."

Vinnie squinted into the glare of the bare bulb, that divot in his forehead catching a smoky shadow. "I gotta pee," he said.

"That's fine." Louis backed up and let his brother past him. "I'm gonna head on into the station," he said. "Do my shower there."

Vinnie leaned over the bowl, the stream pungent and unsteady.

"Hit the bowl, Vin." The noise of water, finally.

"What time are you home?"

"It's next to the clock," Louis said. It was always there, on the yellow strip of paper he'd taped to the wall.

Vinnie did himself up and moved past Louis without so much as a flush, and made his way back to his bedroom. He was older than Louis by four years, but it had been a long time since Louis felt like a kid brother, since Vinnie's mind started to get lazy. He stopped in the doorway and waited for Vinnie to find his place under the blanket.

"Be nice to Delores," he said. "They won't be sending any-one else out."

"Don't they have somebody white down there they can send?"

Louis picked at the paint on the molding. "Don't say that, Vinnie. That's ugly. Be lucky they have anyone at all who's will-ing." He looked over at his uniform draped over there like it was his own body that lay over the back of the sofa, flat, empty, and lifeless. "Delores Jackson is a good woman."

Vinnie snorted and rolled over onto his side. "She's a pain in the ass."

Louis set his jaw, and the electricity reached from his teeth into his eyes. "You're a pain in the ass," he said. And then he closed Vinnie's door harder than necessary, and went to find his shoes, in the hopes that he might get himself to the station before the rest of Stevens County was awake.

11

It was on a winter afternoon that seemed like a million years ago, Nadine making the long walk home from school, her friend Connie in tow. The two of them were playing at smoking like they often did, using pussy willow twigs and the gray clouds of their breath in the chilly air. Sophisticated city women, they pretended to be, strolling between the shops. They were both thirteen. It was already getting dark.

They separated at the corner of Seventh and Spring Street, Nadine going on into her house, where her mother sat alone in the living room with the heavy orange curtains all pulled shut. There was not a single light on in the entire place.

Nadine asked, "Is the TV broke?"

"I come from the doctor," her mother said.

"'Cause of your coughing," Nadine remembered.

"Yeah, well it's bad." She said it as if she were talking about someone else, like a soap opera character. "It's all over in there. There ain't nothing they can do." Then she lit a cigarette and got up from the sofa and stood there for a good minute or so, staring at the television that was not on.

It was bad, in the end anyway. Though she acted like her

time would be up tomorrow, Nadine's mother went on like that for another eight years before the cancer finally took her. And while anyone else might think that extra time was a blessing, for Nadine it was eight years of waiting and worry, and countless mother-daughter fights that always ended with warnings of regret and guilt, of just how sorry Nadine would be once it was all over. And the funny thing was, by the time it really did happen, Nadine had nothing left to regret. There would come a time when she determined it would all have been a hell of a lot easier if she'd been able to walk through those eight years half-blind, that the gift of not knowing what waited for them all would have been too precious to give up.

Nadine had gotten accustomed to Lester's treasure trips, the two or three times a month when he'd disappear for a few hours without much explanation, returning home, sometimes after dark, with a car load of all kinds of crap that he'd picked up someplace for twenty bucks or so. He'd move it all into the shed, usually in the low light of the car's headlamps, with barely a word to Nadine about it all other than the great deal he'd made. Now and then it'd be just a single bag, or yellow envelope, and a quiet transfer behind lock and key, no questions taken because, as far as Lester was concerned, his work was his business. If she didn't need to be told, and there wasn't a great deal she could do about it anyway, Nadine was content living in ignorance.

Typically, she'd wait up for him, curled up with an afghan blanket next to the kerosene lamp, a magazine or a crossword to keep her busy until he came in. On this particular night, though, she was feeling none of it. He'd left hours earlier with the promise of being home by dinner, and she'd cooked up a good pot of stew that now sat cold and untouched in the icebox. She shut down the generator and went to bed. He'd lumber in sometime later, she decided, smelling of beer or gasoline, or both. She'd steel her temper and rub his back, so that he would quit yammering about all the people he'd spent his hours with that she didn't know, and he'd finally fall asleep.

So, when the phone rang and pulled her from sleep, her first instinct was that something bad had happened, because the man never called to tell her he was running late. He was calling from jail, she figured, or maybe it was county hospital trying to track down his next of kin.

"Nadine."

"Lester," she said, "what the hell is going on?"

"You wouldn't believe it," he said. "Hell of a thing." He was stranded in the middle of nowhere by a drained gas tank, and, according to him, he had walked a good half-dozen miles or so to the nearest phone, all wearing his old cowboy boots that were good for everything but walking. Right now, he was sitting in a noisy little bar somewhere off Highway 62. "I'm probably halfway to Kettle Falls," he said.

"Oh Jesus. What time is it?"

"Ten past midnight." He let her groan and stretch and get her head clear, then told her to get out of bed and to take the gas can from the garage. "Take the GMC," he said. "The keys are in the visor."

She didn't know this roadside bar but she knew the highways and most of the road names he rattled off to her. "I'll get there when I get there," she said, and then she hung up the phone and took her time getting dressed, washing her face in the basin and grabbing a handful of Saltines before she made her way out to what Lester liked to call the "garage," really more of a ramshackle firetrap than anything else. It had plank walls and a leaky roof, and a pair of crooked doors that could be closed and latched, and apparently that was all good enough for Lester to pile a bunch of shit inside and give the thing a name.

When Nadine got herself in the driver's side of the bench seat and dropped the keys into her hand, she expected the truck would not start, and she was right. The cranky ignition, the lazy strain of the starter grinding to a mere click. She pulled out the headlamp knob only to see the dullest of yellow illuminate the low grass in front of her.

There was no time to deal with the generator, and the long wait of a battery charge—though it was true that she fought with every nerve in her body the pressure to hurry for him. He had not given her the courtesy of an explanation, or even a clue, of where he was going or what he was up to. He'd simply announced that he'd be gone for a few hours and that was it. Now here it was, six hours later. And there he was, sitting in a rowdy tavern in God-knows-where, probably three drinks in before he even bothered to pick up the phone to call her.

If there was a grain of forgiveness inside of her, it was in the pure fact that he'd had the foresight to leave the pickup with its frontend facing the drive. She popped the tranny into neutral and positioned herself behind the open door and gave it a good, firm shove. The old truck rolled itself gamely. Nadine leaned into it, digging in hard and the thing moved slowly forward, and the ground changed under her feet as she went, the pickup pitching and dipping and rocking with the downward terrain. When she knew she'd gotten to the clearing at the top of the drive, she jumped on up to the seat.

She could barely see the path in front of her, and she knew it would stay that way until she could get the engine going to feed the headlamps. The big camping flashlight she held outside the window gave just enough to let her make out the slight, gentle turns on the way down.

She pulled off the clutch and there was the jolt of the gears catching hold, and a sad cough as the truck seized, refusing to kick in. Nadine cursed at the decrepit thing, giving it a few more feet before trying again. A couple more attempts and the engine finally growled to resurrection. "There's the baby," she said, patting a hand on the dash like it was a pet, continuing to two-pedal it all the way down, gunning the engine with her right and holding down the clutch with her left to coast until she got to the bottom.

Turning out onto the highway, she opened up the throttle and followed the roadway north all the way to Mead, then broke off due east in the direction of Kettle Falls. There were a few forks and turnoffs along the way, through a terrain of scrub and rock so endless it may as well have been Mars. The needle on the fuel gauge jittered between a quarter tank and empty with every rut and divot she rolled over, and right about the time she thought she'd earned the right to give it all up she caught the blue haze of an all-night gas station, just over the next ridge.

It made no sense that it should be there, this dirty, stucco-smeared box out in the middle of nowhere. A pair of sickly-looking pine trees towered at either end of the place, their tops hunched over in sleep or near death. At the far corner of the station, a lone yellow car sat, with a crumpled fender and a plastic-covered rear window. Not wanting to risk the need for a jump out here, Nadine popped the truck into neutral and set the brake, left the engine running, and went inside.

The attendant was an old scarecrow-looking coot, slouched

next to a filter-stuffed ashtray, *Zane Grey* paperback unfolded in front of him. Lord, she knew those books—from her father, from the worn collection on Lester's shelves. Never had she been interested enough to even crack one.

"I feel lucky to see you," she said to him.

He rolled his eyes up at her, nodded, and said it was a sentiment that he got quite a lot this time of night. And when she asked him how far she was from the Hitching Post Tavern, he said, "If you're dead set on going there, just take this road another four miles or so till you see the old burned-out church. Hook a right and you'll be there before you know it."

It was just after two when she pulled into a gravel parking lot outside a sorry-looking dive, a cracker box barely holding itself up under a sagging shake roof. All sorts of clutter hung from the eaves and clapboard siding, the kind of thing someone might do to dress up a dying place to try and make it all look intentional— horse bridles and a few pitchforks, some coiled rope and a scatter of horseshoes. Draped over the front door: a big old saddle.

The lot was mostly empty, and all the neon was dark, with the exception of a single Busch sign that vibrated in the window. Nadine reached down and grabbed the tire iron from beneath the seat and carried it with her across the parking lot to the front door. Taking hold of the handle, she gave it a good pull, only to be met with a firmly set deadbolt.

"Lester!" Her voice was a firecracker and it went in all directions, unanswered. It was cold out here and she hadn't thought to bring her coat from the truck, and as she circled the shingled building and bounced the tire iron against her leg she listened for any kind of sound. It was dead quiet, no Buick and certainly no

Lester to be seen.

"You all right?"

Nadine did an about face, the iron swung out from her side and clenched tight in her fist. A woman stood with her back against the front door, a jacket tumbling from her folded arms like a plaid waterfall. The blue of the Busch sign cast half the woman's face in a ghostly veil, and it looked like she was an older gal. She pushed herself off the door and walked toward Nadine like she knew her.

"I'm guessing you're Nadine," she said. She undid her arms and let the jacket hang down at her side.

"What do you know?"

"I know I heard your name so many times tonight I'm probably gonna start calling my dog after you when I get home." She met Nadine under the hum of the security light, and her face was clear as water now. The hard, soap-scrubbed skin, dry and weathered, silver hair strands drifting like spider silk.

"You missed him by about an hour," the woman said. "My guess is by now he's passed out on a jail cell cot downtown."

Nadine snapped, "Goddamn it," and the woman said, "I'm sorry, hon. I've been there a time or two and it ain't fun."

He had been on the cocky side of things from the moment he came in, apparently. "The beer just turned up the volume," the woman said. "By the time the cops showed up he'd busted three of my glasses and nearly got his ass handed to him by more than a few yahoos in there." She unfolded her jacket and slid her arms inside the sleeves. "Plus, my bartender's a welterweight with a few trophies on his shelf, so I can tell you your fella probably got mighty lucky tonight."

"He's not my fella," Nadine suddenly heard herself say. And it felt right, not a lie, really.

"Well, that's good," the woman said. "I hate to think of him sharing all that charm with someone like you."

Nadine got directions to the station, thanked the woman, and cranked up the engine and drove off down the highway, taking the first hard right and following the serpentine road toward the dull halo of light emanating from behind a band of trees.

The police station sat in an open lot next to a liquor store, both buildings boxy and rugged like they were cut from the same block of wood. She pulled into the asphalt lot and took the spot farthest from the entrance. The long walk to the glass doors was as good on her legs as it was hard on her feet. A sign that read, "Closed except for emergencies," was posted right above a red, plastic button. Nadine considered the button for a moment, then decided that Lester being in the jug, however inconvenient, likely did not qualify as an emergency.

She woke up in a sweat, the air thick and sweltering as the sun blanketed the inside of the cab through the windows. It was almost nine. How she had managed to sleep that long and hard on a knobby bench seat, springs poking through here and there, Nadine had not a clue. She sat up and took time to untangle herself, to loosen up her joints and take in the fresh air of the new morning before going on in to finally see what misery Lester had gotten himself into.

When she walked into the station the woman behind the counter barely looked up at her. She was one of those country girls desperate to be mistaken for a townie, fingernails shined up red like a sports car, hair done up in one of those tight-curled, ratted things. She was planted behind a high counter with the desk cutting her off from the world like she was running a bank in one of those old west towns. Behind her was a few square wooden desks, dark and glossy and tidy with stacks of paper and coffee cups with pencils poking out. Each desk had its own black telephone, the cords curling across the floor like snakes. On the far wall was a wide corkboard, layered with photographs and newspaper clippings, the faces of people in their worst moments looming in the distance, looking back at her.

"You coming in from the pickup truck out there?" Her uniform was like cardboard over her chest, no shape to speak of.

"Yes, ma'am."

"Let me guess." She reached to one side and dug a manila folder from beneath a stack of paper. "Prince Charming."

Okay, that hurt. In any other life Nadine would have turned and walked right out, said she'd meant to be at the dog pound and just got confused. "If it's the last name of Fanning, I'd say yes," she said. "Is there bail to arrange?"

The woman opened the file and rushed a sigh, too early in the day to already be exhausted. She was making this hard. "No," she said. "If you'll claim him and take him, you can have him."

Nadine wanted to know what he had done to land himself in the can, and the woman just said he was *belligerent*. "Belligerent to the point that he very nearly got his head handed to him on a pole. If it hadn't been for that waitress calling us in you might have been standing down there at the morgue instead of here."

They came out through a side door that Nadine hadn't noticed, a sturdy metal thing that groaned when they pushed through it. Lester shuffled alongside a uniformed escort, a handsome youngster who looked like he could have just stepped out of the hallways of the local high school. For his part, Lester looked like he might have just missed the coffin. His shirt collar was torn so it barely clung to his neck, and his left eye was swollen nearly shut.

"It's about damned time," he said. "Did you get lost on your way?"

"Don't you start with me," she said. "How about the next time you decide to get your ass thrown in the jug, you make sure the goddamn truck battery is charged?" She looked at the woman, who stared down at her hands, the edges of a grin barely suppressed. "And while you're at it, you might want to keep a little gas in the damned tank. You're lucky I'm here at all."

"Yeah," he said. "I'm the luckiest son of a bitch in the whole goddamned world, ain't I?"

They drove the entire distance from the jail to Lester's car with barely a word between them, save for Lester's demands of where to turn, and when. By the time they reached the turnout some miles from the tavern, the sun was a good distance over the hills and Nadine had rolled her window down to cool things some, and take up some of the quiet. The rear end of the Buick stuck out from behind a tree trunk.

"Pull up here," he said, reaching behind the seat and taking out a milk jug funnel.

"You want help?" she asked.

"No, I don't want help." Lester climbed out of the pickup and flung the door shut behind him. He only got a couple steps before he stopped, turned around and leaned back in the window. "Look, baby," he said, "I know you could of just hung up that phone and went on back to sleep." His eyes were welled up now, and his lip vibrated like he might cry at any second. Like he was barely out of his trainers.

"Lester," she said.

"It's just been a real shitty night."

"I know."

"Plus, I got a million things still left to do, I can't even—" He drummed his fingers on the door. "You go on home and I'll see you when I see you."

He closed the door and went to the bed and pulled out the gas can, and he looked to her only once over his shoulder as he dragged his feet over the dust toward the car. Then he disappeared behind the ash tree to where she could no longer see him.

12

Louis Youngman laid his Stetson on the counter beside him and scratched out a few more details in his report. The duty nurse had given him the only spare room, two little chairs and a low, papered cot. He leaned against the wall and wrote against his arm while the couple simmered in their seats. Next door, the racket from their son had finally quieted down.

The boy's father had thought it would be fun to have fireworks for his birthday.

"I tried to tell him," the mother said before turning to her husband. "I tried to tell you, Ronny. A six-year-old's party is loud enough without throwing explosions into the mix. And anyways where in God's name did you think you'd find safe fireworks in the middle of April?"

"At the rez," the father said between sips of his coffee. "They sell 'em year-round out there. You know they do that, right, Sheriff?"

Louis said, "Yes I know that."

They sat in that little room, the three of them surrounded by framed cartoon illustrations of people's innards, while the doctor finished up with the boy next door. The youngster, he'd reassured the parents, would retain almost all of what he'd started the day with.

"He's six," the mother said, wiping at her face with her sleeve. She was a petite thing, probably barely a hundred pounds after a casino buffet. "You should of seen how he held up the number the second he woke up this morning—five fingers on one hand, one on the other," she cried. "The sixth one is the most important, you know. It's the pointer," she sniffed. "The steeple."

"Things were fine," the father said, his eyes pooling and red. There was alcohol on his breath, though he was lucid and fairly articulate. "We had a piñata. About ten people showed up, only three of 'em with presents. Things kind of went south from there."

"Soon as that damn lighter came out of your pocket," the woman said.

Louis tapped his notepad against his knee and closed the cover. It was an unfortunate situation, but there was nothing more he needed to do here. He'd put a call into child protective, maybe write a citation for the illegal fireworks. The finger was punishment enough, and both parents seemed plenty broken up about the whole thing. There was no need to break up the family over it.

"Are there any more explosives?"

"God no," the woman said, shaking her head so hard her body rocked from side to side. "I threw every last one of 'em out the window on the way here." She pulled back then, as if she'd just thrown herself into a citation for littering.

The father gave a bit of a laugh, a short cough that he grabbed hold of almost too late. "I guess I didn't notice that before," he said, motioning to Louis's name tag.

Louis snapped the plastic tag with this finger. He'd heard it more times lately than seemed possible.

"Youngman," the man went on. "Old guy with the last name of Youngman. That's pretty damned funny."

"Oh Ronny, Jesus Christ," the woman said. "I'm sorry, Sheriff. Some days I swear he gets out of bed and just leaves his brain there on the pillow."

Louis eased himself back into his cruiser and laid the Stetson beside him on the passenger seat. He drew his seatbelt over his chest and readjusted the side mirror before pulling out onto the highway, steering himself back in the direction of Colville. He went on past acres upon acres of ribbed, parched dirt, the dust having found its way over the road surface in occasional red patches. Up ahead, the white-paneled barns of the old Grauman farm continued to molt out there in the open fields, the gleaming lone silo catching the sun against a cloudless sky, blue as a robin's egg. Everything from here to the Canadian border was kindling dry and itching to go up with the slightest spark. There was no business having fireworks out there, a kid's finger only one of many good arguments against it.

Right around the point at which Blue Creek Road branched off from the 395, his radio crackled awake.

"Sheriff?" It was Holly. "You out there?"

He picked up the handset and held it to his face. He pressed it close and spoke quietly, as if, even in the emptiness of his car, someone else might hear him.

"I'm here," he said. "What's the situation?"

"The situation at the moment, I hate to tell you, is Vinnie," she said. She cleared her throat into the radio. "I'm sorry to complicate your day."

Louis loosened the seatbelt against his stomach. *Jesus,* he said to himself. He'd rather deal with a kid missing his whole hand than have to grapple with anything related to his brother. His patience for this nonsense had run out long ago. Lately, it seemed, he was barely subsisting on fumes.

"You there, Sheriff?"

"I'm here."

"Honey, I know this is the last thing you need, but we've got him down here at the station. Back in holding."

Louis looked up ahead at the roadway as it bent from the pine-riddled hill. The grayed, split rail fencing stretched away from him in dips and rises beneath a lone telephone line that seemed to go on forever.

"What now?"

"Shoplifting," she said. "There's a couple folks who left call-back numbers for you." She went silent for a moment, and Louis pulled off the highway and steered the car into a U-turn, pausing to let a big horse trailer pass by before punching the gas. A white cloud of dust spun behind him as he directed himself back toward Boone.

When they brought him out and sat him in the chair opposite Louis, Vinnie would not look his brother in the eye. His hair was a windswept snowdrift, and a wine-colored crescent lay stamped over his dark forehead like a brand. He kept his head down, his whiskered chin almost disappearing into his shirt collar, the skin hanging beneath his eyes like teabags. He inspected his newly-returned wallet, fingering with chalky nails through the photos and plastic cards and crumpled dollar bills.

"I had a twenty in here." he said to no one in particular.

"Vinnie."

"Where's my goddamned twenty?"

Louis said nothing, sliding forward instead to the edge of his chair.

Vinnie shook his head and stuffed the wallet into his front pocket. He scanned the perimeter of the room, pausing here and there as if he were making a note of each item: the black-and-white wall clock; the bulletin board, layered with yellowed papers; the overhead fluorescent, vibrating like a hive of honeybees. When he had made the entire journey, he gave a slight nod of satisfaction, and only then did he let his eyes rest on his brother.

"Here you are," he said in a near whisper. He moved his wallet from his front to his back pocket and got up from his chair, turning to the front door. "Sure as shit took long enough."

Louis steered his cruiser through town, taking the side streets that formed the grid outside the courthouse square rather than the main arterials. Passing through the neighborhoods had a way of refocusing him, of providing a kind of "reset" when he needed one. Simple, yet determined, the houses on these streets were siblings of the houses on his own street, which were the houses you could find anywhere, in whatever dried-up place you happened to land in Eastern Washington, on the sunrise side of the mountains, be it Boone or Springdale or Ford or any other farm-grown town. Cockeyed chimneys, sagging porches and over-grown lawns, and garages with side-mounted wood doors that never quite shut all the way. No different, and that made Louis feel both relieved and exhausted at once.

"Are you going to tell me what you did this time?" he asked. He gripped the wheel from below, just as their father had done.

"How you got that cut on your head?"

Vinnie put a hand to his temple. He looked out the side window and shrugged his shoulders. "Like you don't already know," he groused. "Want to make me say it like I'm some little kid."

Louis had spoken to Hal Donagan, the store manager, who did not have a great deal to add about the whole thing.

"You're acting like a little kid," he said to his brother. "Impulsive. Stupid."

"To hell with you." Vinnie opened up the glove compartment and began rifling through the stacks of service envelopes and road maps, digging his bony fingers into the recesses.

"What are you looking for?"

"I don't know."

Louis jammed his thumb against the cigarette lighter for no reason other than to give himself something to punch that wasn't attached to his older brother. He was through the letter streets now and was just coming out onto McMahon Street.

Vinnie shut the compartment door and began calling out the makes and models of the cars passing by. "There's a Desoto," he said, pointing a knuckled finger across the dashboard. "I had one of those. Used to pile all the kids in the back of it and drive up to Glacier Lake for the weekend. Remember? Weighed that thing down so much the engine was practically on fire by the time we got there."

Louis tried to recall this. The Desoto, the lake. Vinnie's wife and kids, and the days before Lucy finally packed up the girls and left for good. It was all so muddy and distant. "Who cuffed you upside the head, Vin?" he asked, nodding his chin at his brother. "Was it the security guard? At the Safeway?"

Vinnie rubbed his finger over the swelling bruise.

"Did someone in the jail clock you?"

His brother said nothing.

"If they did, I need to know. We can't be having that kind of thing going on."

"No," Vinnie finally snapped. "None of that."

They turned off McMahon and wound through Cherry Grove, the neighborhood of stucco bungalows and hard-packed, powdery yards with empty swingsets, and half-filled soccer balls littering the edges of curbs. A rust-stained pickup truck crowded the driveway of a corner house, its hood raised, an overall-clad fellow hunched over the grill and almost swallowed by the engine compartment.

"You made me look like a damned fool back there, Vin," he said, "Again, I might add."

"I'm the one who got knocked on his ass."

Lou felt a blooming warmth under his shirt. He cracked the window some, and let the outside spill in, to mix with all the nonsense that hovered in the space around them. "You don't get it, do you?"

Vinnie stiffened, his words barely pressing through clenched teeth. "I get it just fine."

"Do you?" And then Louis said, "So who the hell beat you up?"

"Nobody beat me up, for Christ's sake!" Vinnie said this as if he had wadded the words into his fist and thrown them across the dashboard. "I ran out of that store with a half dozen cashiers and box boys on my ass. Goddamned parking stalls all marked up for those little Jap cars, you couldn't get a real vehicle in there if you tried."

He glared at Louis as if he had been the one to cause it all to happen. The contraband. The chase scene through the parking lot. The skinny parking spaces.

"I cut between a couple rigs and ran head-on into the side mirror of a goddamned pickup truck." He shrugged and looked out the window, toward the rows of cherry trees that pushed back from the road's edge. "They'd of caught me anyhow," he said. "The mirror just made it easier."

Louis turned to get a gander at his brother, at this shiner of his that was suddenly more than just a worry, or a sad embarrassment. He bit down on his lip, holding the laugh fighting to push its way out. *Serves you right*, he thought. *Old sonofabitch.*

They traveled the last distance in silence, down the road as it veered gently to the north, and the Polk Street sign peeked out from a clump of overgrown rosebushes. Louis made a hard right, following the parched lawns and sun-beaten pickets to the clapboard rambler shaded by a big, weeping willow, three blocks in.

A little boy pedaled his bicycle on the sidewalk toward them, a boy Louis recognized from a family of Mexicans who'd moved in down the street a month or so earlier. White tassels swished from the bike's handlebars, a big shiny, pink basket right there in the front, coming straight at them. Vinnie tracked him as they drove by.

"That girl looks like a boy," he said.

"It is a boy."

"What's he doing on a girl's bike, then?" Vinnie wasn't laughing at him. He sounded sweetly concerned.

"It's probably the only one he's got," Louis said.

"Someone ought to get him a boy's bike."

Louis looked at his brother, at the ridiculous worry lines over his eyes. "What do you care, Vinnie? It's got wheels and a seat. He's a little kid, for Christ's sake."

Louis pulled on into the driveway and killed the engine. He

had originally chosen the bungalow on Polk Street so he could be under the streetlights; the lack of prying eyes up in the hills outside of town—for a man who could sometimes be a target for others—was fuel for insomnia. He'd lived alone by choice, the feeling of "shared space" never really allowing the sense of stability he craved. He'd tried this a couple times in his life. Sharing his life with another person. It only ever ended with a litany of regretful words and an ego scattered in pieces at his feet. With Vinnie, it was no different.

The two of them sat there for a bit, just staring at the paneled garage door in front of them. Bits of dried grass spilled out of the gutter like unkempt hair.

"What are we doing?" Vinnie finally said. "Ain't you taking me back to the center?"

"What center?"

"Cedar Glen. The center."

"Vinnie. Come on, already." Louis leaned back and rubbed his fingers into his forehead, felt the rise and fall of his chest as he breathed slowly. "You don't live there anymore," he said. "Remember? They put you out months ago."

His brother pushed a breath of air through his teeth. "Yeah, I know." And yet he stared at Louis confused, those teabag eyes pulling down like a hound. "Bastards."

"There's no one left in this town that wants you under their watch," he said. "Delores Jackson—she's done."

"The hell she is."

Louis said it once more. "Delores Jackson is done with you. I guess you finally got what you wanted on that front, so congratulations."

Vinnie looked down at his hands, spreading them out over his lap as if he were examining the cause of every problem he'd ever had in his life. "I guess I don't know what to say to that," he said.

Finally. The man was without words.

They spent the rest of the evening avoiding one another, Vinnie keeping mostly to his room and Louis cleaning out the weed patch behind the garage and listening to the voices of a batch of kids from down the street, trying to put together in his head what was supposed to happen next. He hadn't heard back from home support and he wouldn't be surprised if they left him and Vinnie to fend for themselves, not that he could blame them. How much punishment did one person have to take?

He slept in fits and starts all night, at one point awakening with the feeling of a great weight pressing against his chest, as though two stony fists were forcing his body deep into the mattress. He shook his mind loose and pulled himself up on his elbows and felt his T-shirt snap from his back, soaked and warm, then quickly cooling to ice in the willful draft of the open window. He took in his breath and counted the beats in his chest and they were like the ticking of a clock, and in time everything seemed to settle back to where it should be.

He lay back down and listened to the sound of Vinnie's snores in the next room, and gazed at the wash of the ceiling as it slowly began to fill with the breaking daylight. Now and then there was the bell-like chirrup of a thrasher somewhere outside. Like him, an early riser but a hell of a lot more optimistic about the day, he imagined.

It was just shy of ten years prior that Louis had gotten the first call about his brother, when things really started to kick up. Vinnie had been wandering through the parking lot of the South Town Plaza in Colville, looking for his car. He was nearly seventy then; Louis was just three years younger and even he forgot where he parked his car sometimes. No, what made this tough was that Vinnie was searching for his old Studebaker—a rig he hadn't seen in almost twenty years.

It was after he'd called the operator to report it as stolen, and the local police had come to take a report, that Vinnie mentioned his kid brother being the sheriff. When Louis showed up and walked Vinnie through the situation, reminding him that he'd put the truck in a ditch back in '52, his brother had tried to laugh it off as the stains of a whiskey hangover. But Louis could tell he was pretty stirred up—the shaking, the circle of sweat that ran from his underarms to his waist.

From then on, every few weeks or so, it was one thing or another with him. Somebody had come into his apartment and moved things around. There was gas missing from his tank. He'd forgotten to pay for the pint bottle found in his coat pocket. After a while the Colville dispatch just started running those calls directly to Louis. After he walked off with some woman's poodle, and then took a swing at her when she came after him, Louis arranged to have him moved into the Cedar Glen home. It was a situation that held up less than six months.

It was still an hour before his alarm would sound, but Louis crawled from the bedclothes anyway and peeled off his sweat-logged T-shirt, slapping the thing onto the floor. Before he could fish a new one from his bureau drawer, before he could put together what this new day was going to resemble for him and his brother, the air was cleaved by the sharp ring of the telephone.

"Hope I didn't wake you, Sheriff." It was Holly, down at dispatch. Was there a time she was not at that station?

"I'm up," he said.

"Us and the birds," she said.

"So I hear." He waited. There was the sound of tapping on the other end. A pen against the desk, probably.

"So the thing is," she said, "I just got a call from the ranger up at Twelvemile Ridge. She's a young gal, pretty new on the job I think. I haven't talked to her before."

"And?"

"Said she came across a body up off Ferry Creek Road. Mitchell's on his way up there now."

"You called Mitch first?"

"Mitch was here when she called."

Louis sat down on the bed and took a pen from the night-stand and listened as Holly threw out one detail after another: the rattle in the ranger's voice, the lousy connection wherever she had called from, the way Holly had calmed the gal down by telling her she was sending the best guys in the county her way. Once Louis was satisfied that he'd written down the most important items from what she had to tell him, he thanked her and hung up the phone, and went to wake his brother.

"I might be tied up the whole day," Louis said. "I'll find someone to come by and check on you later."

"I don't need some stranger to come check on me, god-damn it," Vinnie said, rubbing his hand over his face. "I ain't a baby."

"This is not negotiable, Vin."

Vinnie rolled over onto his side and faced away from his kid brother. "I'll give Hattie a call," he grumbled. "She can come keep me company."

Louis shook his head, slow and heavy. "I don't want Hattie in this house," he said. "Not when I'm gone."

"She's a fine woman."

"I have a file downtown that suggests otherwise," Louis said. "I don't want her here." Vinnie said nothing to that.

Louis knew that the woman would be there by noon.

It was a ten-mile drive over a back-crushing forest service road of ruts and tilled rock before he reached the site. The sun was already out and the dust he brought with him billowed like smoke over Mitchell's cruiser and the ranger's pickup, both vehicles crowded together in a flattened turnout. Mitch stood with his back to Louis about twenty yards off the roadway, stick-like arms moving back and forth, pointing out different places situated among a small grove of Ponderosas. And that sculpted hair of his was always something worth a minute or two. Brylcreem or mineral oil or whatnot, catching the overhead sun like the whole top of his head was shellacked. Louis brought his cruiser to a stop in the middle of the road and the deputy turned only briefly, giving a quick, three-fingered greeting.

The air was thick with the familiar smell of turning flesh and feces, and the curious sweetness lacing through it all. It was an assault on the senses that Louis had learned to stand, even if he had never been able to explain it. In his forty-plus years of law enforcement, he had come upon a human corpse six times and each time the scent was almost the same, no matter if the person was young or old, broad or gangly.

The ranger stood facing the deputy, her arms folded across her chest, nodding to him and glancing uneasily at Louis as he walked to them. Mitch turned to the sheriff.

"Morning, Lou," he said. "This here is Jackie. She's from the station down at Twelvemile."

Louis had been by Twelvemile many times but had not met this ranger. Like Holly had figured, she was a young gal, probably not yet thirty, her hair kept in a long, red ponytail, like a teenager. Too young to be seeing things like this.

"Nice to meet you, Sheriff." She dropped her arms and stepped toward him. Her smile was one of regret, twisted, as if they had all been dropped into an unfortunate situation that she was somehow responsible for.

Louis took her outstretched hand, then turned to Mitchell. "We can take it from here," he said.

"Are you sure?" she asked. Now, disappointment.

"What are we looking at?" He turned back to his deputy.

"It's an odd thing," he said. "I'd be more interested to get your take."

Mitchell King had been Louis's deputy for ten years now and even though he probably knew Mitch better than anyone, there were moments when Louis didn't want to let go of the label completely. That Mitch was part Alaskan native, and even though he never dwelled on it, Louis still found himself wishing for the kind of thing that might show up in a pulpy cowboy story or an old B movie. The listening for spirits and feeling the lick of wind in your hair and holding the sorrow of the earth in your hands as you squatted next to the bloated, ashen body of some lonely old man who had collapsed in his garden days before. The truth was, Mitch was just a guy—a solid lawman and loyal as any fellow could hope for, and there would be no cryptic chants or the waving of smoldering sage, or wise, mystical theories hummed in from the netherworlds. But damn; it would make things a hell of a lot easier if there were.

"I'll just write up my statement and then head on out." Jackie stepped away from the men and walked back to the rear of her pickup, using the dropped tailgate as a desk where she scratched away at a notepad. From where he stood, Louis could see a cloud of flies and the dark mound of something just behind a stand of lodgepoles.

He began to walk toward the site. "Who found it?"

"She did," said Mitch. "Heading to the sunrise, windows down. Caught the smell. She had smelled deer before. She knew this was not deer."

The body was fully clothed and intact so that Louis could easily see it was a male, white, though hard to tell the fellow's age or how long he'd been there. The hair was a dirty brown, shocks of gray on the sides with a face full and round, though it was likely that some of it was because of swelling. Louis was not a forensic expert, but he'd learned plenty in his years, the complications of altitude and climate and humidity on the decomposition of flesh. Two bodies could be dropped at the same time, in the same county, and look entirely different in a month's time.

"What did you find in the way of tracks?" Louis asked.

Mitch shook his head. "What's there is hers, from what I can tell. Straight shot between her truck and the body."

The men gloved up and Mitchell walked the perimeter of the site with his 35mm, the shutter snapping away as he peered down on the body from above and then beside it, squatting close to the ground, gently moving branches and brush to allow the light in.

With the exception of the chalky residue of evaporated sweat around his collar, and under his arms, almost everything about the corpse was tidy: the way the arms lay close to the sides, the shirt buttons secured. Even the trouser cuffs fell neatly over the boot laces. In all, the man could have easily been mistaken for someone who'd simply fallen asleep in the shadow of the Ponderosa and never gotten up.

It was another hour before Orly Downs arrived from Colville in his paneled wagon. Louis had been in Orly's company a half dozen or so times over the years, always in the presence of a corpse—at the base of a staircase, over a tub of cloudy bathwater, at the side of the road at night, air thick with gasoline and whiskey. The first thing Orly always did was reach down and press the eyelids closed, and this time was no different.

Today, Orly was as old as he'd ever been, and he moved as if every minute of his life was a precious commodity not to be wasted. Talk was spare and intentional, and no physical act was without purpose. He lowered himself to his knees and rolled the body from the shoulder, gently, then laid it back down onto the dirt. He ran a bony finger along the collar and tugged it down below the knobby Adam's apple. He reached down and drew up the forearm by the shirt cuff, then paused, as if the dead man was signaling a question.

"Look at this," Orly said, pointing at the fellow's fingers. There was a curious rawness to them, the knuckles chafed, as if they'd been scraped over pavement.

Louis squatted down and leaned in. "That is something," he said, nodding to Mitch. The deputy bent down with his camera and snapped a shot. Louis reached across and took hold of the other wrist, lifting it to get a look at the hand.

"Same," Mitch said. "Maybe a fight?"

"Could be," Louis said. "With a brick wall."

Beyond that, any evidence that had been present was sparse, the man's pockets empty, nothing onsite that would indicate he died where he was found. Somewhere, Louis wondered, there might be a clearer story that existed over a cluster of sagebrush or stretch of concrete, or some cheap motel carpet or, perhaps even, the upholstery of somebody's car. But for now, it was a man lying under a lone pine tree with no wounds other than a little scuff on his fingers.

"Pig in a poke?" Mitch said.

Louis shrugged. They would wait. Wait to see what Orly Downs had to say after he got the fellow back to Colville, to pore over the clothing and cut it from the body and wash it all down, look over every square inch of what was left. Sometimes, as Louis found, there could be surprises.

It was almost one when Louis turned onto his street, only to see Hattie Walton's brown Fairmont with the mashed rear fender parked comfortably against the curb of his house. The front picture window drapes were drawn.

He pulled to a stop behind the wreck of a car and tapped his horn twice before getting out and shutting the door behind him. The boy on the pink bike rounded the corner and pedaled his way toward Louis, and as he got closer, Louis thought of the fireworks kid with the stubbed pointer. They were about the same age, he figured.

"Hey." The kid had waved at Louis before but had never said anything to him.

"Hello to you. What's your name?" The rich smell of cedar and iron-rich dirt hung in the air, and everything seemed so dry and parched, he could not recall when he had set out the sprinkler last. It was a miracle he had a single blade of grass still alive.

"Luis," the boy said.

"You don't say." He looked down at the basket, at the collection of little toy cars and trucks piled inside. "Your sister lets you use her bike to carry your cars around?"

The boy squinted up at him. "I don't got a sister," he said. "This is my bike."

Louis nodded. "Fair enough." And then the boy said, "I gotta go now," and Louis gave a little salute to him as he rode off, those crazy tassels swinging back and forth as he pedaled away.

And then he finally walked up the front pathway and took hold of the porch rail, making his way slowly up the steps, planting his feet heavy on the boards before opening the door and stepping inside.

13

Nadine and Lester had gone to town earlier, for steaks and beers at Tiny's Roadhouse just off highway 16. It was a thing they did every couple of weeks or so. A way to get out of the woods and be among people, people Lester seemed to know in one way or another. Lester had drunk a pitcher on his own while Nadine nursed the same rum and Coke for most of the night. She liked to get a buzz on when she could but, Jesus, Lester was drinking like it was a sport and when that happened it was always a good idea for her to stay on the right side of sober.

It had all been going pretty well, but then Lester started poking at an old onion-nosed lumberjack twice his size, restarting some debate that, judging from the whoops and eye rolls around them, should have been dead, buried and forgotten a long time ago. Nadine couldn't follow the logic in it all, something about a woman named Frieda and a puppy mill in Yakima. It was getting loud and neither side was winning, and the bartender was getting hot.

"I'm not entertaining this tonight," he hollered over them. Then he took Lester's glass from in front of him and turned to Nadine. "Take him home," he said, "before he gets taken out."

Nadine tugged on Lester's belt loop. "Let him win this one," she said. "Let's hit the road."

"I'm not done yet," he said, not even turning to look at her.

"The hell you aren't." She slapped a five-dollar bill on the counter and gave his belt loop a good pull. When he finally turned around his eyes looked past her, glassy and lost. She cupped her palm beneath his whiskered chin and it was then that he seemed to find her, blinking, a goofy smile rolling over his face.

"Well," he said. "Look at you."

By the time they got home he was already half asleep, and he didn't get any further than the sofa before he laid himself down and stayed put. Nadine threw a blanket over him and went on into the bedroom by herself, which was fine by her at this point. Sleep came pretty quickly, and she was nearly into a full dream when the painful bell of the nightstand phone pulled her out of it. One hard ring and then another, and as she leaned over Lester's side of the bed to grab the hand piece, it fell silent.

She laid back down and stared into the dark, wide awake now, her mind a flipbook slideshow of everything she was always trying to forget, of hot summers picking raspberries in the center of a tree-less farm, row bosses with polished walking sticks who made empty but sinister threats of bruises on your legs if you didn't quit yapping and start picking. Of cats that multiplied incessantly and dogs that crawled under porches for the last time in their lives. Of her own poisoned mother, and of Jimmy, in the car, waiting for her to return from the drugstore, ignorant of what was coming his way.

"How many times did it ring?" Lester stood in the open doorway, still dressed in the clothes he'd worn to Tiny's. The dusting of moonlight filled in the dark spaces of his body; his mustard shirt completely untucked, hanging down over black trousers like a loose-fitting dress.

"Once," she said.

"Only once? Are you sure? I thought I heard more."

"It was one call, but it rang two times before it stopped."

He leaned against the doorjamb and raked his fingers through his tangled mop of hair. He was exhausted, maybe still a little bit drunk.

He whispered, "Goddamn it."

"Why's that?"

He reached up and found the propane lamp and brought the room into a low, hissing, yellow light. "I gotta go out for a bit," he said. "I'll be an hour or two."

Was it a friend, she wondered, someone who put their car in a ditch? Another woman somewhere, suddenly lonely for anyone she could find? The onion-nosed drunk signaling a fight? She watched him there in the doorway, and considered the firm grip his hand held on the jamb.

"Do you think you ought to be driving?"

"I don't have a choice." His eyes zeroed in on the car keys still on her nightstand. "I'll be fine," he said. "Don't you worry about old Lester."

Nadine wondered some more, but held on tight to the not knowing. To the hopeful notion that it was all nothing.

Lester went to the closet and dug out his flannel jacket and the pair of striped tennis shoes that he almost never wore. He was talking the whole time, to himself, she assumed, and then he finally sat on the edge of the bed and laid a hand on her leg, rubbing his fingers back and forth over the quilt, an old hand-stitched thing that Lester said had come from his mother before her fingers finally stopped working for her.

"Here's the deal," he said. "It's likely I'm gonna have some-one with me when I get back. Could be two people."

Alright, now. This was something. She sat up in the bed and tried to find his expression in the low light, to trace the map of his face regarding all of this.

"It'd be a big help if you could make up the sofa bed with some blankets," he said. "Put some food out. Nothing fancy." As if fancy could even be a consideration.

"Who's coming?" She decided this was information she ought to have.

"I don't know yet," he said. And when she drew in her breath and cocked her head, he added, "Don't worry. It ain't gonna be a murderer or bank robber or anything like that." He patted her leg and got up from the bed. "I'll give you the lowdown when I get back," he said. And before he walked out, he added, "Sandwiches would be good. Maybe a pot of coffee."

Nadine moved from the blankets to her robe and went to the kitchen and waited at the window, watching as one red rectangle bounced and shrunk from where the car had been to where it disappeared at the bottom of the hill. She consid-ered that Lester likely had no idea he was operating with a single taillight. Then again it would be just like him to ignore something like that.

She dialed up the lantern before going to the pantry and slapping together a few peanut butter and margarine sandwiches. Then she pulled out the can of instant, fingering the plastic lid before finally deciding against it. To make coffee would require a fire, and she wasn't up for the added work and the heat it would create for her. Besides, who in their right mind would want coffee at three in the morning?

After pulling out the sofa bed and covering the whole thing with a couple of moth-eaten, musty blankets she'd dug out of the closet, she wrapped herself up in the blue and white afghan and turned the recliner to face the window, where she would wait for Lester's return.

There was nothing to see beyond the glass but the familiar landmarks her mind had already memorized from that spot. The edge of the porch. The front end of the long, black Plymouth with no hood and a cracked windshield. The crippled, wooden gate just before the dip in the road. They were invisible in the blackness, but she could still see them.

She rocked in the chair, and wondered what might be coming up that drive likely before sunrise. It was a mile and a half hike down to the main highway, which was really nothing more than a two-lane road that wound through a thousand acres of scrub and field, and forestry department-planted pine and fir. Seeing another car on that landscape was a rarity in daylight hours, likely a near impossibility at this time of night. Her head felt heavy and she let it fall back onto the cushion and closed her eyes.

For as long as she could remember Nadine had had trouble making it through the night. Sharp noises, and the touch of hands on her body, real or imagined, often broke her from her sleep, and she might find herself calling out to no one, or hooking her fingers at the air or into the skin of an unfortunate companion. But it had been some time since one of those incidents. While Lester was a man whose faults ran into the dozens as far as Nadine could see, he did not create in her the sense of trepidation, or uneasiness, that she'd grown used to over the years. With him, in this house (except for that phone) she could sleep through the night.

And yet.

What was it about men, she wondered. Maybe she was asking too much, or maybe she just kept catching all the wrong flies. But it seemed like they all had one side they liked to show the world, and another side hiding around the corner, just waiting to jump out.

"Nadine."

She sprang upright in the chair, her leg cramping beneath the weight of her body. Lester stood in front of her, the low light of the lantern behind him casting the kitchen as a collage of streaks and shadows, and unsettling possibilities.

"There's a pair of Chinamen outside in the car," he said. "They're gonna be staying here a couple nights. Till they continue on their way."

"A Chinaman?"

"Two of 'em. And no, you can't tell nobody they're here."

Here was an example, she admitted, where knowing a few details ahead of time would have been good. She rubbed her hands over her face, the skin dry and chalky, then used her fingers to comb through her hair, as if it mattered in the least how she looked right now.

"Do I get a say in any of this?"

"Not unless you got two grand to kick in, you don't."

She stood up and peered out the window, and she could see under the soft yellow of the dome light two faces in the back seat, gazing back at her.

"Are they wanted by the law?"

"They ain't on the run from the cops, if that's what you're asking," he said, and when Nadine took a breath to press him harder on it, he put up his hand. "Let's just say," he added, "that it ain't likely the law is *actively looking for 'em*."

Lester went out onto the porch and waved his arm, and before Nadine could get in another question, the two men appeared in the doorway, each of them holding a lumpy cloth bag at their feet.

Nadine stood with the recliner between her and them and raised her hand in a wave. Of course she didn't know a single word of Chinese, not even *hello* or *stop*. The smaller of the two gave a little forced smile and nodded, but he didn't move from his spot. There was no way of knowing how old either of them was, what with the bad light and all, though Nadine could never tell with people like this anyway. The bigger one did look a stretch older, and she imagined they might be a father and his son. Taking shelter from whatever it was Lester was being paid to help them escape.

"I don't suppose they speak any English," she said to Lester. He gave a lazy shrug and wandered into the kitchen, and the two men said nothing in response. Nadine assumed the answer.

"There's sandwiches in the icebox," she said. "I don't know if they eat peanut butter."

"Why wouldn't they?" he called from the kitchen.

"I don't know. I heard once they don't have it over there. Maybe it'll make them sick." She looked at the little guy again and smiled.

Lester opened the icebox and brought out the plate and a pitcher of water and set it all on the table. He pulled a couple ceramic mugs from the shelf and added them to the spread. "I don't see no coffee," he said.

"Nope," she said. "I didn't get to it."

Nadine moved herself around the chair at last and went to the couple and put out her hand and waited as they each took it and gave it a tired squeeze. "There's food," she said, touching her fingers to her lips. The older man stared at her dumbly, but the younger one nodded, and looked out to the kitchen. Nadine pointed at the table.

"And sleep," she said, sweeping her hand at the pullout sofa as if it was some grand, ambitious creation of hers. When they both looked to the bedspread and the mound of pillows she'd crowded at the head, she announced that she was turning in herself and went off to the bedroom.

She crawled back under the quilt and lay there with the softness of the fabric under her chin, and the noise of cupboard doors opening and closing and Lester's great, grating drone going on and on, who he thought he was talking to, she could not fathom. Finally, after what seemed like a week, he opened the door and creaked into the bedroom.

"Are they eating the sandwiches?" she asked.

"They're picking at 'em," he said. "They're hungry, so it's likely they'll be gone by morning."

"Good."

"I'm talking about the sandwiches," he said. "Not them."

"I figured." She reached over and smoothed the blanket beside her, and he sank down onto it, his back to her, still dressed in everything but his boots. "Do I get the honor of at least half an explanation?" she said.

He growled out a heavy sigh. "We're a stopover is all," he said. "People wanting to pass over the border without all the hassle."

"Smuggling," she said. The sound of it, so filthy and subversive. She turned it over and around in her head. Could there be another word?

"I guess. It's not like they're moving drugs or guns or

anything. They're just folks. Folks trying to make a better life for themself. You of all people ought to understand that."

"Look at you," she said. "A regular Harriet Tubman."

He said nothing to that, but just lay there, his humped shoulders rising and falling in sync with her own breathing. Finally, he said, "Anyway, you can't tell anyone."

"You already said that. And anyway, you're one to be giving orders. Dragging God knows who into the house this time of night. Not saying a goddamned word about it, then warning me off like I'm some child."

Lester flipped himself over with the reflex of a snake and leaned into her face, his breath sour and hot. "I'm not shitting you, Nadine," he hissed. "You breathe one word of this to anyone and I just might lock you in the trunk of one of them old cars out there and never let you out."

At that, Nadine jumped from beneath the covers and stood against the wall near the window. She could see Lester's body propped on his elbow, a reclining shadow with barely enough moonlight to make out those stony eyes.

"You don't need to threaten me," she said. "You already made your point."

"I need to know that you hear me loud and clear."

"I hear you just fine." She walked to the edge of the bed and leaned over him. "And for your information, threatening me is a pretty stupid way of making your point. Cause I can lock shit up in a trunk just as easy as you can, Lester Fanning."

At this, Lester laughed and rolled back over, away from her. "Whatever, Nadine," he said. "We're even then."

She stood there for a good five minutes or so, watching his form find its place and settle into a quiet pose, like a mound of dirt in an empty cemetery. And only when she thought he might finally be asleep did she crawl back under the quilt, keeping her body facing his, her eyes following the plaid of his flannel like tracing the lines of a slow, moving grid.

14

The parking lot of The Burger Shack was littered with empty Styrofoam cups and wadded paper sacks, and stands of teenagers who slouched against car doors and fenders, and one another, as they dragged on cigarettes and stuffed greasy fries into their mouths practically by the fistful. It was the same thing nearly every night and Lord Almighty how Louis hated the whole scene. He loathed the kids for their laziness and misguided entitlement and freedom from worry, and their sheer ignorance of the kind of world that lay ahead of them. One minute they're eating a greasy burger and the next minute they could be riding off down the highway with someone they think they know pretty well, only to be left dead a mere twenty-five yards off a forest service road, in the middle of nowhere, no sensible explanation at all.

"Burger Shack," he found himself saying aloud to Vinnie. "Nothing like Zip's."

His brother looked up from his chocolate milkshake. "This here is an alright shake," he said, "but their burgers could stand in for dog food. Hell. Nobody does it as good as Zip's."

Louis remembered vividly the scent of fried onions, and the tumbling plume of smoke that pumped from the flat roof of Zip's.

The grid of streets that stretched out from that place into the East Detroit neighborhoods, from the shores of the Detroit River all the way out to Grosse Pointe. And then his mind rediscovered the tenth-grade harvest dance, and that long walk from the high school to the pay phone that stood alone outside the post office, just across the street from Randy's Barbershop. He'd still had on him the nickel that Vinnie had given him before he left that night. "Just in case," he'd said. "You never know when you might need to call, and it's a lot more than a nickel if you have to reverse the charges."

"You got Hattie coming by to see you?"

"I do," Vinnie said with an uneasy laugh. He trembled a hand through his wispy hair, like breaking cobwebs. "She ain't a big kick but she's good for company."

"You know she used to be married to Tip Moody." Tip ran the U-Pick wrecking yard just off Wolf Creek Road, and everyone and their brother knew the sideshow the two of them had once been.

"Ancient history," Vinnie said. "Tip gave up on her a long time before he put her out."

Louis took a bite of his burger, dry as sawdust. "I told you I don't like her in the house when I'm gone," he said through the chewing. "She's a bad influence."

"At my age, I'm lucky if I can get any influence at all."

They'd shared five dances, Louis and Shirley Byers, four fast and one slow, when she suddenly fanned herself and said she was thirsty, that she was going to get a drink of punch. Louis said, "By all means," moving to the chairs at the edge of the gym to wait for her. That she didn't come right back didn't bother him at first. That she lingered on the other side of the gym for some time with her girlfriends, even that didn't get on his nerves enough to make any kind of difference. But then she ran off with that creature Brenda Hoyt, and when he waved at them, Brenda just laughed at him and yanked Shirley by the arm. The both of them sauntered off from the gym to the parking lot where he knew Sam Gifford and Shel Tompkins were holed up in Shel's Ford Coupe smoking reefer. They didn't come back all night. That hurt.

Louis made that journey from the school to the post office as if his jacket was concrete, and he called home from the pay phone, with the nickel that Vinnie had insisted he take. *Just in case.*

And it was his brother who came to him, still wearing his ratty bathrobe, not even having taken the five minutes to change into a set of real clothes. He drove Louis straight to Zip's, and sat with him without talking, just holding onto his kid brother's shoulder as the boy cried like a baby into his vanilla milkshake.

The sun had dropped behind the high mountain ridges and everything had that kind of tinny feel, where even the sunflower stems showed gray. The streetlights were flickering up and down the street in fits, as if even they didn't understand the time of day. Louis looked to make sure his brother's seatbelt was locked in before pulling his cruiser from the lot and sailing out onto the highway toward home.

At first, he didn't pay much attention to the sedan, other than the burgundy-colored trunk on the navy-blue body. Even that didn't give him any kind of pause. It was a rare day if he didn't see a car that was in some way patched together, tires of four different manufacturers, quarter-panels coated in primer, grills and bumpers cobbled together with baling wire, rebar, or even rough-hewn wood.

It was his brother who noticed it, about fifty yards ahead, pulling out from the liquor store. "He's winking at you," he said, pointing a finger up the road.

"Who's winking?" And then Louis caught sight of it: a wide-backed sedan—an old Skylark—with its right taillight out.

Any other time he might have let it go, but it was good to let people know about these things. And his brother was right there. If anyone needed an example of responsibility, it was him. Louis reached down and hit the lights and ran on up close to the sedan, so he could get a look at the plates. They went on like that for a quarter-mile or so, Louis cozy with the car, the driver continuing on his way. Finally, he gave a tap to the siren and the driver waved a hand out the window and steered himself to a stop on the shoulder.

"Stay here," Louis said.

"Where the hell you think I'm gonna go, Einstein?" Vinnie opened the glove compartment and started poking through it.

Louis got out and did the long walk from door to door. Besides the mismatched trunk, the car was a patchwork of paint and primer, the rear driver's fender a spackled, matte gray. The driver had the window fully down, his registration and license at the ready. Louis recognized him immediately, the windswept mop and haggard face, wrung through and hung out to dry. The woman in the passenger seat, he did not know, though he could tell she was a pretty gal, and some years younger than the driver. She stared forward through the windshield, not looking at Louis.

"Was I speeding?" Lester Fanning slid his elbow out, resting it casually on the door. "It's forty-five out here."

"I know that, Lester," Louis said. "Were you aware that you have a taillight out?"

This seemed to irritate him, though Louis couldn't tell if it was the question or the circumstances that stuck in his side. "No, I was not."

"It's not a felony," Louis reassured with a grin. He read over the license and registration. Lester Fanning had been on Louis's radar since his arrival in the county some five or six years earlier. While Louis had to admit that the man hadn't done anthing in particular to warrant suspicion (at least not that he was aware of), he always seemed up to something, and the sheriff knew from a few phone calls that there was a history there. Lester was a shifty sort who set off every light on Louis's board—showing up in town at all hours with no consistent schedule, always plenty of cash to throw around. He lived in some primitive cabin he'd thrown together up in Whiskey Hills, and Lord knew there wasn't a whole hell of a lot up there in those woods other than a scatter of seasonal hunting cabins and a few year-round hippie types.

"You have some bodywork done?" Louis turned to look back at the gray fender.

"Just some spot repair," Lester said. "Rust." He kept his hands on the steering wheel, squinting up at Louis as he spoke. Above his lip the skin glistened almost imperceptible, if not for the catch of the dropped sun against it.

"Mr. Fanning," Louis said. "Can you take those keys from the ignition and step out of the car for me?" He moved back from the car and rested his hand on his holster. He was not yet worried for himself, though there was concern for what might be on display for his brother back in the cruiser. This should be nothing—it probably was nothing. But his gut.

Lester climbed out, his hands in front of him. He was a short man, but he carried himself tall, broad in the shoulders, squat legs and arms, everything in that rectangular shape. And that hair so unruly and thick as a mop, everything swamped with the dank odor of cigarettes, stale and heady.

"Am I in trouble, Sheriff?" he asked.

Louis walked backward, slowly. "I'd like you to open your trunk for me if you would."

"What do you need me to do that for?"

"Lester," the woman said from inside the car. "Don't make trouble."

Lester leaned down and looked into the car, then looked back at Louis with a grin and a slow shake of his head. He said, "Since the lady protests, I will do that, sir. Though I don't believe it's warranted." He moved with Louis's pace, his hands visible and steady except for the rattle of the keys. "I do believe I have the right to refuse. But I'm a man who is respectful of the law and the work that you fellows do." He put the key in the lock and popped the trunk. "Far be it for anyone to say that Lester Fanning does not comply when asked."

The trunk lifted like a drawbridge and Louis took from his pocket a pen light and shone it down into the space. With the exception of an old wool blanket that lay folded against the back, the trunk was empty and spotless. He focused the beam at the lamp housing where a pair of wires hung loosely from the connector. He reached in and pinched them between his fingers.

"Here's your trouble," he said. He held the wires up and turned them from one side to the other, the frayed, copper fringe shining in the light.

"Would you look at that," Lester said. "I must have snagged them when I was mucking around back here." He stepped back from Louis and rested his body against the fender. "I'll be sure and get that taken care of first thing in the morning."

"You'll want to curtail your night driving," Louis said.

"I'm heading home as we speak."

Louis went back to his cruiser and climbed inside, reaching

across Vinnie to the glove compartment. Fishing out a scrap of paper, he wrote out the name and tucked it down into his shirt pocket. "Lester Fanning," he said aloud.

"Who's that?" Vinnie asked.

"That's him." The Buick sat for a second while Lester fiddled with his papers and then it slowly pulled back out onto the highway, the single red stripe shrinking until the car disappeared around the bend.

"You sure carry yourself out there like you're somebody," his brother said. "Like you're a somebody among somebodies."

"World of lions, Vin," Louis replied. "Doesn't pay to act like a lamb."

"That's what Dad always said," Vinnie nodded. "He said that."

"Yes, he did." And then Louis started up the car and eased out onto the highway and drove the last few miles to his house on Polk Street.

15

"Haven't you read that thing a dozen times already?" Lester hovered at the base of the porch steps, his hand cupped over his forehead in a lazy salute. Nadine let the magazine drop to her lap.

"Don't get on my case, Lester," she said. "It's hot."

"I'd be happier to see you taking a walk around the perimeter. Maybe check on the rabbit traps."

"*You'd* be happier?" She laughed at him. "By all means let me help you with that."

The truth was, there were plenty of things in Lester that Nadine still felt good about, the same things that pulled her into his pickup truck that day. His eyes, of course—too often Nadine found herself handcuffed by the right shade of blue. The way he cupped her breasts from behind when he held her, the sensation of his unshaven face on her neck, tender more often than simply coarse. And the dozen lines that he recited like some actor in an old movie, the kind of guy with a rain-soaked fedora and a smoldering cigarette hanging from his lip. Not possibly real, except that they felt so genuine in the moment she could have folded them up and kept them in her pocket for the rest of her life.

"I've connected with people off and on all my life, but lady, you've got your hooks in me."

"I could fall asleep to the sound of you."

"I'd put my heart right here on the table, but I think you already stole it."

Enough of it all still felt good, and the house was warm and still had all the right smells. And as cutting as he could be sometimes, he usually came back to the good, and he didn't expect a lot from her, and it was all enough to cancel out most of the bad. It was better than it could be, that much was sure.

She took the usual path from the house to the near meadow, hugging the underbrush at the base of the trees, where the cage traps were. Lately they sat empty, sometimes probably due to uninterested rabbits, other times because Nadine had intentionally skipped over with the bait.

She had found herself fascinated with the first meal of rabbit and peas that Lester had prepared for her. She hadn't eaten rabbit before and the presentation of the whole thing seemed so exotic. The smoky-sweet taste of the meat, and the fact that he'd captured it just for her. She was in the midst of a romance novel, love in the deep woods, a place lost in time. And it stayed like that for a while, Nadine growing to look at the rabbit situation as a sort of competition, a quest to discover all the ways there were to cook the same animal. She'd keep the traps set and ready, and she learned how to skin the things with the skill and precision of a surgeon. But now, well into the second season, she was sick of them, and it seemed like there wasn't a way in the world to cook rabbit that would hide the gaminess. More and more, all she wanted was chicken.

In a cloud of Oregon grape near the cedar grove there was a commotion of sorts, a rattle of leaves, and Nadine knew right away what was happening. She could see the thing before she even reached it, flailing in a semicircle, its little unlucky foot caught in one of Lester's nasty snags.

She'd always hated those snare traps, and even when she wanted rabbit she would often sabotage the snares when she found them. The sight of a rabbit cinched by the neck, the dirt and groundcover torn up in a wide circumference made her furious.

"How would you like it," she asked Lester, "if someone suddenly took you by the throat? Held you there so you couldn't get away?"

"You say it like it ain't ever happened."

No, Nadine decided she'd rather deal a solid club to the rabbit's head herself, knowing it would be an instant death, than be a party to suffering. This terrified creature, wild-eyed and shaking, the foot swelling but not swollen, wrapped with the wire. She looked back toward the house, but Lester was nowhere.

"There's no need for cruelty," her grandfather would say to her, steadying the rifle butt against his shoulder. His eye settled to a wink, peering into the distance. "Be accurate and it'll be over for her the instant she hears the sound of the shot." And he'd squeeze his finger and there would be the crack, and Nadine would flinch, opening her eyes in time to see the doe fall to the ground.

She peeled her T-shirt over her head and laid it over the little rabbit like a blanket, pressing gently into the warm body, holding it in place with one hand and working the snare with the other. There was a weak fight and a few squeals of protest that always seemed such an unlikely noise to come from such a fairy tale thing.

Her fingers tugged at the wire and the little foot kicked and twitched, and when it was free, she yanked her shirt away like she was some magician. The rabbit sprung loose from her, disoriented and random at first, then straightening out and bounding off into the understory, a haze of yellow dust in its wake.

"Be smart next time," she said, then laughed at the irony. "Says the princess living in the castle tower." She stood and brushed off her jeans and went ahead and continued on her patrol, her T-shirt hanging from her pocket like a flag. The light breeze brushed over her naked skin and she imagined that if her mother would not have approved of her walking topless through the woods, she'd surely have smiled at the distance she achieved in hurling that damned snare trap out into the far cedar grove.

16

There were days when Louis remembered the clouds vividly, the rusty water stains that seemed to float across his ceiling from one side of his bedroom the other. He remembered the way they had tumbled themselves into old faces with mouths swayed open and howling, and how his mother's breath brushed his ear with a voice that sang low. "There, little one," she'd said, and then there was the blessed coolness of waterlogged terrycloth, draped over his forehead and chest. He shook until he might come apart at the joints, his teeth tapping a rhythm in his head. His skin burned, the bedsheets soaked beneath his naked body.

"We need to get him into the tub." His father, in the doorway, a figure like Jesus. "Get the fever down."

"It'll break soon," his mother said, the words falling in pieces. "Don't be rash."

The clouds drifted until they found one another to dance against a yellowed sky. His body was weightless, traveling above his bed and across the bedroom on down the hallway, past the framed photos of faces both familiar and not, rigid figures with vacant eyes in sepia-tone, watching as he soared past.

He recalled a sensation of tumbling then, and the sound

of Vinnie's voice from somewhere calling out, "What's wrong with Lou?" And there was the smell of his father's aftershave and worry-sweat, and then the feeling of a thousand needles being plunged into his body and the rattle of ice against porcelain. He screamed and fought, for the edges of the tub, for the strength to pull air back into himself, all while his mother leaned against the closed door and cried into her fists.

For the third time that week, Louis made the drive up Highway 16 to Twelvemile, and on up the forest service road to the lonely spot beneath the pines where the man's body had been found. He pulled onto the shoulder and got out to walk a wide circumference once more, covering both sides of the roadway even wider this time, pushing over a dead log with his shoe just because it was something he hadn't done yet. But there was nothing new, nothing but sand and scrub and the occasional tawny flash of a sagebrush lizard jumping from the shadow of a porous rock. It made no sense whatsoever, that this John Doe would come all the way out here on his own and lay down in that sandy bed. Of course, someone had brought him there, but why make the trip and risk it? Orly Downs had called in the medical examiner from Spokane, who reported the cause of death as *inconclusive*. "No trauma to speak of," he'd told Mitch over the phone.

"They're leaning toward heatstroke," Mitch relayed to Louis. "Maybe even hyperthermia."

It had been hot, but it was spring, not like an August heat, and they weren't in the real desert. Louis had been through Death Valley once in mid-June and that was enough to make him understand how people could get sidetracked and collapse within eyesight of their own car, only ten minutes away from water and air conditioning. It hadn't been more than eighty in Colville that week.

It was almost one by the time Louis stopped by the house. Hattie's car was parked at the curb, the driveway wide open for him. As usual, the drapes were closed. Louis came up the steps with some noise in his walk, taking the steps harder than needed, giving a cough here and there. Like a parent, he supposed, warning off a pair of teenagers cozied up on the sofa. He didn't know what the two of them had between them and he didn't want to know. He opened the door and let the daylight fall over the room.

Vinnie was in the recliner, a half-eaten sandwich in his hand and a crumb-specked plate on his lap. On the other side of the room, Hattie sat on the sofa, her legs curled under her, that dirty-gray hair of hers pulled back with a rubber band. There was a big glass of something dark on the little side table next to her elbow. Water pooled from the base of the glass onto the unprotected wood.

"It's a Coke," she said. "Straight up." She stared ahead at the television, some soap opera with women in dresses too fancy for just sitting around, drinking coffee at a little round kitchen table.

Louis looked to his brother. "Did you take your pills?"

Vinnie nodded, and Hattie added, "I made sure of it."

The dispenser sat on the counter, the Tuesday AM compartment open and empty. Beside the stove was a football-sized chunk of beef, trussed in string and dusted in green flakes, squeezed into a rectangular pan.

"Is this meat supposed to go someplace?" Louis asked.

"It's going in the oven, when this show is all done," Hattie called back. "I got some potatoes peeled for you, too."

He leaned over the round pot sitting in the sink, at the clutch of white, stone-like things looking up at him from the milky water. The counters were clear, and a blue hand towel lay neatly folded over the oven handle. There was a nice smell in the kitchen, like cinnamon and brewed coffee. No hard liquor that he could sense.

He went to the refrigerator and counted the cans of beer in the door, then fished one from the rack, popping the top and going to the living room, where a car loan commercial was now playing loudly on the television. It seemed like everything that was on the tube during the day had to be shouted.

"You ain't got work?" Vinnie asked.

"I always got work," Louis said, taking a drink. "I'll be gone soon and then you all can get back to your show."

"I don't care about that," Vinnie said.

Hattie went into the kitchen with her purse on her shoulder, and took the roast from the counter, sliding it into the already warm oven. Louis considered that she ought not be doing any of this, and he did not like that she was cooking his food in her way. Helping herself to the refrigerator and cupboards, and to the toilet. Yes, that, too.

"This isn't necessary," he said, following her back in there.

"I know that." She bent over and peered at the clock dial, turning it slowly. "You want to know how he is?" she said. "When you're not here to watch him?"

"I suppose," Louis said, and he did.

She stood up. "You suppose." Then she crooked a grin and gave him a little shove with her shoulder. "He's still Vinnie," she said.

"A pain in the ass," Louis said, taking a drink from his beer.

Hattie laughed. "He's called me Lucy once or twice, but I don't mind that, and he corrects himself when I call him on it. He don't remember the names of his old tavern buddies. Probably a good thing. He gets confused over the TV. Forgets all the shows I know he's watched a hundred times. But mostly all he wants to do is talk about the old days, anyway. He could do that in his sleep."

"God knows he remembers every damned detail of them," Louis said.

Hattie nodded in agreement and turned up the oven dial another notch. "Vinnie told me about the guy from the other night," she said quietly.

"What guy?"

"The one-taillight guy."

Louis peered into the living room at his brother, who continued to gawk at whatever stupidity was playing out on the screen.

"If you're gonna let him in on anything, you might as well invite the world," Hattie said. "It was Lester Fanning, right?"

When Louis didn't answer, she pushed air through her closed lips. "I wouldn't trust that sonofabitch to walk my dog," she said. "He comes into the wrecking yard every so often. Tip swears that for every part he pays for, he probably pockets two. Slippery bastard."

"So, you know him pretty well."

"We don't *know* him," she corrected, with a half grin and a wink of her eye. "We just know him."

She reached into her purse and produced a lone cigarette. "I ain't been up there at his place, but I hear people say it's something of a wrecking yard in itself. A little bit of everything, including a different lady friend every few months or so."

Louis knew a good deal of this already. Lester's name was often mixed in with miscreants Louis had had dealings with—shoplifting, drunk driving—the kinds of things that yielded court dates and fines that needed chasing down. Up to now, there hadn't been anything yet about Lester Fanning to warrant a good deal of attention, but he was often there on Louis's list of wonders.

"He likes to play at being Mister Nothing-To-See-Here," she went on. "But believe you me, that man's got his fingers in all kinds of pies." She dropped her purse onto the counter and continued to dig around inside it.

"Such as?" Louis took the cigarette from her fingers and set it on the counter next to her purse.

"For starters," she said casually, "he's a fencer. But you probably know that."

"Fencer?" He'd not been aware of this, and her assumption that he did only compounded the embarrassment.

"Yeah, a fencer," she said, looking down at that cigarette. "Not like a picket fence kind of fencer. A mover of stolen property. Piddly stuff, though—the kind of stuff addicts take: TVs, stereo systems. I'd bet my left eye that every pawn shop from here to Spokane has at least ten things with Lester's fingerprints all over them."

Louis leaned back against the stove and considered this. He'd need to dig through the dozen or so burglary reports over the last couple of years, see what he could draw from it. Maybe make a run up to Whiskey Hills.

"I'm surprised you didn't know."

"Well, I didn't."

"It ain't really a well-kept secret."

"I guess I must be the town idiot, then."

Hattie gave a soft laugh and swatted her hand at him.

"Anything else about Lester Fanning that I ought to know but don't?" Louis asked.

"Oh, I'm sure there is, but I ain't in the habit of spreading unsubstantiated gossip and hearsay," Hattie answered, picking up the cigarette and tapping it against her wrist. "But I'd think any kind of poking around under that fella's bed is bound to turn up something."

"Why do you say that?"

"Because that's the kind of person he seems to be."

"And you know him," Louis said through his teeth.

She nodded, gave him a wink, and lit up the end of her smoke with a flame that was big enough to start a forest fire.

17

The story she'd told Lester was mostly true, with a few crucial details taken out, the holes filled by her imagination. It wasn't the first time that she'd reshaped a story for a man, and she knew it wouldn't be the last.

What Nadine told Lester was that she had been a couple of days into a weeklong vacation with Jimmy, who was not yet her husband. The plan had been for the two of them to drive from Seattle to someplace near Itasca, Minnesota, to visit a cousin of his, a big family of alcoholic Catholics that she had no desire to see in the first place. But she went along with it, she told him, because that's what couples do. Nadine was a better driver than a passenger, but Jimmy was never one for sharing, not even the steering wheel. He was happy to share his secondhand smoke, though, going through one cigarette after another, with the windows rolled up, singing along with the radio even when he didn't know the song and couldn't hit the notes. They'd done three road trips like this already and each one had ended with a two-week separation starting the moment they rolled back into their own driveway.

On this trip, they had barely reached Boise when Nadine

decided she was finished once and for all. Jimmy had settled on a radio station some twenty miles earlier, one of those Mexican Hombre Music things, and Nadine's head started pounding about five minutes into the mariachi.

"It'd help if you turned off that noise," she said. "And crack a window for Christ's sake."

He gave her a side-eye and dialed down the window barely a notch, ignoring the radio.

Nadine rolled down her window about halfway, the racket of the wind tumbling in to muzzle at least some of the music. A Rexall sign rose up over the ridge at the next exit.

"I need a bottle of Excedrin," she said. "Pull off here."

Jimmy threw his head back and howled, "Seriously?" then steered hard from the highway, winding his way through a rope of roadway, finally bringing the car to a stop a good distance from the front of the drugstore.

"Make it quick!" he snapped as she opened the door. "I'd like to make it to Montana by dark." He then rolled down his window all the way, and kicked up the trumpets another notch.

Nadine had on her favorite pair of jeans and a button-down blouse, and not much more if you didn't count the hoop earrings and the cheap, gold-plated promise ring that she slipped into her pocket after she went out the side door with her brown leather purse weighing on her shoulder, sixty-seven dollars in her possession and a credit card that was already overextended. She told Lester that she had thought she'd just be making a point when she went out that door, that Jimmy would get tired of waiting and see that she was not in the store, and he'd circle the block a few times looking for her. But then she felt herself suddenly put out her arm and raise her thumb and within a few moments, Lester Fanning practically ran his pickup off the road to get to where she stood. He leaned out the passenger window, a mop of sandy gray and brown in need of a cut. And that radiator grill smile, a single tooth missing along the top, near one side.

"Where you headed?" he had asked. This part, he remembered.

"It's complicated," she said as she climbed in next to him and looked into the side mirror as they pulled away, the neon Rexall sign dropping below the ridge.

In the months since she had been with Lester, living in that ramshackle house, Nadine had rebuilt the chicken coop using lumber they'd salvaged from a collapsed barn near town, and she'd repaired the diesel generator three times, once in the middle of a downpour that hit the tin roof so hard she thought she might go crazy with the racket. She could figure things out if she had to; it wasn't hard to do. As resourceful as Lester was, he was no use as a handyman. Maybe he'd built all this under the watch of a more skilled craftsman, or perhaps he'd just given up by the time Nadine came on the scene. Whenever she asked how he'd ever managed to survive without her, he'd just laugh and say, "I did a lot of things before you that would make that pretty head of yours spin off its shoulders, lady."

Now he sat in a parking stall out front of A&L Auto Parts while she stood against the wood counter, a single clear light bulb in front of her. The old gal behind the register was a weathered thing, probably Nadine's mother's age or close to it. She'd colored her hair a crazy shade of orange that most definitely was not her own. But it was something to look at, that much was true. She picked up the bulb and turned it over in her hand, holding it by edge of the plastic casing.

"Where'd you get this?"

"Off the hook back there. It's a taillight. For that Buick out front."

She glanced at the window, grabbed a ringed binder and began flipping through the pages.

"I'm guessing it's the right one," Nadine said. "I'll know for sure as soon as I get out there."

Then there was the sound of Lester's booming tone from outside. Nadine turned to see a guy bent down into the driver's side window. He practically had his head inside the car, and yet the two of them were talking so loudly that Nadine could hear them all the way inside, though she couldn't make out what they were saying.

"Cash or charge?" the woman asked. She slid the bulb across the counter to Nadine.

"Account," Nadine said. "Under Lester Fanning."

The woman stopped and gave Nadine a look. The smell of solvent lingered in the air, sweet and fragrant. Behind her, a ridiculous array of tubes and fan belts hung like skinned, black pelts.

"Lester, huh?"

Nadine looked back outside. The man had stood back from the window. He was a greasy sort, with hair shiny and hanging loose over his profile so Nadine could not make him out. He was practically shouting as he thumped a finger into his palm.

"He's right there," she said.

"You family?"

"No," Nadine said. "But I am staying up there."

"By choice?"

Nadine cocked her head. What kind of question was that?

"Never mind," the woman said. "Me being nosy. That's what I do." She grabbed a bound book and opened it, and scratched a pen across the page. "Tell Lester he's due to settle. Sooner's always better than later."

"He's right out there," Nadine said again. "I can have him come in."

"By mail is just fine." She waved a hand. "Or he can come in when Edwin's here."

"Are you sure?" Nadine said. She tucked the bulb into her pocket and pulled on the heavy glass door.

"I'm sure," the woman said. Her voice was sharp enough to split firewood. She sucked in her breath and gave Nadine a smile and put out her hand. And then she closed the book and pulled a newspaper from somewhere behind the counter, snapping it open and thumbing through it, a newspaper that Nadine could see was well over a week old.

PART THREE

The Ogre does what ogres can,
Deeds quite impossible for Man,
But one prize is beyond its reach:
The Ogre cannot master speech.

About a subjugated plain,
Among its desperate and slain,
The Ogre stalks with hands on hips,
While drivel gushes from his lips
—W.H. Auden, *August, 1968*

18

Rodney and Otis sat in the living room on opposite sides of the cherry coffee table, their hands resting on their knees like schoolboys. Rodney's shirt collar scratched at his neck, and his trousers bunched in places he was not willing to adjust in front of Otis. They were his "church" clothes, though his family hadn't been to any kind of church since coming to Hope. His mother had insisted he dress up nice. It was a special night.

"What's this guy like, anyway?" Otis shifted in his seat and tugged at his collar. He wore a white button-down shirt that still showed the creases from its life in the package.

Rodney had been sweeping out the warehouse for a good four months or so, yet had only spoken to Charlie Kruger twice. And even those moments had been just in passing. But he had seen the boss around the shop, and knew the man's face, and the hollow baritone of his voice as he drew out his words, as if vowels were to be savored as gifts from the gods. The sustained "O" of Rodney's mother's name could carry to the farthest reaches of the warehouse. "Ro-oohse!" he would call out. The rest would be nothing more than a rumble of words, unintelligible.

"He's alright," Rodney said. "He drives a big car."

"Is that so?" Otis leaned forward suddenly, his fingers raining on his knees like keys on a piano. "What kind?"

"I don't know." Rodney didn't know cars too well, other than Otis's Bonneville. And the Impala that had been out front of course, once upon a time.

"Is it a Cadillac? Or maybe a Monte Carlo. Does it have a front end that goes on forever?"

"I said I don't know what kind of car." Rodney undid the top button of his shirt, offering a welcome breeze against his chest. "This is stupid," he said. "It's just dinner."

"On that," Otis said, "you and I agree." He stood from the high-back chair and went into the kitchen, where Rodney's mother was working the pots and pans and the cupboard doors like they were drums.

"By the way," he heard her say to Otis, "I don't want you drinking."

"At all?" Otis said.

"Ideally."

Then there came the rattle of bottles on the refrigerator door. "Jesus Christ," he said. "You'd think we were having dinner with the goddamned mayor."

From where he sat, Rodney caught a blink of movement through the open drapes as a long, silver sedan stuttered to a stop against the curb, like a railcar pulling into the station.

"He's here," Rodney called out.

Otis flew into the living room and huddled against the wall, peeking out the window from its edge like he was a five-year-old looking out for Santa Claus.

"Looks like a Lincoln," he said, snapping the drapes back. "Figures."

Rodney's mother opened the door and called out *hello*, and

Kruger howled her name as usual.

Otis looked over to Rodney. "Ain't they just a couple of chums?" he said.

Kruger carried a bottle in one hand, and as he walked up the front steps his suit jacket swung back and forth from his barrel stomach. His face was vivid pink behind a curled mustache, and he nodded to Rodney when he caught sight of him.

"Little man," he said.

"Hello Mister Kruger," Rodney answered. He didn't need his mother's shoe against his shin.

"Mister Kruger," Rose said. "This here is Otis." She motioned behind Rodney. "Otis Dell."

Kruger walked past Rodney, his hand reaching out. A shine of metal and stones winked from his fingers, no less than three impressive rings leading the handshake. The two men greeted one another like men do, hands melted into a single fist, arms pumping, eyes locked in some unspoken competition.

"Is that a Lincoln you got out there?" Otis asked.

Kruger looked over his shoulder as if he needed a reminder. "Yes sir," he said. "Continental."

"Damn fine car," Otis grinned.

"I couldn't afford a yacht," Kruger said, "so I settled on her."

"I did the same thing." Otis nodded at Rose and winked.

"Aren't you the comedian?" Rose reached out and Kruger gave her the bottle. She turned it in her hand and looked over the label. "Very nice," she said, smoothing her thumb over the paper. Rodney knew for a fact that his mother didn't know one kind of wine from another. "It's all just sour grapes to me," she had said to him once.

Kruger turned and peered into the living room, his reddened eyes scanning the walls from one end to the other. He craned his thick neck, the flesh spilling over his collar. It looked to Rodney like he was lost, or maybe searching for something he'd left behind at a previous visit.

"I always wondered what it looked like in here," he finally said. And when Rose cocked her head, he smiled and added, "Curious, I guess. Ever since I was a boy."

Otis said, "It's been around that long?"

"The Collettis—they were this big, Italian family—they lived here when I was your age," Kruger said, glancing at Rodney. "Nice people, but good lord, were they ever loud. You could hear one of those girls of theirs from a half mile away, whether she was fighting with one of her sisters, or just talking to herself. Anyway, the rumor that rumbled among us kids was that something happened one night between old man Coletti and this brand-new teacher of ours. She was a pretty young thing whose name I couldn't come up with if you paid me. I do remember she'd just moved here from Chicago, though." He looked at Otis and winked. "Anyway, the wife, she didn't take too well to the news as you would imagine. Apparently some words got said in a public place, in a way that was too messy to get out of. Shortly thereafter, the whole brood picked up and moved away in a single weekend."

"That's something," Rodney's mother said. "I can't imagine."

Kruger offered up a big, horsey nod. "The house sat here empty and boarded up for quite some time after that," he said. "Somewhere around '68, I'd guess, old man Kovac bought it."

Otis said, "Sounds like a Jew name."

"Otis," Rose said. "Don't be like that."

"I'm just thinking out loud," he said, tapping his shiny forehead. "I didn't know we had a Jew for a landlord."

"Why would you?" Rose said. "It's not even a detail worth

sharing." She reached around and put her hand on the small of Kruger's back, and he seemed to stand a bit taller when she did this.

"Let's eat, shall we?"

She had bought a tablecloth and fancy cloth napkins for this, though she apologized for having what she said were the wrong glasses, though they were the same tumblers they always used. As she tipped the bottle with a trembling hand, the red licked up over the rim some.

"If it'll hold what I'm drinking, it does what it needs to," Kruger said. He raised the glass in the air before taking a drink. Rose laughed softly and Otis said, *Amen*, tipping the glass to his mouth and staring up at the ceiling with raised eyebrows.

They all piled their plates with roast beef and green beans, and scalloped potatoes that Rodney knew had come from a box, and at first everybody ate and nobody talked, with the exception of an occasional compliment from Kruger.

"The meat is perfectly cooked."

"This is just like my mother used to do it."

"It's been awhile since I had such a meal, Rose."

Rodney's mother would smile behind her napkin, or whisper a sheepish, "Oh now," while Otis would nod, his cheeks distended and flushed. He took a hard swallow and turned to Kruger.

"So," he said. "How long have you owned that outfit on Charlotte?"

Kruger wiped his napkin over his mouth. "The store was my father's place first," he said. "He opened it in '39. A lousy time to start a business."

"Why's that?" Otis cocked his head and shoveled another forkful into his face.

"Why's that?" Kruger grinned. "The Depression, for one.

And then the war shortly thereafter." He turned and winked at Rodney. "Of course."

"Of course," Otis said, giving an unconvincing nod. "That crazy goddamned war."

"God bless, he somehow made it work," Kruger went on. "He was a crusty old S.O.B., and I mean that in the best way." He took a gulp of wine and blinked a glance at Rose. Otis took up the bottle and reached over, adding a few splashes to Kruger's glass.

"I grew up in that place," Kruger continued. "Started working in the warehouse when I was his age," he said, nodding his chin toward Rodney. "After Mom passed in '65, the old man lost whatever interest he had in the place. So I took it over. Figured I couldn't do any worse."

Rodney's mother stared at her plate, now and then glancing up at Otis during the monologue. It was clear she had heard it all before.

"He passed on a few years later," Kruger said, circling a chunk of bread along the edge of his plate. The rings on his fingers caught the overhead lamplight in glitter-like bursts. "I sold off the old house here in town and built my little place up there on Prospect Hill. And here we are."

"You never got married?" Otis asked.

"Otis," Rose said. "That's personal."

"It's all right," Kruger said, touching her on the shoulder. "It's a tendency of some to wonder."

"And?" Otis insisted.

"To be frank," said Kruger, "I don't spend a great deal of time even thinking about it." He then turned his attention to Rodney. "You're doing a fine job in the warehouse," he said. "Prompt. Efficient. Good traits for a young man to have."

"You need to hit the corners a little better, though," Rose piped in.

"Now then," Kruger said, turning one of the rings on his finger. "The finer details will come."

"It's all about the details," Otis said.

"I know that," Rodney said.

"A job worth doing is a job done good," Otis added.

"I know that, Otis," Rodney said, his voice rising. His fingers started to itch. This dinner was running a lot longer than any dinner he'd ever had.

"I don't want to be nosy," Otis then said to Kruger. "Those rings, they're something."

"Oh, Otis," Rose said. "For crying out loud."

Kruger reached over and opened her hand for her, then slid a ring off—the biggest one—and set it in her palm. "That's a ten carat gold piece there," he said. "Three-quarter carat rose cut in the center. Got it about seven years ago from an old Russian jeweler on a trip through San Francisco."

"Any occasion?" she asked.

"Indulgence," he said. "I've got a few. This is just one of many."

"Rings or indulgences?" Otis asked.

"Yes and yes," Kruger said, tipping the wine bottle and emptying the last drops into his glass.

Rodney pressed his feet to the linoleum and ground his chair back. His mother turned to him.

"Are you asking to be excused?" she said.

Otis said, "We're still eating."

"It's alright," Kruger said. "No boy his age should be stuck listening to a bunch of talk about business and personal vices."

Rodney's mother waved a hand, and Rodney pushed himself

the rest of the way from the table, and ran off to his bedroom.

He sat on the edge of his bed for some time, the hum of conversation continuing in the other room, the cut of laughter and the occasional rattle of ice against glass.

Rodney slid his hand beneath the mattress and drew out one of the magazines, a Detective Comic, still in its plastic wrapping, protected from filthy hands and childish, undisciplined excitement. Safe. The hero swinging from one building to another, his black cape practically filling the entire cover, was Batman—though he was called *The* Batman in this issue.

Rodney considered taking it from its sleeve, this thing that was older than he was, older than Otis—maybe even older than Mister Kruger. He ran a single finger over the cover, the thin plastic shifting and creasing under the pressure. He could do it. He could take it out and read it, and fold the pages, tearing a couple loose if he wanted to. He could throw it away in the trash and nobody, not even Otis, would miss it.

The evening light began to settle. Rodney screwed the bulb on his nightstand lamp, and then there came a merciful lull, with the business of thank yous and good nights. Rodney got up from his bed and stood at the window, watching as Mister Kruger walked to his silver car, a little lighter and unsteady on his feet than he had been upon his arrival. He walked around the rear end of the car to the driver's side, where he stood with his hand on the roof, his eyes looking back toward the front door.

"Hey." Otis was there at the bedroom door, behind him. He had changed into a dingy white T-shirt, which hung from his body like a shop rag. "Go help your mother with the cleanup."

"Isn't she on the porch?"

Otis screwed up his face at Rodney. "Why the hell would she be on the porch?" he said. Shaking his head, he gave a whispered laugh, and thumped on down the hallway to the bathroom. "Ain't she on the porch," he said once more. Outside, Kruger's giant car was gone.

When all was washed and put away, the last remnants of Charlie Kruger flushed down the drain, Rodney lay on the sofa watching the final stretch of a movie he had seen several times before. It was a cops-and-robbers flick, with the criminals on a cross-country run, heroes though they had killed a few bystanders along the way. His mother and Otis sat at the kitchen table together in darkness, except for the single tiny bulb over the stove.

Otis was nursing a beer while Rodney's mother moved a cigarette from her lips to a glass ashtray, a dancing vine of blue smoke rising to the ceiling. They were talking, but Rodney could only catch snippets, and only when things seemed to come to a flashpoint.

"How should I know?" His mother's voice. "If you're so brilliant..."

"He said so." Otis now. "You heard him."

They went on like this for some time, and when they got tired of the chairs or the conversation, or had run out of beer perhaps, or she had finished her last cigarette, they got up from the table and went past the living room to the bedroom.

"Don't stay up too late," his mother said.

"Just till this is over," Rodney answered.

"When's that?"

"Twenty minutes." He had no idea, really.

Otis disappeared into the bedroom and started opening and

closing drawers, and rattling the clothes hangers.

"Hey," she said to Rodney.

"Yeah."

"Look at me."

Rodney rolled to his side and turned his head to his mother. She stood there leaning against the door jamb, a sleepy smile drawn over her face. The day had been endless for her, and she wore every minute of it like a rain-soaked, woolen coat.

"Thank you," she said.

"For what?"

"For being nice to him."

Rodney shrugged. "He seems nice."

"He is nice," she said. "Not everybody gets to see that side of him." Then she kissed the air and said good night, and slipped into the bedroom where Otis was quiet now, closing the door behind her.

19

It was the first time a woman had been a part of the mix. She was young, eighteen at best, and accompanied by an older man wearing what looked to Nadine like pajamas. He was nearly bald, with only a light downy patch circling around the back from ear to ear. The girl spoke to him in whispers and tiny gestures, huddling against him as he nodded and smiled a gentle crescent moon. After a few moments, he patted her on the shoulder and she moved a step or two away from him, and the two of them stood with hands on the porch railing, gazing out over the expanse of the cluttered land. The old man said something, then tottered down the steps to pace around the property with his hands clasped in front of his body, studying the piles of rusted junk that Lester had dropped everywhere. He looked over them as if they were discovered treasures, ancient artifacts from some long-dead civilization.

In time, the girl turned her attentions to Nadine, keeping to her like a horsefly, pointing out things and chittering at her in what sounded like some secret code, a tumbling nonsense, the girl occasionally laughing at her own words. What could Nadine do with that? So she took up a one-sided conversation of her own, spilling complaints about Lester and the house, of the winter that would clench those very hills in just a few short months. The place needed more work than one person could possibly do, but Nadine supposed that was just the way it was going to be as long as she stuck around.

"I don't know how he ever survived on his own up here," Nadine said as she and the girl crowded into the henhouse, the air tinged with grit and fluff and fans of incoming sunlight. Nadine handed over the basket, and the girl went right over to the nesting boxes at the far end and started plucking eggs from the straw like it was her daily chore.

The girl looked at Nadine and held up a single egg. A lone, downy feather had lit on the side of her head, a white starburst against the inky black of her hair.

"Egg," Nadine said.

"Egg," the girl repeated, and then she grinned and said, "Les-ter Fan-ning," as if she were picking the syllables from a jumbled pile of words.

"Lester Fanning," Nadine said, and then she moved her hand in an outward movement from her body, as if she were smoothing it over a distended gut. The girl laughed at this, curling her hand to her mouth and turning away from Nadine.

Nadine started doing this with everything. At first it was fun, in a Miracle Worker kind of way. Nadine the teacher, the girl trapped in a world in which she could not communicate. They wandered the circumference of the house, and Nadine would point out things. *Tree. Squirrel. Mushroom.* As exhausting as the charade quickly became, Nadine was glad for the hard barrier of understanding between them. She couldn't even explain to herself the reasons for sticking around, much less to another person. For every moment she found herself ready to descend that mountain and climb into the first truck she could throw herself in front of, there was another moment that grabbed hold of her. A voice telling her it wasn't worth it, that it was her problem, not his. After all, hadn't she decided long ago that while there was probably no such thing as a truly good man, the world was at least likely made up of a number of halfway-decent ones? That all she had to do was stand ready until they showed her there wasn't enough decency to make it all worth the effort? For all his swagger and self-centeredness, and the occasional ridiculous ultimatums, Lester was no better or worse than any man she'd ever been with—or would ever be with.

Jimmy had hovered around *decent* for some time, long enough for him to have promised to maybe marry her, someday, to have spent a bit of his paycheck on the little pawn shop ring which he gave to her over hamburgers at that little diner in Yakima. He hadn't hit her or anything like that, even when she made him so mad he pulled the car off the road and stomped fifty paces off into the rows of someone's apple orchard. But he could hurt her with words; that was for damned sure. Comments and assumptions about her education, or lack of, touting his community college degree as if it was a fucking PhD. "You wouldn't last in college," he'd say to her. "You got to be willing to think."

He would say that kind of nonsense to her while he used that precious education of his to sell carpet remnants for his uncle. That and peddle dime bags and single joints between the dumpsters that crowded the alley behind the shop. They drove around in a ten-year-old station wagon and lived out of an old widow's basement, but it all would have been just fine with Nadine if he hadn't pushed her as far as he did.

"I told Lester that Jimmy and I had been on our way to Itasca," she said to the girl, taking a broom from the corner near the henhouse door. The girl set the egg basket on the shelf and reached out to take the broom. Nadine balked, but the girl took it from her anyway and began raking it along the floor slowly, keeping the dust to a low cloud. Nadine went to the feed bin, and sank the scoop into the meal. "But the real story was that we were heading to some dealer he knew in Idaho Falls." She went to the far end of the house and poured the feed into the tray. Instantly, her legs were swarmed by a dozen chickens, warbling and pecking at the floor around her. "He had probably a couple thousand dollars' worth of grass in the trunk. Plus at least one pistol that I knew of."

The girl moved from one end of the house to the other, gently moving the broom in and among the hens without so much as raising a single feather from them. It was getting warm in here now, but Nadine didn't want to open up the door just yet. She liked the intimacy of the space, of the two of them in there talking, without the men hovering over them. Whatever they might be saying to one another, it was for their ears only.

"The part about the Mexican music was true," she said. "And the headache. Both of those I could have dealt with, but then he yelled at me from his window all the way across the parking lot." Nadine moved out of the girl's way as the broom found its way to her. "I can't remember if I told Lester that part, but yeah. He yelled at me that I was a fucking idiot, right there in front of everyone at the Rexall. And that was it."

Nadine then opened the door to the outside and the rush that forced its way in was a blessing. A couple more hens scurried in, wings beating at the air. Down the hillside, the old man was poking around an aging pickup truck that was half-covered in blackberry brambles.

"I called the cops on him," Nadine said. And the joy that

came with simply saying that aloud swelled in her throat like a balloon. "I grabbed that phone inside the door to the drugstore where he couldn't see me, and I dialed those numbers and told the woman on the other end that there was a drug dealer in the parking lot and that he had a gun on him, and they'd better hurry because he was about to leave and do some serious shit."

She laughed at that, and took the broom from the girl and swatted the pile out the door in a giant plume of dust. "And then I went out the side door to the access road out the back and stuck out my thumb, and as fate would have it, Lester Fanning just happened to be driving by at that very moment."

They walked back to the house together, the girl holding the basket of eggs like it was a baby. Lester was waiting for them on the porch, a dewy beer in his hand.

"They're leaving tonight." He turned to the girl. "You're leaving tonight!" he shouted, as if the barrier in the language was merely volume. "Go help her pack so she understands," he said to Nadine.

Nadine had an almost painful curiosity about these people who turned up from places she knew little about, and would never see. What were they running from that was so bad they had to separate themselves by an entire ocean? What was it that was so bad that Lester Fanning and his palace of wild rabbits, split firewood, and rusted cars was their savior?

She picked blouses from the clothesline and handed them to the girl, and she cobbled a story in her head that would explain her, and the old man. They were chased from their village for a crime they didn't commit. No, she thought. Maybe they knew too much for their own good, and they were staying one step ahead of assassination. It was something she eventually did with each set of visitors. Imagine that they were something they certainly were not. Deposed royalty, or spies perhaps, who secretly understood every single word she said, yet locked them tightly away with all of the other secrets they had collected over the thousands of miles they'd traveled.

"Thank you," the girl said. It was like the words of a small child, the repetition of a set of memorized sounds followed with a smile and the expectation of reward.

"You're welcome," Nadine said. And when the girl said, *You're welcome*, Nadine said it again. "You're welcome."

"You're welcome," the girl replied back, and then she said, "*Bu-ke-qi. Shee-Shee.* Thank you. *Bu-ke-qi.* You're welcome."

"*Shee-Shee,*" Nadine said. "*Bu-ke-qi.* You're welcome."

20

Rodney and Otis sat in the living room watching a bowling match on television that Otis had settled on. Out in the kitchen, Rodney's mother worked by herself, knocking pots on the stovetop and turning the faucet on and off, muttering the whole time to nobody in particular. There was more noise than usual out there, and if Otis caught this, he gave no evidence of it. His eyes didn't move from the screen, from the scatter of pins and the pumping fists of thick-mustached men.

"Rodney," his mother suddenly called out.

Otis broke from the show for a brief moment, giving Rodney a look.

"Come help me wash this pan," she said, tapping the side of a roaster. It had been lasagna, and she had overcooked it. Cleaning that pan would be an ordeal.

"Can't it soak?"

"Come in here and keep me company." Her voice was elevated, high and birdlike. Forced into something that was not her at all. "It sure gets lonely in this kitchen by myself, you know."

Otis said, "Go on to Mama," and jutted his chin out at him. Rodney gave Otis a twist of his lip and shuffled over to the sink. He let the water run and dropped in some soap, moving his hand over the topography of the pan bottom. His mother remained next to him, sponging the countertop in slow, circular movements that hardly resembled any real cleaning.

"So?" she said.

"So what?"

"So, how is school?"

"Fine." When did she ever care about school?

"Who's your teacher again?"

"Miss Carr."

She whispered, *Miss Carr*, and then she started swirling the sponge again. "Otis says there's a teacher at the school who has a wooden leg," she said. "I never heard that before. Have you?"

Rodney had never heard anything of the kind. A wooden leg. He ran through the faces of every teacher he knew, and tried to picture them walking in the halls, across the playground toward their students all lined up against the wall. There was no one he could think of who could have a leg made of wood.

"It sounds like a lie to me," he said.

"It might not be true, but I wouldn't go so far as to call it a lie," she said. "It could be that Otis is just teasing."

"Same thing," Rodney said, "A lie is a lie."

"Teasing is supposed to be fun, like a joke. Lying is"—she paused—"deceptive. Wrong." She stopped with the sponge and turned to face him. "Let's say that someone told you to keep the truth from me," she said, "or to give me an answer that wasn't true, even though I asked you point-blank." She pointed the sponge at him. "*That* would be lying."

Where was this coming from and, more important, where was it going?

"Sounds like a couple of old ladies gossiping." Otis had

come into the kitchen and pulled a chair from the table and slid into the seat, his legs stretched all the way to his filthy socks.

"She said you told her someone at my school had a wooden leg," Rodney said.

"That's what I heard," he said. "Some woman named Brown or Green, or something like that."

"There's no one at my school with a color for a last name."

Otis snorted. "Oh you're the expert all of a sudden?" he said. "You've been in this place not even a year and you know all about who works at that school and who doesn't."

The lasagna pan was clean now, but Rodney kept on scrubbing.

His mother dropped the sponge in the sink and turned around to look at Otis. "I get the feeling sometimes there's some secret between you all that I'm being kept out of," she said, "What do you say to that, Rodney?"

Otis said, "What do you say to that, Rod? Mama wants to know what secrets you're keeping from her."

Rodney could feel eyes on him, like spider legs on his neck. They'd had a deal, right? Rodney had done what Otis had told him to do, and he hadn't whispered a single word to anyone else about it. Every night he lay in bed with the payment for that loyalty hidden less than a foot beneath him. What was Otis trying to do here? Test him?

He picked up the pan from the sink and handed it to his mother. "It's all done," he said. He wiped his hands on his jeans and kept his eyes locked on hers. "I don't have secrets."

"You'd better not," she said. "I went through this enough with your father; I don't need to relive it now."

She glanced quickly at Otis, who laughed and said, "I don't know what you think could happen right under your nose that you wouldn't know about."

"Yeah, well, I notice you've got a lot of pocket money lately. And what about all that stuff in the garage? I don't think I've ever seen so much crap in my life. Why anyone would be willing to pay good money for it, I'll never understand."

"I'm a resourceful man," Otis said. "I'm a mover and a shaker. You should be happy."

"I'll be happy when I know what the hell is moving and shaking under my own roof," she said. She took the pan and dropped it into the lower cupboard with a pointed racket, then stomped from the kitchen and to her bedroom, slamming the door behind her.

Rodney wiped down the counter and turned to leave, but Otis was right there, standing in his way. His arms hung loosely at his sides, fingers wiggling like he was typing on a typewriter. Rodney stepped to one side, and Otis mirrored him. A simple curl raised at one side of his mouth.

"What?" Rodney took a step back. "I didn't say anything."

"Good. You'd be smart to keep it that way."

Rodney pushed off from the counter and moved to circle past Otis. He didn't get one step beyond before Otis grabbed hold of his arm.

"That night…" He squeezed down, his fingers working themselves into the muscle. He leaned in close, his breath hot against Rodney's ear. "You didn't exactly come away empty-handed."

"I didn't ask for anything." He pulled back against Otis's grip, but those fingers held tight.

"You sure as hell didn't refuse what you got, either."

Rodney pulled back again. "You're hurting my arm," he said. "Otis—"

There was the sharp sound of the bedroom door clicking open, and Rodney's mother's voice calling down.

"Otis. Come and talk. Please."

Otis reached over and gave Rodney a little shove in his shoulder. "I guess you can't pick the rose without getting pricked by thorns," he said with a wink. "Don't stay up too late reading."

21

Nearly the whole of Boone still lay sleeping as Louis drove himself into town, chimneys smokeless and windows blackened, streetlights flickering over empty streets still littered with last night's tossed beer cans and burger wrappers. To the east, the Iron Range was barely visible, with only the drowsiest of blue opening up over the ridge line.

The heater began blowing warm over his hands at last, just as he steered himself into the station lot. He held his fingers to the vents, letting them thaw as he leaned forward and stared up at the old ranch-style building, at the security light as it stuttered blue over the clapboard. The faint layer of frost on the shake roof was not something he had expected, though he wasn't surprised by it. For a brief moment, the scene pushed him back into January, when the freeze would have stayed up there all day and Vinnie still had that little room of his own over at Cedar Glen. Before things had gone to hell.

Louis let himself into the station, his key fighting the old lock like he was busting into the place. The waiting room had its Tuesday morning haze of pine cleaner and floor wax, with the blinking of Holly's phone message light casting a rhythmic orange over the walls. He ignored the wall switches, instead going straight to his office in darkness, where he snapped on his little desk lamp and unrolled the morning *Tribune* beneath its glow. In this moment, in this place, it wasn't about last night's news or the brewing coffee in the kitchen next door. It was about the quiet, the solitude. Too often he found himself forgetting what it was like to be all alone, without the constant burden of some other soul in the next room draining the life out of him. He thumbed through the usual articles about gas shortages and the souring economy, drawing out the sports section for a deeper study to be done at a later time.

He had emptied his first cup of coffee when his serenity was violated by the swing of the front door and the mumble of Holly's answering machine cycling through the calls. The harsh fluorescents snapped on and spilled in, soon followed by footsteps. Mitchell poked his head into the office doorway.

"There's a message from some gal up in Blind Horse," he said, that hair of his catching the new cut of sunrise breaking in through the window. "Says she came across a bag of something we might want something to do with."

"Why's she calling us? Tobias isn't more than fifteen minutes from there."

Mitchell shrugged. "Maybe she figured it was too important to hand over to a part-time fella," he said. "Wanted the big guns."

"Tobias is a sturdy lawman."

"Barney Fife," Mitchell grinned. When Louis didn't respond, Mitchell wagged a thumb over his shoulder. "I'll go ahead and run up there if you want."

Louis leaned back in his chair and smoothed his palms over

his eyes. It was early still, quiet to the point of sleeping. The drive might do him some good. He took his hat from the rack and turned it over in his hands.

They took Louis's cruiser, Mitch hugging shotgun, the window cracked just enough to bring in a whistle of cold from outside. The mustard fields were lit up now from the asphalt to the ridge, an endless plane of gold as far as the eye could see, occasionally interrupted by Volkswagen-sized boulders, prehistoric remnants of the great Missoula floods.

"I'll never get over those," Louis said, nodding to a lone sphere off in the distance.

"It sure would have been a sight to see," Mitch said. "Forty foot wall of water, they say. Coming at sixty miles per hour."

Louis glanced down at his speedometer and considered this fact. They were moving at a good clip.

"How's Trudy?" he asked.

"She misses you. Wishes you'd come out for dinner sometime."

In the early years, Mitchell and his wife were always trying to get him to come up for a meal or whatnot, excuses to sit on the porch of their big, pitched cedar house drinking wine and staring down at the green ribbon of the Columbia, as it lazily wound its way through the craggy basalt columns. They'd talk about Mitchell's teenage years reeling in sockeye off the Kenai Peninsula, and Louis would unpack the old stories of him and Vinnie working to build the Grand Coulee Dam, back before the war, before he threw in the pickaxe for the badge and Vinnie ran off to Tacoma, where he'd spend the next decade or so burning a whole slew of bridges.

"Tell her I said I'll try and make it out before too long."

Mitch gave a quiet laugh. "I'll tell her you said that."

What Louis couldn't—or *wouldn't*—say was that he could never really find a way to get settled in that house, with the two of them and that daughter of theirs chirping about vacations and church and school, things so foreign to him. After the same few conversations were exhausted, Louis was always mapping his steps to the exit, an escape from his role as the proverbial third wheel, a possible suitor for Trudy's widowed mother, or some gal or another from the bank or the hair salon, prospects always described as having the best senses of humor, just a few years younger than Louis.

"The greatest wonder is in Uncle Sam's fair land . . ." Louis made no attempt to find the tune, just spoke it out like it was a poem. "It's that King Columbia River, and the big Grand Coulee Dam."

Mitch nodded. "Woody Guthrie."

"Woodrow Wilson Guthrie," Louis said.

The sun was well in the sky now, and Mitch had let the window creep down a little further, so they had to raise voices to hear one another over the incoming wind. Mitch thumbed toward the north. "I read somewhere that the power company paid him to write that. Try and sell the public on the big dam."

"It was a different time."

"Yes, it was."

"You say that like you remember." Louis glanced over to Mitch, whose eyes were fixed away from him, just staring straight out at the fields.

"I remember what my folks told me," he said. "What they still tell me. I don't suggest I know better than you, Lou."

They left it there, and took to filling the rest of the space with work, of Mitch's recent call on the Wyatt twins, and the shiner Cecil had given Calvin. It was a woman who'd come between them this time, and Mitch mused that it seemed a better reason than a motorcycle, as the previous call had been.

It was almost eleven o'clock when they pulled into the rutted lot of the Hitching Post Tavern. It was the same crippled shack Louis recalled from an ugly biker brawl a few years earlier, the outside walls draped in the familiar ragged horse tack and rusted shoes, the whole place seemingly held together by its slowly peeling coat of filthy white paint.

"Good things happen here," Mitch quipped.

"Now and then, I guess."

Louis pushed his way in through the front door, and waited out the momentary haze of coming from sun into sunless. Inside, it was tavern-thick with the smell of last night's smoke and spilled beer, and today's after shave vs. underarm. A slow dance ballad groaned from the jukebox, the layers of slide guitar and a remorseful woman. From the back, the crack of billiard balls knocking against one another.

There were less than a half-dozen people in the joint, most of them belly-pressed to the bar. They turned to look at Louis and Mitch, but paid no real attention, not enough to put down their bottles and stop talking. The bartender was almost as weathered as the siding outside, with a ducktail swept back from a face like a drawn curtain. He looked like he'd not moved from behind the bar since that hair of his had been a thing.

"What can I do you gentlemen for?" His voice was unexpected, soft like a woman's, and Louis wondered what kind of trouble that might have brought him over the years. "A couple of beers?"

Louis thumbed his badge, and the man cocked his head and said, "You ain't local then, if you're letting that stop you."

"We're looking for Yvette," Mitch said.

"There ain't nobody named Yvette here," the bartender answered. And then they all stared at one another. A couple of billiard balls knocked in the back. Finally, the bartender said, "We got a Yvonne."

Mitch took out his palm notebook and flipped the pages. "Is she working now?"

"She's in the can at the moment."

They took a booth, Louis setting a couple of Coke bottles on the table between them. Mitch looked at his watch and asked about the state of things at the Youngman household.

"Hell, I don't know," Louis said. "It's a slow leak with Vinnie. Like a nail in his tire."

"That's a hard thing to watch happen," Mitch said.

"And that woman." Louis took a drink from the bottle, a drop falling from the bottom onto his trousers leg. "I can't seem to decide if its good to have her around, or if one of these days I'm gonna come home to find my place in a pile of cinders."

"Hattie's had her bad patch," Mitch said. "Hell, we all saw that play out. But she's in a better place now." Mitch pushed him some more on that, suggesting that Hattie's company might actually be a good thing. "I imagine she could be a help to him," he said. "There's a lot someone can do if they're willing to just sit around and talk. What's his recall?"

"Here and there," Louis said. "He can tell me all about a stray dog he came across in 1932, or the number of catfish we got on a single day when we were kids. But I'll be goddamned if he can't find his way through the same grocery store he's been going to for the last five years."

Mitch leaned over, his elbows propped on the table, a topography of concern over his forehead. It was a shame, he said. He'd had an uncle who'd lost his world in that way. "It was slow at first," he said. "Almost like someone had pulled a little tiny plug from the back of his head."

"That's what it's like," Louis said.

"Till the end," Mitch added. "I don't want to bring you down."

"No worry of that," Louis smiled. "I'm already on the ground floor."

"Yvonne." It was the gentle voice from behind the bar, and Louis looked back over his shoulder to see a woman coming from the back room, wiping her hands over her jeans. She wore her hair in a single, thick braid down her shoulder, and a red flannel shirt that fit her like a cattle rancher. Square and sturdy, Louis thought.

The bartender nodded his chin toward the booth and Louis raised a hand, as if there were a dozen old cops in the nearly empty place.

"Oh Christ, hold on," she said, and then she disappeared into the back again. A dull ache was starting behind Louis's eyes; he was already wishing he'd just let Mitch come here on his own. Somebody busted into a phlegmy laugh, one of the coots sitting at the bar, and the bartender said, "Settle down you two or I'll have to put you out on your heels."

Yvonne reappeared, carrying a sandy leather satchel. "You got here pretty quick." She laid the bag on the table like it was captured game, a shot pheasant or a rabbit.

Louis fingered the laces at the top as Yvonne stood with her legs pressed against the table's edge, her arms folded over her chest, eyes ticking between Louis and Mitch.

"What have we got here?" Mitch asked.

"I figured you'd know." She glanced over her shoulder to the bar, at the gin-blossomed faces looking back at her. "Why don't you all count the ice cubes in your glass?" she snapped at them. "Jesus."

Louis drew open the top and looked down into the bundle of crap inside—envelopes, folders, loose papers—all stuffed in as if someone had had to go somewhere with no time to waste. He pulled out an envelope and thumbed through the contents. It was writing he didn't recognize, some letters familiar, others unlike any kind he'd ever seen.

"The morning cleaner found it a couple weeks ago and stuck it back in the office. Didn't tell nobody about it." Yvonne said. "I only noticed it in there yesterday when I was looking for a lost set of teeth."

Mitchell laughed at that and Yvonne said, "You think I'm joking." She nodded her chin at the papers. "Anyway, after taking a gander inside I figured it was more than just a local yahoo's shit."

"Passport," Mitchell said, and he pinched out a small, red booklet.

"Russian, ain't it?" Yvonne reached over and tapped it with her finger. When both men gave her a look, she said, "What? You think I was born in this place? I know a thing or two about the outside world."

Louis flipped through to the photo, to the familiar face that stared somberly back at him. The full, rounded jawline, the bridge of the nose that fanned out like it had been pressed. He passed it to Mitch.

"Oh well, now." He looked back up at Louis, then glanced

over to Yvonne.

Louis said, "You have any idea how this got here, Yvonne?"

She shrugged. "Nobody remembers this guy," she said. "Someone like that, talking Russian like he probably would have. You couldn't hide that shit."

Louis thanked her and asked her to keep quiet about it, at least around anyone who didn't already know.

Neither man said anything more about it until they were back onto the clean asphalt of the highway. It was then that Mitchell finally asked about the papers, and Louis said he didn't know what to make of it, but that he could try to track someone at WSU, that they probably had a professor there who could translate. Mitchell said that was all fine and good, but what he really wanted to know was what Louis's gut told him, as if Louis's instinct had ever been any kind of divining rod.

He reached over and took up the passport, looked at the man's face again, working to superimpose it to the one that had gazed vacantly up at him in the pines. The knuckles grated and dried like little strips of rawhide. Russians didn't just show up in Stevens County like this.

"My gut is, this fellow didn't come into the country all by himself. He was likely brought over up at Kettle River."

"Smuggled."

Louis gave a heavy nod. "Smuggled over and then something went sideways."

"What would he be doing up in Twelvemile, though?"

"I'd guess that it happened somewhere else," Louis said. "Twelvemile was just a dumping spot. Probably hoping he'd be picked clean before anyone found him."

Mitchell seemed to consider this, his fingers curled into his palm, picking at one fingernail with the other.

"Well this sure turns a funny page, doesn't it?" he said, looking up at Louis.

"How's that?"

"In all my years wearing this badge, I've never had to deal with an actual murder."

22

On that September morning, after a long bicycle ride through a hard, unrelenting rain, Rodney sat in a crowded classroom that reeked of wet wool and unwashed underarms. If Miss Carr, his teacher, noticed the smell, she gave no sign, but instead casually walked up and down the aisles reading aloud from a textbook opened at her chest, something about Thomas Paine, and the idea of government being both lousy and important. "Necessary evil," she called it. She went on like that, her voice a metronome, the classroom a sea of eyelids and jaws slowly losing battle with gravity. Suddenly, she stopped midsentence and turned to face the door.

"Rodney," she called out, her eyes trained on the window to the hallway.

He straightened in his seat. What had he done?

"Otis Dell is standing there in the hall." Miss Carr turned her head toward Rodney. "I'm guessing he's here to see you?"

From where he was seated, Rodney could see nothing against the door glass but the reflection of the white sky from the opposite window. Chairs groaned under the weight of the other kids as they craned their necks to try and get a look at the man in the hallway.

"Why do you think he's here for me?" he asked. "He's not my dad."

"I thought he and your mother ..." Miss Carr stopped then as her cheeks flushed, and a wash of pink spread down her neck to her chest. "Perhaps you should go and see what he wants."

Rodney scanned the faces around him, some still gawking at the door, the rest staring him down, this silent majority agreeing with Miss Carr that, yes, he had better go and see what Otis Dell wanted.

His scarecrow body was resting against the lockers opposite the classroom door, like he belonged there. His hands were in his pockets, and he sported a yellow baseball cap with a picture of a hammer on the front, the bill pushed down so that it practically hid those black eyes of his. Hair fell out from the edges of his hat like burnt grass, and the work shirt he wore did not even have his own name stitched on the front.

"What're you doing here?" Rodney asked, closing the door behind him and moving out of sight of the window. Otis did not belong there. By that classroom, in that school. Nowhere.

"I figured we'd play hooky, you and me." Otis took his hand from his pocket and held out a scrap of paper. It was a note of some kind, with his mother's name scratched at the bottom.

"That's not her handwriting," Rodney said.

"They don't know that," Otis grinned.

"Who's Leroy?" Rodney asked, stepping back and nodding to the stitching on Otis's shirt pocket.

Otis looked down and rubbed his thumb over the patch. "Leroy's a guy who wears the same size shirt as me." He pushed off from the lockers and began to walk down the hallway in long strides. "Trying to be a nice guy here," he said over his shoulder.

"But whatever. I don't give a rat's ass what you do."

The boots on linoleum were like fists beating against the walls. In the classroom, Miss Carr's voice had started back up, ticking away facts and dates and sleepy asides. At the end of the hall, just before the double doors, Otis stopped and put his hand up in the window light. One finger, then two. Three.

Rodney grabbed his backpack from his locker and slammed the metal door shut, the snap of two dozen eyes looking up at him from the classroom as he left. He ducked past the office and out the front door, climbing into Otis's Bonneville just as he kicked it into gear, and the two of them pulled away from the curb with a roar of the engine and tires screaming like a kicked dog. They shot through the neighborhood streets, avoiding the downtown core, hardly slowing for the countless intersections they crisscrossed along the way.

Rodney held his backpack to his stomach, watching the blur of houses through his window. His bicycle was still chained to the rack next to the gym doors, and he had left his notebook on his desk.

"Where are we going?" he asked.

"Crazy," Otis said, tapping his fingers on the steering wheel.

"Mom doesn't know you took me."

"I didn't take you. You walked out on your own two legs."

"She doesn't know."

"And she won't. Not unless you blab to her." He looked at Rodney. "You gonna do that?"

Otis spun the wheel hard to the right, and they doubled back onto McMahon Boulevard, heading out where the warehouses and stockyards sat on the far end of town. "Let it ride, kid," he said, slapping Rodney on the knee. "It's gonna be a hell of a day."

They cruised past the old brick buildings that stuck to the edges of McMahon, the tall, thin-paned windows blinking the late morning sun. People lingered in doorways or against the fenders of parked cars, some nodding their chins at the Bonneville as it went past, as if they had been expecting a drive-by. As if, whatever big secret there was going down, they were all in on it.

Otis swung the car around and reached over Rodney's lap into the glove compartment. He fished around in there for a few seconds, finally coming back with a pair of mirrored sunglasses that he slid onto his face. And at the end of the block he pulled off the road, into the parking lot of the Fine Boy Drive In.

They took a spot some distance from the window. Otis told Rodney to keep his ass in the car and wait, that he'd go on over and order for the two of them. He strutted up there like he always did, like the world was waiting on him, and he stood at the window talking up the girl who probably lived her days behind that register, under a folded paper hat. Otis leaned on his elbows and pushed his head into the window opening some, and the girl moved back, turning to one side as if she was talking to someone else. Before long a man came out from the back with a cup in his hand and gave it to Otis.

"You're welcome for the milkshake." Otis swung the cup over to Rodney's hands and squeezed his shoulder. Then he took a look at his watch and leaned back in his seat, staring out the window into the empty parking lot. The way he had that cap pushed up on his head made Otis appear to be a different person, as if he should be throwing a baseball with Rodney, or teaching him to fix his bicycle. The line of his whiskered jaw pulsed, and when he glanced at Rodney, he smiled through tobacco-stained teeth, as if there was some great need to reassure that the two of them were indeed there together, like buddies. That there was not a hidden reason for this whole thing.

"Am I going back to school or what?"

"Do you want to?" Otis asked.

Rodney didn't know that he wanted that, and he said so.

Otis cocked his head and pushed his knee against Rodney's. "Well shit, boy. If you don't know then who the hell does?" He looked at his watch again. "Tell me about that teacher I saw through the window," he said. "She wouldn't be bad to look at all day."

Rodney thought of Miss Carr still in that classroom, still reading that book, or maybe passing out dittoed maps for everyone to fill in with the wrong names, noticing but not caring about the abandoned notebook on his desk. He had not thought of her in that way, though. Like Otis was suggesting.

"She's all right," he said.

Otis said, "She's got nothing up top, though." He patted his chest. "I had a teacher when I was your age, Mrs. Tallow. Now that was a woman. The hands in that class were like pistons, boy. Going up right and left just so she'd come over to you. Lean over your desk to help. Those things'd be right up against your face before you knew what was what."

He laughed and then looked over at Rodney. "Don't tell your mother that story, either." And when Rodney didn't say anything to that, he continued. "There's things she won't understand, Rod. Stuff she just can't, being a woman and all. Things like ditching school now and then. Having a milkshake at ten o'clock in the morning. Certain things we might keep just for ourselves. Things . . . things we might, say . . . hide under our mattress." There was a snake grin on his face, the lips stretched to the edges, lines raked into his face. He jabbed his hand out and said, "Deal?"

Rodney didn't respond, but Otis took his hand anyway, and

did the shaking himself. Then he fired up the engine and drove off from the diner. They did not turn back in the direction of the school, but rather steered onto the county road that would take them north up into the hills toward the Indian reservation. Otis turned on the radio and punched at the dials until he settled on a country western station, a low band of static crackling beneath the yodeling singer.

By this time Rodney had decided there would be no point in asking any more questions. Otis had the day mapped out and any further needling would only end in a fight, with Otis shouting and Rodney in tears.

They wound through spreads of cheat grass and spruce-pocked groves, and past skinny roadways that split off the highway to snake toward lone, sun-beaten farmhouses. On they went, the radio still swaying, whizzing by tilted fence posts connected by taut lines of barbed wire, and when they came up over a saddleback in the road, a Gas n' Go sprang into view, curly letters and a faded picture of a hot dog on the plywood sign. Otis turned off, bringing the car to a stop in the gravel lot, next to a giant pill-shaped propane tank.

"You know what a Lincoln looks like, right?" he said, producing a scrap of paper from his pocket, handing it to Rodney. "It's a big, long car."

"Like Mr. Kruger's." Rodney said. He remembered.

Otis thumbed the paper. His jaw pulsed and twitched, and he looked at Rodney as if he had struck the nail precisely where it should have gone. "I guess he did have a Lincoln," he said. "Yeah. Like Kruger's."

A pickup rolled in from the highway, coming to a hard stop at the fuel pump. A Paul Bunyan guy climbed from the driver's side door, barrel-chested with a charcoal shock of a beard. He stepped from the running board to the ground, took a sweep of the lot, and lumbered on into the minimart.

"I got this thing I have to do," Otis said, "and I need your skills." He leaned back in his seat and pointed through the windshield. "You see that road there?"

Rodney stared out at the thin, white line of dust that wound its way from the paved road up into a landscape of mustard-spotted hills. He said, "Yeah I see it," and then looked back to Otis. He was leaning into Rodney now, his hands practically against the boy's legs, as if he thought Rodney might jump from the car any minute and break into a run.

"I gotta go off somewhere for a little bit," he said.

"Where are you going?"

"Somewhere, I said." He pointed to the far edge of the parking lot. "You see that phone booth over there?" Just over the curb, under the umbrella of a hearty maple, was a blue-and-silver box. A rickety old picnic table sat nearby, squeezed against the maple trunk. "Now, if you see a big old Lincoln happen to turn up that road after I'm gone," Otis went on, "I want you to pick up that phone and give the number on that paper a call. You let it ring two times then hang up." He leaned onto one side and dug his hand into his jeans pocket and brought out a dime, laying it on Rodney's pants leg.

The coin was filthy with grease, and the paper smeared with numbers that looked as if a child had scrawled them out. Beyond the blue-and-white phone booth lay a vast field of purple-specked flax, a single wheel move sprinkler parked in the center. From somewhere deep in his gut Rodney felt a tumble. *Maybe,* he thought, *I'll just throw up, right here in Otis's car and it'll all be done.*

"Don't get yourself coiled up in a knot," Otis said, sweeping a hand over Rodney's hair. "The chances of you even having to make the call is almost zero."

"Zero?"

"Almost." Otis checked his watch. "Now, tell everything back to me."

"I heard you," Rodney said.

Otis leaned into him. "Tell. It. Back. to me."

Rodney took hold of the door handle and stared up at the white ribbon road cutting its way between those low brown hills, and he repeated everything Otis had said to him, about the car and the phone number, and the number of rings, two, before hanging up.

Otis studied him, a look of sleepy satisfaction as Rodney droned out the replay, and when it was finished, he leaned across the seat and pushed open the passenger door. No sooner had Rodney stepped out into the parking lot did Otis punch the accelerator and drive off, his Bonneville lurching straight up the dirt road into the hills.

Rodney kicked a rock across the parking lot, where it arched past the phone booth and disappeared into the sea of flax. He walked over and settled onto the splintered bench, the table beside it peppered with powdery bird shit and fallen maple keys. The sun's light pushed through the leaves and flashed in and out of his periphery, but Rodney could see the empty road stretching to and from town, the gentle dips in the topography where a car could easily hide from view if it wanted to.

In the store window was a clock reading just after eleven. He would be in math class now. Mr. Byers was likely standing at the chalkboard working out a problem and showing every-one the proper steps, something that Rodney would now have no idea how to do.

There was a crackle of tires on the gravel and a car rolled into the lot, pulling up right next to him, at the phone booth. It was a little orange Japanese car, with a sheet of bunched plastic covering the hole where the rear driver's side window should have been. The door swung open and a woman climbed out, fish-white legs pouring out of a pair of cutoff jeans, the soft fringe wrapped tightly around her thighs. She slapped her purse down on the hood and snapped back the flap, digging through the bag like everything she ever owned in her life was inside it.

Rodney stood up and moved toward the phone, fingering the dime in his pocket. The woman snatched up her purse and looked up at him, eyeballing him like he might draw a gun on her at any second.

"Are you using it?"

"I might," he said. He knew that was an answer that meant nothing, but there was nothing else he could really say.

She rolled a shoulder and moved past him, slipping into the box and dropping several coins into the slot, then punching away at the numbers as if each one was an ex-boyfriend.

The activity from the highway continued to be unremarkable, and a faint haze of white dust lifted in the hills where the Bonneville had disappeared. A couple cars that were not Lincolns cruised past, headed in the direction of Hope. There was a chittering in the maple branches, a couple of red squirrels circling the trunk and carrying on with one another like an old, tired married couple. Like Rodney had seen a few times in his own kitchen. A few more whirlybirds floated down, spiraling out onto the patchy, yellow grass.

From behind Rodney the growl of a beefy engine swelled, and a boxy pickup truck pulled in heavy, the cab rocking back and forth. On the door was the stenciled outline of a horse, rearing up on its rear hooves, front legs arched forward, black paint on white. The driver brought the truck to a stop next to the fuel pump, a clang of bells ringing out as it rolled over the cables.

The woman squawked into the phone with her back to Rodney, and there was anger in her voice, the pitch rising and falling in hard kicks. "He *promised*," she said. "A million times already." It went on like that for some time, the shouting about this man and a baby, someplace, and a pile of bills that sat on the counter at home, all unpaid, not the least bit of care that the ugliness of her life was being flushed right out into the parking lot of the Gas n' Go.

"You're a fair distance out of bounds."

Rodney's stomach gave a knock, like an electric shock. He looked up to see the familiar white flattop and curled mustache of Charlie Kruger. He stood just outside the shade of the maple canopy, those ringed fingers of his bare now, thumbs hooked over his glossy black belt. His blue-striped tie fluttered in the breeze against a pillow stomach.

"Everything okay?"

Rodney looked over at the pickup again, at the same horse stencil he'd seen every single day for as long as he'd been going to the feed store. How had he not recognized it when it had pulled in?

"Are you with her?" Kruger asked, nodding toward the woman in the booth.

Rodney shook his head. He could not come up with any words to explain what he was doing here, by himself, next to a phone booth in the middle of nowhere. "Otis," he finally said. The name fell out of his mouth like his body was ridding itself of a virus. "Otis." Once more, just to be sure.

Kruger looked around. "Where is Otis? Did he go off and leave you?"

"He forgot something," Rodney said. "He'll be back soon."

Kruger ran his hand along the top of his head, the thick, white turf springing back as he passed over the surface. He watched Rodney closely, eyes searching, the loop of his mustache twitching just so. He turned and looked over his shoulder, at the roadway that rolled up into the hills.

"I'm okay," Rodney said.

"All right then," Kruger said. "If you say so." Just as he began to walk back to the pickup, he stopped and looked back over his shoulder once more. The flesh of his neck spilled over the collar, his eyelids reddened and tired, and yet—a sense of kindness there. "Is this something I ought not mention to your mother?"

Rodney glanced back at the woman in the booth, who was, once again, digging into that purse of hers. What would his mother do if she found out where he was, with Otis? There had been secrets—too many. *I went through this enough with your father*, she'd told him. *I don't need to relive it now.*

Rodney had no answer for him.

At that, Kruger climbed up into the cab and fired up the engine. He did not put any gas in the tank or get anything from inside the store, but he rolled down his window and put out his arm, and gave Rodney one last look before pulling away from the pumps. He paused only briefly at the exit before crossing the highway and steering on up the dirt road, into the sage-covered hills.

The woman stood outside the booth now, the cord stretched as far as it would go. Rodney moved close to her and held the dime in his fingers, so she could see if it she looked at him. Which she didn't.

It had not been a Lincoln, but it was Mr. Kruger, and maybe that's what it had been about all along. By making the call, who was he helping most? If Otis was up to something—and Otis really was probably up to something—would the call send him running for the hills or would he crouch behind a tree or a closed door, just waiting for Mr. Kruger?

By doing nothing, though, he'd be leaving the unexpected, the possibility of a nasty surprise. And if he'd learned anything from all those *House of Mystery* stories, surprise never turned out well.

Rodney leaned to one side to catch the woman's eye and, when she finally did look at him, it was a tossed glance, the kind of thing given to a mere distraction. It was only when he moved into her direct line of vision, practically sitting on that orange car of hers, that she finally gave in.

"Oh Jesus," the woman yelled, putting the handpiece to her breast and expelling an intentional, heavy sigh. "What is your problem, kid?"

"I need to use that," he said, nodding to the phone.

"Too bad. I'm using it."

"You can't hog."

"Watch me," she said, and at that, she snapped the booth door behind her and spun around, turning her body completely away from him.

A tumble of white dust rose above the roadway, heading further up the hill. Rodney pushed through the station door, the man behind the counter giving him a reflective look at best. "Can you believe it," the man said. At the opposite end of the store, an old codger moved packs of Marlboros from a carton into an open glass case. "Apparently he drove a little Volkswagen bug. That's what they knew about him. Drove a VW bug, and wore a fake cast on his arm. To trick the girls into going off with him."

The guy looked to be something of a hippie, stringy hair past his shoulders and a grassy brown beard that he had tied off with a tight red rubber band. He leaned against the back counter, tattooed arms folded over his chest, his fingers tapping out each punctuation. "A gal I used to date swore to God she met him up at Vail, at the ski lodge there," he continued. "Said he had cast on his arm, that he tried to get her to carry his gear to his car. Acted all sad sack and charming. But there was something about him that didn't sit right with her."

"Intuition," the old man loading the cigarettes said. "Probably saved her life." He opened up another carton and began pulling out packs.

"Son of a gun." The hippie guy looked over at Rodney. "You lost, my friend?" Behind him, tucked to the corner near the window, was a chunky black rotary.

"Can I use the phone?" Rodney asked. "That lady won't hang up." His shirt had started to stick to his skin, and there were the beginnings of his own sour odor starting up. "It's kind of important."

The cashier leaned forward and looked out the window. "Phone hog?" he said. "God, I hate phone hogs." He reached over and took the phone and set it on the counter. "Keep it local and keep it short."

Rodney brought out the scrap of paper and unfolded it on the counter. There were no low numbers, the dial just turning and turning forever in slow motion with each digit. He finally finished up on number eight, and there was a clicking sound before the first ring finally broke in. The cashier leaned himself against the back counter again and stared out the window. The second ring sounded, and Rodney set the hand piece back in the cradle.

"That was short." The man behind the counter took the phone and returned it to the spot behind him.

"He said he's coming," Rodney announced, nodding to the phone. "He's on his way, now."

"That so," the cashier said. "You didn't say nothing." He furled his lip and searched Rodney's face like it was a riddle. Like Rodney's mother had done, that day in the kitchen, with all the talk of one-legged teachers and keeping secrets.

"I did so say something." Rodney watched the man's eyes, the lids drooped, unsatisfied. The guy tipped his head toward the old man and Rodney took the moment to escape, turning and pushing through the door to bolt across the lot to the backside of the maple tree where he crouched on the small patch of weed grass and waited. Waited for whatever might eventually come down from those hills.

Three cars and a pickup truck came and went before the woman finally slammed the phone down and stomped out. Rodney did not look at her except to curse at the tail end of her car as she tore out of the lot.

The longer he sat there under those leafy branches, the greater the story unraveled in his mind, of what might be happening up in those hills. He expected any minute a parade of lights and sirens tearing up there, and the sound of his mother's voice, the piercing wail on the other end of the telephone when she found out where he was.

And then the cotton clouds began to lift from the high hill and the Bonneville rose briefly into view at last. It dipped then reappeared again as the roadway descended to the highway. The car did not stop when it reached the intersection, but sailed directly over the roadway into the lot, coming to a hard stop in front of the maple.

"Get in the goddamned car!" Otis screamed at Rodney through the open window. The top side of his head was wet and shiny, a small trail of red running down from his ear. His breath was winded and breaking, his eyes bulging as if they might squeeze right out of their sockets.

For a moment, Rodney could not move. His feet were spiked to the ground, his brain sending orders that his body could not receive. It was only when Otis leaned into the steering wheel, clenched his eyes shut and gave off a grisly, mournful wail, that Rodney snapped out of his trance.

He ran around the back end of the car and jumped in, but then it was Otis who just sat there, rattled breathing tight in his chest, his fingers drumming on the steering wheel, his back arched over and eyes panning upward.

"Otis," Rodney whispered. "Your head . . ." The blood was at his collar now and soaking into the fabric.

Otis kept rolling his fingertips over the wheel. He looked from one end of the highway to the other and then he reached back and pressed his fingers into his hair and brought them back, all blood and nerves. "Oh Jesus," he said. He gave a fugitive look to Rodney then settled back in his seat. "This is just fucking great," he said, and there was a sad tremor in his voice, as if he might collapse into tears at any moment. Spinning the wheel hard to the right, he slammed the gas.

They had gone at least twenty miles, the car moving like ocean waves as Otis alternated between rocket speeds and a near crawl. They were heading north; Rodney knew that much—farther outside Hope than he'd ever gone before. All the while, Otis continued to scan the left and right vistas, muttering to himself with each directional that came into view.

"Where are we going?" Rodney finally asked.

"Where we're *not* going, you mean." Otis whooped a throaty laugh, eyes clicking like a bird's from the horizon to the mirrors, to the gauges. "We're sure as shit not going back where we came from."

And that was it—the punchline that had been a mere, fleeting thought to Rodney when he left school that morning. That Otis's appearance in the hall—and the slow drive through town, the milkshake—could have been nothing more than an impulsive whim, an effort toward some desperate kind of *friendship* on Otis's part.

As if he had been kicked from the inside, it all burst forth. Tears and mucous and gasping for air that wouldn't come, ugly and hideous, and the more Rodney fought to contain it, the harder it forced its way out of him. It broke against him like a pounding surf, his breath coming to him in only in choppy, stingy rations.

And just like that his head snapped to the side, the blinding crash of Otis's hand against his face, striking him just above his mouth.

Rodney shook clear and shrunk back, retreating as far from Otis as he could, his body crouching against the door, hands curled to his mouth. He looked over at the bloodstained hand still raised, just hovering there in the space between them, those fingers shaking, ready to go again.

"What in the holy fuck happened?" Otis screamed at him.

"You had one simple thing to do!"

"I did," Rodney cried out, his voice breaking. "The lady . . ." In his mind she was still there in that phone booth, laughing and swearing about some boyfriend, and their baby, while she kept stuffing dime after dime into that slot.

They held steady for a time, sticking to the road beneath them and meandering through a sparse forest of pine and red-spotted shrubs, and Rodney could see in the distance the towering GAS sign, red, white, and blue letters shouting over the trees.

Otis slapped the dashboard and eased up on the accelerator, swerving the car into the lot and steering them past the red Fire Chief pumps to the back of the building, just outside the toilets. He made a hard stop a few feet from the split, weathered siding and threw open his door. Leaning out, almost laying himself onto the ground, he sucked in a chestful of air and pushed it out through his teeth, a pitched whistle.

"You better go on in there," he said. "It'll be the last chance you get for a while."

Rodney pushed on the door with Otis right on his heels, crowding him into the small bathroom. It was a one-person outfit, a rust-smeared basin bolted to the wall and a single toilet sitting all by itself in the corner.

"Don't worry," Otis said. "You got nothing down there I'm interested in."

Rodney turned himself away from Otis as much as he could. Behind the sound of his zipper he heard the click of the lock behind them. He stood over the bowl and watched his stream roil the water, and scanned the graffiti around him, the phone numbers and words about sex and women, and war and drugs.

After what may well have been the longest piss Rodney had ever taken, he finished up and flushed it all away and did up his pants before turning back to the door. Otis stood there at the mirror with the flickering fluorescent lighting against his face, shadows and cuts gouging a kind of death mask over him. He held a small stack of paper towels against his head, and mooned at his reflection, as if the face looking back at him was someone he had never in his life seen before.

"Go get my hat from the car." He reached behind himself and pulled the door open, and kicked it to the wall.

Rodney went to the back seat and fished around until he found the yellow baseball cap with its hammer picture and salt ring over the rim, and he brought it to Otis, who now stood slouched against the cinderblock just outside the bathroom door. He snatched the hat from Rodney's hand and slid it down over the paper towel bandage, tucking everything up inside like he was putting on a wig.

"Wait for me in the car," he said, wiping his hands over his jeans. Then he limped around the corner of the building to the little payphone that was mounted to the outside wall of the station. It was something to see, that was for sure. The way Otis jammed that handset against his ear. The way he held onto that cord, and pounded those numbers like he was killing ants. And he stayed that way the entire time, not once looking back to see if Rodney had actually gotten in the car, instead of turning tail and running off into the apple orchards that fanned out behind them.

Otis danced in the sun, moving his weight from one foot to the other, waving an invisible lasso over himself then dropping it gently, brushing it lightly over the outside of that yellow cap like he was dusting pollen. There was a sharp cry from off in the trees, a hawk maybe, and Otis turned around finally to look back at the car. The phone pressed right to his mouth and those lips moved like he was shouting at someone, his eyes locked perfectly to Rodney's. His mouth froze, and he pressed a finger to his opposite ear. Listening, now. Once more he put his hand to his head and that mouth started up again, rattling a few more things into the phone before he finally turned and dropped the receiver onto the hook.

He came back to the car, kicked and beaten. "We're going north from here," he said. "We gotta be invisible for a few days."

"What about Mom?"

"What about her?" He squeezed his eyes shut. "Your mom's fine."

"That was her? Just now, on the phone?"

He looked at Rodney with eyes narrowed. Deep channels ran from his nostrils to the edges of his mouth, and he stayed like that for a long time, hardly moving, a face carved from an old tree trunk.

"I said she's fine," he finally said.

And with that, he cranked the engine and launched the Bonneville out onto the highway.

23

They sat there in the booth, the three of them, picking at burgers and nursing ice water in red plastic glasses. Hattie and Vinnie took up one side of the table, their backs to the window, Hattie just helping herself to his French fries like they were her own.

"I always wanted to ask you something," Hattie said to Louis. "But I don't want you to get all knotted up over it."

Louis shifted in his seat.

Vinnie said, "Here we go."

"Vinnie says you never got married," she said. "From where I'm sitting, I'd say that's a damn shame."

He was a lifelong bachelor, and he knew the kinds of stories that might kick up. There had been women he had loved in his life and, if he was honest with himself, a few men he'd grown awfully fond of, but not in the way folks might raise eyebrows over. There were plenty of things he understood about men and women, though few he'd ever experienced full on. He always thought it would happen unexpected, but here he was, almost seventy.

"I have a hard enough time sharing space with him," Louis said, nodding to Vinnie. "I think I realized a long time ago that I don't always make the best company."

"In other words," Vinnie said, "he don't like people."

At the far end of the parking lot, as a lone woman had set up a tent and was sitting in a big rocker underneath, fiddling with something in her lap. Around the tent was a perimeter of colorful, gaudy blankets hanging from strung lines like laundry, the kind of things you'd see covering windows in the welfare rentals in town: horses rearing up on hind legs, Elvis in profile, three different kinds of Jesus. A breeze was picking up, the blankets rippling on their lines like caught fish.

"I had two wives, the first in Detroit and the second in Tacoma," Vinnie said.

Hattie straightened up. "I thought you said you was only married once."

"I said I had two wives. I never said they was both *mine*." He gave a belly laugh and elbowed Hattie good-naturedly, but she said nothing. Still, he kept at her and nudged her again, and she finally gave up a laugh of her own, elbowing him right back. The two of them looked over at Louis then, like they were up to something sneaky right there in front of him.

Just then, a little car pulled up to the tent in the parking lot, and Louis watched as a woman got out. She walked right over to a queen-sized blanket with a picture of a buck drinking from a pool that was as blue as a robin's egg, and grabbed hold of the blanket's corner, like she was examining a pelt.

"So," Hattie said, side-eyed to Vinnie. "You gonna bring it up or do I got to?"

"Jesus," he said. "I was on my way there." He took a drink of water, the ice bunching against his lips.

"Bring what up?" Louis asked. The possibilities could stretch from here to Canada.

Hattie would not take her eyes from Vinnie, and the old

man kept his chin down, looking up at Louis, a dog waiting for permission to move.

Hattie finally spoke up. "He wants to shack up," she said, helping herself to another French fry. "We both do, I guess."

Vinnie leaned back in his seat as if Hattie had put out a fire at his feet. Cool relief ran down his face.

"Your place, I'm assuming?" Louis said to her.

Vinnie nodded, putting his hand on Hattie's leg. "No reflection on you, Lou."

The woman outside now had three blankets draped over her arms, and the trunk of that little car popped open, a trunk that looked so small it couldn't hold one of those things, much less three. She folded the blankets up into a bunch and shoved them into that space. Louis could see she was having a hard time, bending down and crawling partway in to move things around.

He reached over and took one of the fries himself. "You still work with Tip over at U-Pick?"

Vinnie blew smoke across the table and tapped a clump of ash into the tray. "Who are you talking to?" he asked. "What's Tip got to do with this?"

"Now and then," Hattie said. "He ain't fired me yet."

Louis stirred the fry into the pool of ketchup, slowly, less interested in eating it than the movement. "No hard feelings, then," he said. "Between you and Tip, I mean."

Hattie rolled her eyes. "My days of romance with that man are but the snows of yesteryear," she said. "Tip couldn't care less if I move one man or twenty into my place."

"That's not"—Louis looked over at Vinnie, at those eyes of his, half empty and roaming from his own knotted hands to Hattie's, fingers entwined.

"You can check up on me if you want," Vinnie said, not

looking up from the table. "Send one of your lookouts if it'll make you feel better."

"Hattie," Louis said. "Think you could meet me at the U-Pick tomorrow?

Vinnie said, "Why do you want to go to the U-Pick?"

"I can meet you," she said, ignorning Vinnie. "I'm there anyway."

At last the woman outside got into her car and pulled away, stopping at the edge of the lot. She moved her head from side to side, waiting for the half-dozen or so cars to pass by before finally pulling onto the highway, no turn signal to be bothered with.

24

Lester held both beers by the necks, neither of them cold. Nadine took one, pulling her feet under the chair so he could scoot on past her.

"He'll be here in a couple days, if he makes it at all." Lester sank into his rocker and took out a cigarette, lighting it up and tossing the match off the porch into the dirt. "It's a different situation this time," he said. "This Otis Dell character is bad news. I want you to stay clear of him."

Nadine tipped the bottle to her mouth, took a full drink before answering. "If he's so bad, why is he coming here?"

"I can handle him."

The chickens were acting up behind them; something was likely lurking near the hen house, a raccoon probably, or a coyote. Nadine had secured the pen, so she knew it was tight as a drum.

"Should I expect something out of him?" she asked. "Maybe keep a knife on me or something?"

Lester pushed air through his teeth. "He ain't like that," he said. "He's an asshole and a liar. He might put his hands on you if you let him, but it's nothing a good knee to his balls wouldn't take care of."

Nadine took another drink and stood up from her chair, taking the four steps down to the dirt. She stood there for a good minute or two, watching the branches of the far pines dip and spring back, a gray sparrow darting in and out of the grove, hopping from one tree to the next.

"I don't need this kind of headache, Lester. This is turning out to be as far from *simple* as it gets."

"Jesus Christ, lady." He snapped his cigarette butt onto the ground near her. "I'm not wagging my tail at the thought of him here, either. But it won't do either of us any good if I turn him away."

"What do you mean by that, *Won't do us any good?*" She never saw Lester as a man who did anything he didn't want to do.

He shook his head at her. "It ain't gonna be more than a few days at best. I promise."

She felt her body sink, the weight of defeat sliding down her bones. "Should I even bother asking anything more?"

"The less you know, baby." He raised his bottle to her. She could use another one of those, warm or not.

"I guess I'll make up the sofa, then," she said.

"No." Lester swung open the screen door and held it there. He turned and looked back to Nadine, letting his gaze fell over her for as long as he'd ever done, until Nadine couldn't take it anymore and looked away. "There's a mattress in the back of the Dodge," he finally said. "Put some blankets in there for him."

"That old van?"

"I don't want that sonofabitch setting one foot in my house." Then Lester went inside, letting the screen slam hard behind him.

25

They had traveled through fields of tall cornstalks and the criss-crossed acres of clipped grass that stretched out forever, to the low hills that wrapped them on all sides. Otis looked to be trying to stick to country roads that wound through old farmland with roadside signs warning of God's word and the evils of drunk driving. Cockeyed fence posts connected strings of sagging barbed-wire.

At one point, shortly after he swilled down an entire can of Coke, Otis steered off to the shoulder and vomited a brown fountain out the open window onto the pavement. "Well damn," he said, wiping his sleeve over his mouth. "I didn't see that coming." The stench filled the car, of cola and the nastiness of everything else that had come up with it.

The cars passing by had their headlights snapped on now. Rodney hadn't realized until then that dusk had already begun to settle.

"Are we gonna get a motel?" he asked.

"A motel," Otis said. "Look at you. The little prince." He knocked the car into gear and meandered back onto the highway, leaning over the wheel and scanning the horizon like he was looking for birds, or flying saucers maybe. This went on for a good five miles or so, until he finally took a left branch off the route onto a downward running access road.

Rodney asked, "What's here?" but Otis ignored him, still hugging that steering wheel, his eyes rolling from hill to field now.

"Otis," Rodney said.

"Otis," he echoed back to Rodney, then suddenly he fell against the driver's side window. The Bonneville started to drift, the rise of the nearby shoulder looming toward them. Otis's eyes fluttered and his breathing hissed through a hard-bitten jaw, the white foam of spit pushing through his lips. The casting of fields came up over the dashboard and Rodney grabbed hold of the wheel, bringing the car back into its lane. He managed to push Otis's foot from the gas, enough of an interruption to allow a rolling stop against the graveled shoulder, inches from the split rail fence.

Rodney slid the gearshift to *P* and fell back into his own seat, his shoulder pressed firm to the door. Otis looked to be coming around, his breathing more settled, hands moving over the steering wheel as if he was rediscovering it after a long sleep. It was when Otis shifted himself in his seat that Rodney saw the dark bloom that now spread out over his lap.

"There's water spilled on me," Otis said, running his hand over his crotch. He looked up at Rodney. "What did you spill on me?"

Rodney told him he hadn't spilled anything, but he could not bring himself to say anything further.

Otis dabbed at his lap with his fingers and surveyed the view that stretched from one window to the other. The blood on his forehead had begun to crust over now, the tiny cracks breaking up the heaviest of it.

"I called the number," Rodney said.

"What?"

"I said I called that number, even though it wasn't a Lincoln."

Otis pulled his chin to his chest and searched Rodney's face like he was hearing all of this for the first time.

"If it was Mr. Kruger I was supposed to watch for, you should have said so."

Otis dug around in his shirt pocket and took out a pack of cigarettes, sliding one from the pack, bent and beaten. He punched in the dash lighter and thumbed toward the glove compartment.

"Open that up."

Rodney did as he was told. A small revolver dropped into the cradle of the door, almost toy-like, with a cylinder about the size of a Ping Pong ball. Rodney looked over at Otis, who sat there grinning at him as if he had caught him red-handed in something. Maybe with one of those skin magazines of his.

"Go ahead and pick it up," he said.

Rodney wanted no part of this thing, but Otis insisted, pushing on Rodney's elbow. "Pick up the damn gun," he demanded. "Feel how heavy it is."

Rodney lifted the pistol like it was a dead animal, holding the grip between his thumb and forefinger. And it was heavy in spite of its small size. Otis said, "Hold it like you mean it," and then Rodney took it in his palm, running his finger along the trigger guard, turning it over in his hand, from one side to the other.

"It's a nice piece, huh?" Otis nodded out the window. "Point it, point it out there. Out into the field."

Rodney kept it where it was.

"Don't be a puss," Otis said. "Point it out the window and see what it can do. There's no one around. But hurry the hell up."

Rodney leveled the barrel so that it pointed in the direction of the far distance, and he knew that Otis would not leave him alone until he did it. He squeezed down on the trigger, and there came the hard kick before the crack of the gunshot even registered.

"Sonofabitch!" Otis said, and then he gave a kind of animal howl before snatching the revolver from Rodney's hand and stuffing it under his seat. And as if nothing had happened at all, as if there hadn't just been a bullet fired from this car, he slid the Bonneville into gear and pulled out onto the highway, the weight of acceleration whipping Rodney into his seat back.

They drove in silence for a good while, Otis staring straight forward, wild-eyed, chewing on his lip, only once or twice glancing in Rodney's direction. Finally, he reached over and smacked Rodney's arm.

"Do you know what an accessory is?" he asked.

"You mean like a crime?" Rodney had seen this in stories. People who helped roll the body up inside the big carpet or dig the hole in the woods, or wipe up all the blood from the bathroom floor.

"Yeah. Like in a crime."

Rodney said yes, that he knew what an accessory was.

"Good," Otis said. "Then I don't need to say anything more."

And he didn't, not for a long time. When the sun dropped completely behind the far ridge and the roadway began to bleed indistinctly into the shoulders, Rodney suggested headlights, and Otis snapped them on without a word. There was a strange warmth that came from the glow of the dashboard lights, and Rodney felt a certain security in being able to see that there was plenty of gas, that the engine temperature was in the middle. That they were not going a great deal faster than they were supposed to.

Otis turned into a forest service road, bringing them up above the highway into the curtain of trees. The headlamp beams slid over pine trunks like piano keys, and Rodney thought there were moments when he saw eyes in there looking back at him, eyes of men and monsters.

In time they came to a turnout and Otis pulled into it, laying on the brakes and killing the engine.

"Here's your motel," he said. "You can have the back seat all to yourself and I'll stretch out up here."

Rodney opened the door. The air outside was cool but not cold, and there was much in that car to make him think he would not be getting anything close to a good night's sleep.

"Do you have a blanket or anything?" he asked.

Otis laughed at him. "A blanket," he said. "You might turn up a hand towel back there if you're lucky." He gave Rodney a shove against his leg. "You and me, we're fugitives now, in case you ain't figured it out yet. No blanket is the least of our troubles."

Rodney climbed into the back and pushed the candy wrappers and empty soda cans onto the floor and laid out over the bench seat. An excavated flannel shirt, draped over his torso, did a lousy job of anything other than stinking like Otis. In the front, Otis soon began to rattle the interior with his snoring, breaks of snorts and whistles, and the occasional dead space after the heavy rush of exhale. In those moments Rodney did not think Otis would take another breath in his life, just a stone silence, outside of Rodney's own heart knocking in his head. And then there would come the sudden gasp, and Otis would suck in a roomful of air, as if he'd just surfaced from a deep-sea dive.

It wasn't long before the windows fogged over thick like cotton. Rodney reached up and rolled down the window, and the space was filled with the gift of fresh air that had never touched Otis. He leaned out and took in the scent of juniper and sage and, maybe from far off in the distance, the smallest hint of wood smoke.

The car settled and rocked slightly as he straddled the open window and lowered himself gently to the ground. Outside it was nearly full dark, but from where he stood he could make out a hint of openness, of the roadway in front of him, and he walked slowly from the car up the slope of the drive, the packed dirt and ruts guiding him forward. Overhead, the night sky was a view up into the underside of a colossal umbrella, a million pinholes poking through. A single point of light drifted from star to star in a straight line, and Rodney knew it was a satellite up there. But for a brief moment he imagined it might be a spaceship, an alien craft way up there looking down upon them out there in the middle of nowhere.

"What in the hell are you doing?"

Rodney looked back at the car, at the dull stripe of yellow, the illuminated interior of the Bonneville. The stick silhouette of Otis ambled up the roadway toward him, arms drifting at his sides in broad circles.

"I had to go pee," Rodney lied.

"All the way up here?" Otis came within spitting distance and stopped. He put his hand over his brows as if in salute, then looked back in the direction of the car. A little unsure, Rodney thought. As if perhaps he ought to have felt for that gun before he got out of his car.

"Did you look up?" Otis said, tipping his head back almost

to his shoulders. "Look at how goddamned clear that sky is. There must be a million stars up there." He stood up tall and straight, lifting on his toes like he was trying to reach for them. "I wonder if maybe there ain't some Jack up there on one of those things looking right back down at us. Maybe a couple of Martian fugitives just like you and me, kid. Standing on a Martian road looking up at the Martian sky. You ever think that?"

"I guess." Of course Rodney had wondered this.

Otis went on. "I think sometimes a fella could live a thousand years and still never do a single thing worth a damn, something that would make a real difference, anyway. Not in a universe of a million stars. Think about it. One minute we're here taking in air, the next we're nothing but worm food, rotting under a pile of dirt. Gone and forgotten."

"Anyone can make a difference," Rodney said. "It doesn't take a thousand years."

"Says you." Otis moved a little closer to Rodney, shuffling a couple little steps and leaning into him, like he was preparing a secret. "I don't wanna talk about what happened back there," he said, almost a whisper.

"You mean with Mr. Kruger."

Otis shook his head and then he produced a lone cigarette from his shirt pocket and fired up the tip, his face lit in an orange hiccup. For an instant, almost like a snapshot come and gone, it looked as though he had been crying.

"I said I don't want to talk about it," Otis said, his voice like split wood.

"I didn't say—"

"Don't push me, goddamn it!" He reached down and took up a rock then, and hurled it through the air, the impact against the tree trunk like a gunshot in the night.

Rodney jumped back and Otis took a swing at him, grazing his sleeve with his open hand. "Get back to the car," he ordered, then he turned and stumbled his way down to the Bonneville, the windowlight flickering now from the inside, as if lit by candle.

26

It was in the late afternoon when the man Lester had warned her about finally came rolling up the drive, his face staring up through mirrored sunglasses like he was some giant housefly. He leaned in close to the windshield and Nadine could see there was someone next to him, a kid, it seemed. When the car came to a stop and the man climbed out, the kid did not follow.

"You Otis?" Nadine asked. She stayed a safe distance up on the porch, her arm firmly around the post.

Lester pushed through the door behind her. "You dirty son of a bitch," he said, stomping past her, down the steps and straight over to the man, clapping him hard on the shoulder. "Christ almighty, you smell like an outhouse."

"It's been a hell of a time," Otis said.

Lester nodded at the kid in the passenger seat. "I see you got company."

"Yeah, well. Things kind of spun out."

"That's a detail I'd have liked to know about ahead of time," Lester groused.

Otis said, "I guess it slipped my mind." And then Lester

reached up and smoothed a thumb over Otis's forehead, over the crusted patch over his eye. Otis winced, and slapped Lester's hand away.

"Looks like you had a conflict," Lester said. "That slip your mind, too?"

Finally, the passenger door swung open and the boy climbed out. He was a skinny thing, mostly arms and legs, barely a teenager, if at all. His face was a mosaic of freckles and dirt, and he stood there as if he was waiting for someone to tell him what he ought to do next.

Nadine took the steps to the bottom of the porch and motioned to him. "You want something to drink?"

Otis said, "I'll take a beer."

"I wasn't talking to you," Nadine said. The boy said nothing, and Lester hooted a laugh, and punched Otis in the shoulder again.

Nadine said to the boy, "Come on in with me." And when he didn't move, she walked toward him and put out her hand. And though he was too old for hand holding, he reached over and took hold of hers.

They went up to the porch together and she gave him Lester's seat, and then she went inside and pulled a Coke from the cooler, still halfway cold. He took it without hesitation, offering a quiet "Thank you" as he popped it open, drinking down nearly half the can in one take. Nadine took the seat next to him and tapped him on his knee. "What's your name?" she asked, and when he told her, she said, "I have a sense, Rodney, that you and your dad are in some kind of trouble."

"He's not my dad."

Nadine nodded, a pinch of relief at that bit of news. "What is he, then? To you, I mean?"

"He's nobody. Him and my mom"—Rodney stammered. "They're"—and then his voice trailed off.

Down the slope at the car, Lester and Otis stood at the open trunk, Lester with his hands on his hips and Otis touching that bloody patch on his head.

"What happened to him?" Nadine asked.

Rodney shrugged. He took another drink and looked back at Nadine. There was something hiding in there, in those eyes of his, something that he was holding onto tightly. She knew that look. Hell, she'd been there—desperate to share the burden but terrified to hand it over. He leaned in close to her, a wary glance toward the car.

"Can I call my mom?"

"Nadine!" Lester was at the front of the car now, thumbs hooked in his trouser pockets like an old farmhand. "Go to the garage and pull out that big green suitcase for me, would you?"

Nadine got up and took the steps down from the porch, and she did not turn to go up the path to the garage, but went to Lester instead. He dropped his head back and let out a rattled sigh. "Here we go."

"He wants to call his mom," she said. She looked down into the car's trunk, at the mounds of linen in there. They looked like pillowcases, lumpy and knotted. At the edge of the space was what looked like a kid's suitcase, the red stitching of a cowboy and his rearing pony over a white panel. Lester stepped between Nadine and the trunk.

"He does, does he?" Lester looked back at Otis. "I don't suppose that's an option?"

"I'd say it ain't a good idea. Not right now, anyway."

Nadine kept her focus on Lester, not saying anything at first, just dipping and craning her neck to try and catch his eye.

Finally he looked up at her, and cocked his head.

"You heard him," he said with a half grin. "Not a good idea."

"Is that so?" she said, then she turned to Otis. "You kidnap him or something? What'd you do to him?"

Otis drew his chin back, as if she'd slapped him across the face. "I didn't do nothing, lady," he said. "I didn't do nothing," he repeated.

"He's just a little kid, Lester." Nadine leaned in real close to Lester, almost to the point of touching. "Can't you see he's scared out of his gourd?"

Otis cut in. "I said he's fine," he snapped. "I'll take care of it. I'll take care of everything."

Nadine looked over her shoulder at the boy, who leaned back in Lester's chair now, his eyes closed, the empty Coke can lying on its side at his feet.

"Just like you've taken care of everything up to now?" she said.

"Lady, you don't know shit from shine-ola." At that, Lester swung his arm from his side, cuffing the back of his hand squarely against Otis's forehead. Otis stumbled back, catching himself against the rear fender of the Bonneville.

"Goddamn, Lester!" he hollered. "Like I don't already got issues with my head!"

"Don't forget who here is the guest, and who's the host," Lester said. "You'd be wise not to get on the wrong side of this woman here." And with that, he said, "Suitcase, Nadine," then moved on back to the open trunk and started moving who-knows-what from one place to another inside there.

27

It was eighteen minutes after twelve when Louis pulled his cruiser onto the rut-laden lot that fronted the U-Pick salvage yard. There were four cars parked up against the tall fence, one of them Hattie's root beer-colored Fairmont. He snapped up his field jacket and leather gloves from the passenger seat and pushed on in through the heavy steel door. Tip Moody looked up from his rollaway chair behind the plywood counter, his thick fingers working a pocket knife at an apple.

"How do, Sheriff," he called out. A long, snaking red peel wound over his lap and onto the floor. "What brings you here on this fine day?"

"Meeting Hattie."

"Oh, what kind of trouble has that woman gotten herself into now?"

Louis laid his gloves on the counter and fished his arms through his jacket sleeves. "No trouble," he said. "Not that I'm aware of, anyway."

Tip curled his lip so that his missing tooth-hole peeked through. "Hattie!" he hollered. "The police have come for you." He looked at Louis and gave a little lift of his eyebrow.

Hattie appeared from the back carrying a set of hubcaps like it was a stack of pancakes. "You're late," she snapped.

Tip said to her, "What are you up to now, lady?" He gave Louis another eyebrow crook. "You know she's supplied about ten percent of them totaled cars out there."

"Ha ha, you sure are a kick in the pants, Tiparillo." She shook her head at Louis. "And people wonder why I cut you loose."

She and Louis went out the back door together, to the expanse of the yard where long-forgotten cars lay stacked like cordwood, mashed, flattened roofs, branches of rust spreading over the hulking piles in creeping orange veins. Every car in the place was a story, of course. A fanfare birth off the factory line in some rust belt state. That joyous run over a long stretch of interstate, handled with kid gloves in those first weeks like it was a newborn babe. Maybe there was a family trip to the mountains, or a long haul to the ocean, the noise of hollering children, a precarious pass over a rain-soaked highway. No matter the story in the middle, all of it ending in a horrific tragedy, blood and glass and broken bones. It was something to consider that for each metal carcass in there, a person's day, or perhaps their entire life, had been ruined in the blink of an eye.

"I already looked it up," Hattie said. "You were so late I figured I might as well make use of the time." She led him past the smooth, cracked ground, among makes and models of rigs that spanned decades, some built in factories that didn't even exist anymore. Along the perimeter of the yard the more usable units sat parked, a vast car lot crowded with its mangled inventories. Crippled vehicles with holes where doors should be, sliced upholstery showing through, fenders ripped from the frames. Mechanical roadkill, all of it being slowly picked clean.

"Bullseye." Hattie thumped Louis on the arm and pointed

to a sedan about a half-dozen cars from the end of the row. It was a burgundy Skylark with the telltale gouge of a tree or telephone pole kiss at its front end. Where the trunk should have been, an empty space stared black up into the sky. There was no evidence of the old lid anywhere nearby; nothing leaning against or lying next to the car. Louis knew that people typically pulled the parts and took them home to do the install in the space and comfort of their own garage. But for the bigger stuff—doors, fenders, trunk lids—it wasn't unusual to just pull on into the yard and do the work there, pitching the old piece to the side, to be compacted later.

He dug his hands into his pockets. "Looks like whoever it was that swapped it out must have hauled the old one away with him."

Hattie snorted. She walked from the car and stood in the drive, hands planted on her bony hips like it was a piece of her own car that had up and disappeared. "He could of," she said with a shrug. "But I doubt it."

They started at the closest cars, both of them haunching down and leaning one way or the other to try and get a glance underneath. Louis ducking into the narrow spaces between bodies that had been dropped haphazardly in place. There were the piles of twisted metal, only the littlest bit parts still left deep inside them. An engine block from a '52 Nash, maybe. The steering column of a mid-forties model International—things like that. About five minutes into all of this, Hattie called out.

"Here it is," she said. She waved Louis a few rows in, back to the skeleton of what had been an old pickup truck. She took hold of the blue tarp that had been draped over the bed and yanked it free, the sweep of a magician in some great reveal.

It was, in fact, exactly what he had wondered about all this time, what he imagined he might see. If what might have happened with the Russian indeed did happen to the poor fellow. In the center of the trunk panel were two or three raised points, like rocks had been thrown from the backside. But not rocks at all. These dents were less specific. They'd been made not with a hard object or concentrated force, one that might create a pinnacle, or a central point. These were softer, divots surrounded by a wider circumference. As if pressed, or pounded with a rubber mallet, rather than a hammer.

He took hold of the lid's edge and flipped it, setting it down on the outer rim of the truck bed. Squatting down close, he leaned in tight to the gray fabric insulation on the underside, torn and loose, hanging like skin from a rotting fish. It did not take long before he spotted the rust-colored smudges, blotted in and among the linty fabric.

"Damn it to hell," he said. "I'm gonna have to call for someone to come pick this up."

"If you say." Hattie hovered over him, her shadow a slender stripe over the panel. "Should I keep this from Tip?"

"I need you to not say anything to anyone," Louis said. He stood up and turned to face Hattie. She held her arms folded at her chest, gazing at the trunk as if it was a discovered fossil, an artifact of something she had absolutely no concept of.

"Nobody?" she asked.

"Nobody."

28

The sky was cut into ribbons of purple, the mosquitoes out and feeding like they were starved. Rodney slapped at them when he could, but his hunger outweighed his annoyance, and the spread of sandwiches and potato chips was the best food he'd had in days.

Otis sat on the bottom porch step with his knees pressed together, a paper plate on his lap, picking at a slice of bread. "You got any mayo in there?" he said over his shoulder.

"Who are you talking to?" Lester stepped down and took the plate from Otis's leg, and tossed it out onto the ground. "Walk with me to the shed."

And the funny thing was that Otis didn't say anything at all to that, he just sprang to his feet like he'd been poked with a stick. For a quick moment he looked at the ground, where his supper lay scattered over the dirt. Then he simply walked on down that boot-made pathway, between the sap-specked pines and those rusted-out cars that lay dead behind everything.

No sooner did they disappear through the trees did Nadine come out onto the porch. She pulled a folding chair from the wall and sat down beside Rodney, holding two Oreos out onto his plate.

"How are you holding up?" she asked.

Rodney squinted up at her, at the way she twisted a cookie in her fingers, turning it like she was opening a jar.

"I'm fine," he said. "Better than Otis."

"Amen," she said over a whispered laugh. "From where I'm standing, I think we're all doing better than Otis."

Rodney took a bite of the cookie and let it stay in his mouth awhile, tasting the choclate while he leaned back to watch a flurry of moths knock against the porch lamp. It had cooled down quite a bit, and he thought of how nice a blanket would feel around him then. But then the last thing he needed was to be wearing something on his body that he hadn't been wearing before. To create a thing that would give reason for Otis to ask him about. He shoved the rest of the cookie into his mouth and brushed any evidence of it from his shirt onto the ground.

"You're up to something," she said. "The two of you."

"Why do you think that?"

"Because nobody comes up this drive unless there's a hundred miles of shit behind them, pardon my cuss."

Rodney peered through the trees. He could see the dirty white paneling of Lester's shed out there, the door swung wide open, no clear sight to what lay inside. The great mystery happening in there between Otis and Lester.

"I already told you," he said to her. "I don't know all of what he did. But it doesn't really matter anyway."

"Why would you say that? Of course it matters."

"No," Rodney said. "Because I was with him at the start of it all. I was with him, so it's partly my fault."

"Oh that's a crock of bullshit," she said. "That sounds like something Lester would say. That fellow Otis is the one driving the train, kid. You're just hooked to the end is all."

Rodney took the second cookie from his plate and held it out to her.

"Look at you," she said, taking it from his fingers. "The only gentleman in this place."

"Nadine!" Lester's voice raked through the trees. "You put the bed together yet? It's getting dark."

"I rest my case." She stood up and brushed off her lap. "I could use a hand if you're up to it." she said to Rodney. "It won't be the Four Seasons but we'll make it something you can fall asleep on."

They carried armloads of musty blankets, burrs and grass collecting to ends that dragged behind them. After they piled it all into the back of the old van, Rodney stuffing the best of the pillows into the corner, Nadine sat down on the floor's edge and leaned in to the cab.

"Give a holler if something comes up." It was a tone so low it was nearly a hum. "If something happens, I mean."

"What's gonna happen?" Was she talking about wild animals? Were there grizzlies out there?

For a moment she didn't reply, and he wondered if they just might be in the middle of bear country after all. "I'm sure nothing," she said finally. "But that rear door opens outward if for some reason you need a quick exit." Then she laid a flashlight onto the blankets and stepped out onto the dirt, making her way through the tree shadows on back to the house.

Otis had stripped down to his undershirt and sagging briefs, and he waved Rodney to the bedroll against the back of the van. The space was nothing but mattresses, a jigsaw of yellowed rectangles, the occasional cloud of stain bleeding through. The flashlight beam pierced through windows to dart among the pine branches.

"We'll find the shower for you tomorrow," he said. "You smell like shit."

"We smell the same," Rodney said. Perhaps Otis had forgotten about pissing himself.

Rodney crawled to the back and slid under the wool blanket, bunching it up to his chin just before Otis cut the light. There was the noise of rusted springs and the gentle bouncing of the rig as Otis seemed to struggle with his own bed there by the door. And throughout all of this he was talking, to nobody it seemed, under and over his breath about Lester and his woman, and of money and things owed, and unappreciated. Somewhere, sometime in the midst all that mumbling, Rodney dropped off.

29

"You'd follow a man straight off a cliff if that's where he led you."

Her mother never had any use for the men Nadine brought around. There was always something wrong with them: too short, bad skin. They drank too early in the afternoon, or they went out too late at night. She'd heard stories about them from ladies at work, or their tattoos looked suggestive and aggressive. It got to where Nadine gave up on introductions, just walked right past her mother wherever she might be, busying herself with the kinds of nonsense Nadine swore she would never do. Stitching things that should have been thrown out long before, polishing silverware that nobody ever used. Scrubbing vegetables that were perfectly fine as they were. And as right as her mother was about those men, Nadine would never give her credit, not in a million years. And besides, Nadine always managed to stop just shy of the cliff.

With Jimmy, she had known what the trip was about. She had helped with the weighing and double bagging, packing it tight into the sports bags—basketball teams, all of them. He hadn't appreciated her, though, and while she could forgive an oversight here and there, she found that she had her limits. Even her mother would attest to that.

"You've always been a hothead, Nadine," she said, as her daughter threw the last of her clothes into the plastic garbage bag. That time it was Armand waiting at the curb in his little German coupe. "God forbid someone should give you the smallest bit of criticism."

Nadine stomped through the house to be heard and slammed the door behind her so hard that old Mrs. Hulburt stood up from her garden bed, craned around her holly bush to try and see what in the world had just happened.

Now, Nadine looked up from her spot on the sofa, from the open magazine on her lap, at the sound of steps coming up onto the porch. It was well past dark, the single gas lamp barely illuminating her reading much less the room itself. She had left the front door open, the screen the only thing keeping the outside where it should be. The figure, dark and lanky, stopped at the threshold.

"Nadine." It was, of course, him. His hand pressed against the screen, moving itself like a disembodied object up one side and down again.

"Otis."

He stepped back from the screen and ran a fingernail over the mesh. "Is Lester around?"

She turned the magazine onto its face, as if she should somehow hide what she'd been reading from him, this man she could not see. "He's sleeping," she said. She stood up and stretched, uncurling her arms from her sides like a mantis. "I was just about to—"

"I wanted to thank you, Nadine," he said. "For letting us hole up here. I'd bet a hundred dollars if you had your way we'd be at ten different places before we'd be here."

He leaned against the jamb, the profile of his face against

the screen now. "You got a Coke or something?" he asked. "I could sure as hell use a Coke."

Nadine took a step closer to him. With his face pressed like that into the screen, he looked like one of those bank robbers who had forced a pantyhose over his face, his features flattened and childlike. He pleaded with her, with that marble eye of his.

She went into the kitchen, to the ice box where the soda sat stacked near the back, where Lester kept them. She wasn't going to wake him to ask.

"It's warm," she said, passing it through the door. "I can't start up the generator till tomorrow."

He thanked her, and took the can with a trembling hand, his fingers brushing lightly against hers, and her stomach did a little turn. He popped the top and took a healthy swig and then she said, "Otis. How do you and Lester know each other?" She stayed close to the door, her face pressed to the screen now.

Otis suppressed a belch, turned his head to the side and blew it out. "He didn't tell you?"

She shook her head.

"We shared time in Montana State."

Nadine caught herself. "Prison?"

"It wasn't college," he said. "He never told me what he did to land inside there, if that's your next question."

Nadine looked over her shoulder at the bedroom door again. As if she could see in there, at Lester sound asleep in that bed, sucking air through the pillow.

"I guess you didn't know." He laughed softly. "It was a long time ago. I was practically a kid, running with the devil, you could say. Stole the wrong car and got myself sent up for three years."

"Some people might say that any car stolen is the wrong car."

Otis laughed again. "Where were you when I was eighteen?" He ran a finger over the edge of the screen. "Lester, he sort of—" he paused then, giving a kind of humming sound, like trying to find the beginning of some forgotten song. "He sort of took me under his wing, I guess you could say."

Nadine said, "Lester, the caretaker."

He stepped close to the screen then, and Nadine could see him clearly for the first time. He was shirtless, his body haggard and pasty, his hair in all sorts like a toddler just hauled out of bed. His mouth drew down hard, lines etched from his nose practically to his chin.

"Lester takes care of things, all right," he said. "When he wants, and how he wants."

There was a rattling sound behind her, and the bedroom door swung open. Lester stood there with his hand on the doorknob, his naked torso leaning out through the opening, all hair and tattoos and scowls.

"What are you up to?" he said.

"Me?" Nadine smoothed her hands over her jeans, as if she had been doing something with them.

"Yeah you," he said. "Who else is there?"

She looked back to the front door, through the screen to the empty porch and the quiet night. To the soft sound of bare feet padding quietly in the distance, over sod and dirt, like a runner's heartbeat.

30

Vinnie had stuffed what clothes were his into an old Samsonite, and then surveyed the house for whatever else seemed familiar or interesting. Next to the suitcase was a single cardboard box with a curious variety of things, half of which did not belong to him.

Louis pulled out a couple of candlesticks, a windup alarm clock and an old framed photo of him and Vinnie as boys, standing at a lake somewhere, Louis couldn't remember. Vinnie presented an impressive bass by its gills.

"What are you doing there?" Vinnie asked. He held a fistful of Louis's neckties in his hand.

"These are mine, Vinnie."

"The hell they are." He came over and draped the ties over the sofa arm, taking the photo from Louis. "I picked up the frame here from the Pay 'n' Save over on Sprague Avenue," he said.

"Vinnie—" Louis closed his eyes and gave himself a breather. Logically, he knew none of this mattered. They were *things*, nothing more, and chances were he'd wind up with it all before long, anyway. But still, it got under his skin in the way that only Vinnie could make happen.

"Where was that at?" He nodded his chin to the photo.

"What, you don't know?" Vinnie laughed softly, shook his head at his brother's short-circuited recall. "It was Cricket Lake, up near Mead, remember? The same summer I got this." He held up his arm, turned it so the scar caught the light from the table lamp. Louis remembered the scar but goddamn if he could bring back what exactly had happened.

"Right," he said anyway. He took the photo and studied it some more, those cheeky faces smeared in dirt. The way Vinnie's chest puffed out like a turkey, holding that bass as if it was the greatest thing to have ever happened to him.

Louis laid the picture back in the box, along with the candlesticks, the clock and the ties, rolled neatly into a tight coil. "I'll give Hattie a call now," he said. "Let her know you're ready." And before the hour was up, Vinnie was gone.

It had been nearly a week, and Louis couldn't shake those last moments when Vinnie shuffled down the walkway and climbed into Hattie's Fairmont. He'd paused at the door and looked up at Louis, scanning the house as if he'd just been released from prison or something; the only thing missing was a final salute, or maybe a defiant middle finger. It had been his brother's choice to leave, there was no denying that, but Louis couldn't help thinking that he'd pushed the decision along, having never gotten a decent hold on the resentment and irritation, the old coot being under foot and nerve every waking moment.

As he rolled out of his drive and watched the house shrink behind him, the windows all black and cold, Louis tried to turn over that sense of liberation that had been waiting for him all that time, the relief of being alone again. But it was nowhere to be found.

It was just after seven when he pulled into the station. Holly's VW was in her usual spot, the stubby, yellow Beetle crowded under the low branches of the cedar. It was the only place in the lot that guaranteed shade for the bulk of the day, and she'd claimed it as hers the minute she came on board, timing her arrival well before the earliest of early birds.

This morning she was already at it, standing at the bulletin board, shuffling papers around, sticking pushpins in flyers received through the mail drop. There was a wild-eyed drugstore thief thought to be heading east with his underaged girlfriend; a hippie fellow who'd walked off from a work camp over in Yakima; a kid missing from out of Wyoming, likely kidnapped, information to follow.

"Always running," Louis said.

"Why can't folks just stay put?" Holly said, pulling down a yellowed sheet of paper and wadding it in her hand. "It'd make it a heck of a lot easier to catch 'em, wouldn't it?"

"Yes, it would, as a matter of fact."

Louis went straight to the coffee pot and fished his mug from the stack, stealing a cup while it continued to brew.

"I'm gonna hole up in my office," he told Holly. "When Mitch gets in, have him give me a holler, will you?"

"It'll be the first thing out of my mouth when I see him."

He had the folder laid out on his desk when Mitch poked his head in through the door. There were yellowed papers, thin as tissue, text unreadable what with the blots of bleeding purple ink and script that looked to Louis like a child's jumbling of random letters. In the center of it all he unfolded the passport. Staring back at him, that face, almost exactly the way it had looked up at him under the pines. Eyes vacant and tired, the face a roadmap of lines and folds from his hairline to his chin, nothing whatsoever to suggest that the man had had a single bit of joy in his life. Louis had seen plenty of passports in his life and while they could never be mistaken for a Sears portrait, one could typically get a sense of hope. A passport usually meant something good lay ahead, a journey somewhere better, perhaps. This one, in its grainy black and white, head bent forward as if he'd been hit from behind just before the flashbulb, was more like a mugshot for a man about to step before the firing squad.

"Holly said you're antsy to see me," Mitch said.

"'Antsy' is a bit much," Louis said. He waved Mitch in, motioning for him to close the door behind him.

"You getting sleep?" Mitch asked.

"Some."

"You don't look like it," he said. "Missing Vinnie, I suppose."

Louis laughed at that one. "If it wasn't for all the little clean spots on the shelves where he swiped things from me I wouldn't even notice." He picked up the passport and turned it to face Mitch. "If it's all the same, I like to bounce a little something off you," he said. Mitch didn't say anything, so Louis went on. "This fellow. He's taking up an awful lot of head space."

"The Russian."

"There's something about it that I can't seem to let go of."

Mitch took the passport from Louis and thumbed the page. "You sound anxious."

Louis turned in his chair to look out his window, to the bank of trees that shielded his view of the highway. "I feel like there's a story out there," he said. "It's got a beginning, middle, and end that I've somehow cobbled together in my mind, and I don't know if it's just this crazy old man's misfire, or if it's the most obvious goddamned thing there ever was. I already got myself halfway convinced, but I want to be closer to damned sure before I do anything further with it."

"Okay," Mitch said, pulling a chair up to the desk. "I'm listening."

31

Rodney stood in the shade of a crooked larch while Nadine worked a load of laundry, humming a tune he knew, but couldn't name. It brought back memories of his mother singing along with the radio in their kitchen back in Hope, when she still sang to herself, while his father sipped a beer at the table. Rodney pinched the towel around his waist and bunched the oversized, smoke-scented T-shirt of Lester's that Nadine had given him to wear. He looked down the open slice of the gravel drive, through the trees and tufts of sage brush, the rocky landscape rolling all the way to the highway. In the distance, farmlands spread flat sheets of green, and a single water tower poked through a cloud of treetops, proof of a town somewhere over there.

Lester and Otis had been in the shed most of the afternoon, digging around and moving boxes, the noise of knocking metal and glass tumbling out and over the hills. They kept the door shut the whole time, even though it had been hot enough outside that the towels pinned to the line a half hour earlier were already stiff as tree bark.

Nadine drew a sheet from the barrel and twisted it into a long white snake, cloudy water falling over her arms.

"So, tell me," she said, nodding her head back at the shed. "What's his story, anyway."

"Otis?" Rodney said, and then he shrugged his shoulders. "He's just some guy my mom—" He stopped, not entirely sure how to finish.

Nadine smiled so her teeth just barely showed through her lips. "I get it. You could easily say the same about Lester and me if you wanted to. He's my question mark." She draped the sheet along the clothesline and clipped the edges, the low sunlight shining through like it was a movie screen. "He mean to you?"

Rodney looked through the trees to the shed. Someone had propped open a side window halfway, but he couldn't see inside. "I'm not scared of him or anything."

Nadine went back to the barrel and turned a spigot near the bottom. A stream of water poured from the nozzle, running in a tiny, gray river down the slope into the weeds.

"What about Lester?" she said. The front of her blouse was wet, and Rodney could tell from the way things settled that she was not wearing a bra under that shirt. He had heard his mother say things about women who did that. She asked, "Does he scare you?"

Rodney considered this. He'd not had reason or opportunity to feel one way or the other about Lester. Not yet. "He scares Otis," he said finally. "He acts different when Lester's around. Funny. When he talked about him, too, before we got here."

Nadine looked at the ground and nodded, as if she were pairing two things in her mind. "He took the phone out," she said all of a sudden. "When I asked him about calling your mom. I went into the kitchen not twenty minutes later and the whole thing was missing from the wall."

"Did you ask him?"

She coughed out a laugh. "I don't need to," she said. "It's just the sort of thing he does. I don't know why I was surprised."

The sky behind the tree line was sinking into purples and grays, and Rodney could see the flash of what looked like night birds zig-zagging from branch to branch with no clear pattern.

Nadine went to the farther line and pulled the clips from Rodney's clothes, from the load they'd hung together earlier. "Here," she said, bringing them to him. "They're dry enough." She turned her back to him and continued her work down the line. A tiny shape flickered above her, in a darkening space between the trees.

"Bats," she said.

Rodney didn't like the sound of that, though he knew enough not to say anything. He didn't want her to think he was afraid. "They don't hurt people," he said, and the upswing in his tone made it a question, something he hadn't intended.

"No," she said, folding a sheet over her arms. "Unless they're rabid; otherwise they're harmless." She added the last of the laundry to the basket and turned to look at the sky, her hands planted on her hips like a superhero. "We had one find its way into the house one time," she continued. "It was all kinds of hysterical, more scared than anything. Cute little guy, like a little mouse. Lester was gone at the time and I knew if I didn't help it to find its way back out again, he'd kill it once he got home."

"How come?" Rodney asked. "Did it have rabies?"

Nadine shrugged her shoulders. "It didn't matter. Lester assumes the worst in any critter and he'd just as soon kill it than help it." She bent down and picked up the basket of laundry, and rested one edge on her hip. "He's sour that way."

Rodney finished dressing under the towel, and then Nadine took it from him, adding it to the basket. "Anyway," she said, "between the broom and this exact towel right here, I managed to get it close enough to the door that it flew out on his own."

"Escaped," Rodney said.

"Into the night."

They ate on the porch again, Otis still banned by Lester from setting foot in the house. The bugs were frenzied, and Rodney imagined be might take in half the swarm with his spaghetti by the time he finished. Lester and Nadine sat in the chairs against the wall on the porch, a layer of sweat over their faces shining like oil. On the porch step below Rodney, Otis shoveled in noodles, his shirt stuck to his back like paint. The air was thick; even the humming porch lamp made everything feel hotter.

"When did you get that Skylark?" Otis asked.

"A couple years ago," Lester said, taking a bite of bread. "I traded a gutted Winnebago for it."

"You need to decide on one color for it," Otis said, and then he laughed so that noodles hung from his teeth like a stringy beard.

Lester looked over at Rodney, twirling his fork on his plate round and round, letting his eyes roll over the boy's arms and his shirt, on down to his shoes.

"What do you know, little man?" he asked.

Rodney swallowed a mouthful of noodles, the food settling in his gut like concrete.

"I don't know," he said.

"I think you do," Lester said. His eyes narrowed, and he leaned over onto his knees. "I think you do."

"What year is it?" Otis suddenly boomed.

Lester gave him the side-eye. "What do you care?"

"It's a '70," Otis said, answering his own question. "I'll bet you didn't know that once upon a time a certain fella tried to get into business with none other than Henry Ford." He stuffed another forkful of noodles in his mouth. "Ford told him to go straight to hell," he mumbled with his mouth half full, "and just to show him what was what, the sonofabitch turned around and started his own car company."

"So the hell what?" Lester spat.

"GM, that's so what. Now you got your Skylark there," Otis said.

Lester gave a breathy whistle. "To think I lived all these years without having that little nugget of information." He reached his leg out and gave Rodney a nudge against the back. "Did you know that, sport?" he said. "They teach you that at school?"

Rodney slid forward, hugging the edge of the step. He shook his head.

"Well, what kind of tidbits do they teach you?" Lester pressed. "Enlighten us with your knowledge."

"Lester," Nadine said, getting up from her chair. "Enough." There was silence as she reached down to take Rodney's plate, then Otis's. "It's late." She took Lester's plate last, picking up the brown bottle at his feet by sliding her finger into the long neck. "Come on."

"Who gave you the keys to the kingdom?" Lester asked.

She said nothing to him, and he stood up, saying, "See you boys in the morning," before swinging open the screen door and letting it slam shut behind him.

Nadine took hold of the post, just waiting there above Rodney. When he turned to look up at her she was gazing down at him, her hair loose and falling over her shoulders, much like his mother's would sometimes do, before she'd cut it all off.

"Good night, Rodney," she whispered. Then she slipped through the front door and into the house, the sound of dishes tumbling into the sink, and then there was that song again.

Rodney and Otis made their way to bed, Otis stopping at the outhouse, where he proceeded to sing a cowboy song over and over while he did what was needed. By the time he got to the van, Rodney was already under the covers, wedged against the back doors. The windows had been left open all day and the space was a cloud of mosquitoes, humming in Rodney's ears and piercing any bit of flesh they could find.

"We can't stay here much longer," Otis said. "Lester's hospitality never lasts but a few days at best."

Rodney said, "Are we going home then?"

Otis gave a heavy sigh and slid the side door closed. "I got some ideas," he said.

He was quiet then for a bit, and Rodney wondered if he was expected to ask Otis about those ideas. But then he started up with that cowboy song again, and Rodney felt his body start to settle into his blankets, the cradle of sleep taking him under.

Just as quickly he was pulled from his sleep by a painful high-pitched wailing, and in that curious space between the cry and the awakening, Rodney imagined it was his mother calling out. He bolted upright, unable to untangle where he was as the darkness around him bound his eyes. In time, he found the back-lit window squares edged with fog, and the deep and guttural breathing and smell of Otis Dell, and the confusion lifted from him.

"You awake, kid?" Otis was sitting up in his bed, the ashy moonlight washing over his heaving silhouette.

"Yeah," Rodney said.

"You awake?" he repeated. His voice shuddered as he spoke, almost like they were riding over a long gravel road together. It was a strange feeling, Rodney thought, to hear Otis sounding like that. Like he was afraid.

Rodney sat up and studied the windows, searching for standing shadows, or perhaps the whisper of branches that could have frightened Otis. There was nothing outside but blackness.

"I ain't a murderer," Otis said. "If someone tells you I am."

"What are you doing, Otis?" Rodney asked.

"I didn't mean for it to happen," he went on. "I didn't plan on it. He was there." Otis swallowed hard, like a drop in an empty bucket. "The phone never rang and then he was just there."

Rodney considered what must have happened next. "Was it Mr. Kruger that hit you on the head?" he asked.

"I didn't have no choice," Otis whispered, as if it was a secret. "He got in the first hit. At that point it was him or me then, right?"

There was a strange feeling that came from those words, from the desperation that seemed to fill the space inside that van, anguished and suffocating like Otis himself. He wanted an answer from Rodney.

"Did you kill him, Otis?"

Otis didn't say anything at first, and Rodney could see that the shape of Otis had turned now and was facing in his direction. He stayed like that for a good half minute, the shape moving in and out with the breathing.

"I'd say no," he said finally. "Not really, not when you look at it real close." He laughed, a squeaky noise that labored behind his breathing. "I gave him a good shot to the jaw is all. The stairway behind him—that's what killed him."

"But you hit him."

"He was standing too close to the top step. It wasn't my fault." Otis leaned over to Rodney then, his breath sour and raw. "You hear me?"

Rodney pulled back so that his body pressed against the metal side panel, the cool seeping through to his skin, as Otis slid the side door open, flooding the van with the gift of oxygen and moonlight. He swung his legs out and stood up. His under-clothes glowed blue as he walked away from the van, a ghost moving further into the clearing. And just as Rodney drew in his breath to call out to him, Otis's body folded in place, bending sideways like a closing pocket knife, collapsing onto the ground.

32

"Something happened to Otis."

Nadine felt her body kick, and she opened her eyes to see a slim silhouette in the open doorway of the bedroom. It took her a moment to ground herself, to piece together the words that had awakened her.

"What did you say about Otis?" she asked. "What's wrong with him?"

"I don't know." Rodney leaned against the edge of the doorway and wiped an arm over his face.

They stood there in the clearing between the van and the outhouse, three points surrounding the body as it lay in the patchy light like a dropped marionette, the arms and legs bent in unlikely angles, the eyes gazing vacantly straight up at the moon.

Lester leaned down and touched the neck and cussed two to three of his usual words before making the call that he was good and dead. "Must of been that knot on his head," he sniffed, standing and folding his arms over his chest like he was the detective at a crime scene.

Nadine retied her bathrobe around her waist. "Better go hook up the phone, Lester. We have to call someone."

Lester put his fingers to his forehead. "No, no, no!" he snapped. "Jesus, woman! If you don't realize half the state is probably looking for Butch and Sundance here, then you're even more stupid than I already figured."

Nadine felt her skin tighten. "Don't call me stupid, Lester."

"Don't act it, then." He walked around Otis's body and gave Rodney a shove. "Get your shoes on, kid," he said. "This pile of shit laying here is half yours."

Nadine stood there thinking of how she might go with him, go with Rodney to the van and whisper for him to run, to follow the drive downhill until he got to the highway. He could crouch down among the sage, and wait until a set of headlights came up over the ridge. The driver would surely stop for a kid, she imagined. Take him straight to the police station if he asked them to.

But Lester had hold of her wrist now, and he was leading her to the house. It was only when she fell behind, her bare feet catching on every rock and root, that he let her go.

"What are we doing?" she asked. Her voice hooked in her throat.

Lester stopped, turning on his feet to look at her. She could not see his face under the shadow of the eaves, but of course she could see him plainly. She knew the way his eyes had narrowed at her, and the look of his teeth as he ground down on his lip.

"Otis Dell is gonna take a trip down the rabbit hole," he said, clear as day.

"This is crazy, Lester!" she pleaded with him. "That's a human out there!"

"You're being generous with that," he said. He moved toward her, and there was now something in his hand she couldn't make out, long and cylindrical, and he slapped it against his leg like it was a riding crop. "He's a criminal," he said. "You know that."

"You never told me he was."

"Did you just say don't call you stupid?" he said. "Well, I'm giving credit where credit is due, honey. You knew it, and you gave him safe harbor right alongside of me."

She said nothing to that.

Rodney walked alongside holding the flashlight, Lester struggling with Otis's legs, one pinned under each arm, Nadine cinching her hands behind Otis's neck in a sort of full-nelson.

"Hold that light steady." Lester's breathing was all over the place.

"I'm walking down a hill," Rodney said.

"I don't give a shit if you're rolling down it. Hold the fucking light steady or I'll crack you over the head with it."

"Lester," Nadine said. "Jesus."

Lester suddenly let go of Otis's legs, as if the dead man had suddenly found a hidden pocket of life and offered one last kick.

"Give me the goddamned thing." Lester snatched the flashlight from Rodney's hand and panned it over the ground to the square of plywood that shone pale under the yellow beam. "Go down there and pull that piece of wood back," he said, giving Rodney a hard shove that sent him stumbling.

Rodney steadied himself, then made his way down the hillside. At the plywood he turned and looked at Lester and Nadine, his face twisted in a confused expression, mouth cockeyed, eyes staring back with pupils shrunken to pinpoints.

"Pull it back," Lester snapped.

Rodney reached down and took hold of the corner of the

board, moving it back with broad, heavy steps. Once he was a safe distance away, he collaped onto the grass.

"It stinks in there," he said.

"You think it smells bad now," Lester said, "give it a week." He turned to one side and spit something onto the ground, then handed the flashlight to Nadine. "I got it from here."

Rodney stayed back against the tree as Lester walked the body to the edge of the well. There he seated Otis's body against his legs as if he was a child, as if, any minute, Lester would start to rub his shoulders, or stroke his hair while singing one of those cowboy songs for him. Instead he called out, "Make a wish," and shoved Otis away from him, letting the body fall freely into the darkness.

Rodney shifted himself against the tree bark. The sound of his back against the trunk was like a whisper of secrets Nadine could not stand to hear.

"Come here," Lester said, waving the light at Rodney.

"No."

"Get over here," he said. It was not a hard order but something unsettlingly sweet, like a scatter of apples sinking into the ground beneath the branches of a tree.

"Lester," Nadine said. "Leave him alone."

"Look down in here," he said to Rodney, panning the light into the pit. "You can't even see the bottom. It's like it goes on forever, I shit you not. Like, somewhere in the middle of China, that sonofabitch just flew up from a hole in some Chinaman's backyard." He laughed, a rattle of phlegm kicking from deep in his chest. "Now drag that board back over it," he said, nodding to Rodney.

"I'll get it." Nadine took a step forward. Lester put a hand out.

"I told him to do it. Most of this is your baggage, kid. Now get off that tree and put the board back."

Rodney moved slowly forward, taking the corner of the plywood in his hands. He slowly pushed the wood closer to the hole as Lester's eyes narrowed on him, and his mouth formed thick commas at the edges, curling and trembling as if he were anticipating something at any moment.

"Oh, for Christ's sake," Nadine said, pushing past Lester and taking one side of the plywood, and heaving it over the opening. "Go and wait up at the house, honey," she said to Rodney. "We'll pick apart this mess when the sun's up." She handed him the flashlight and held it tight in his hand, and explained that she and Lester would be fine, that they knew the way back in broad daylight or pitch black. "You know," she said. "Just like the little bat."

Rodney held her gaze for a moment before turning away. Nadine watched the light fan out over the ground, getting smaller as Rodney made his way up the hill, until he was gone.

"I want your word that you're not going to do anything," she said to Lester.

"What in the hell are you talking about?"

"With him. With the boy."

Lester laughed softly, and Nadine started from the sudden touch of his hand on the back of her neck. "What do you think I'm gonna do?" he whispered. "You think I'm cold-blooded? Is that what you think?"

Nadine didn't say anything as she pulled away from him.

"Answer me," he said.

"I don't know if I trust you so much." She put her hands to her stomach and it felt like something was spinning in there, like a rabbit caught in a snare.

"When have I ever done you wrong?" he asked, almost in a laugh.

Nadine discovered the image of a big Rolodex in her head, one card after another of Lester's misdeeds. "You really want me to go there?" she said. "You want to open up that can of worms?" Before he could leak out another of his smart retorts, she turned to go, letting her feet feel their way in the dark up the hill, where the house loomed in silhouette against a star-choked sky.

33

If his memory was true, Rodney knew he could get to the highway in half an hour at best, if he stuck to the drive and moved fast. But it was dark and there were trips and dips and deep ruts, and even with the small beam of light in his hand, he couldn't cover much distance before catching his shoes on the ground and nearly falling into the earth.

His body moved in fits and stumbles and his heart knocked inside of him until he thought it would break through his ribs. Somewhere behind him Lester would eventually figure out that he had gone, and he would come for him. There was no doubt. How many people, he wondered, might be driving the highway this time of night? He didn't even know what to do if he even made it there.

He thought of his mother, asleep all the way back in Hope, in that bedroom of hers with the door closed tight. Or maybe she wasn't sleeping at all, but instead sitting at the front window wondering if her son might ever walk up those steps again. He could see her, with her mud-brown hair down over her face, cheeks scrubbed to red. She would have no need for Otis. Not anymore.

Somewhere in the distance, off to his right, the brush moved, and the tapping of little feet sounded, growing faint, as whatever it was ran away from him. There was a stabbing in his side, and his legs felt like they would fold underneath him at any step.

His father had actually taken him fishing with the lure Rodney had found that day at the lake. He had been waiting for Rodney at the house, after school, the doors to his Impala wide open and waiting like two arms. Rodney threw his school bag up onto the porch and the two of them went to the same lake, and Rodney watched as his father baited the hook and clipped the little red and white ball to the line and cast it out onto the glassy surface in an artful, high arc, snapping the reel in place.

"Now keep your eye on the bobber," he said. "If it drops below the water, give it a little tug." He unfolded two lawn chairs and they sat together until the mosquitoes found them, and Rodney's stomach started to poke from the inside. They didn't catch any fish, but the lure was baitless when he reeled it in. He had forgotten all about that.

The roadway veered to the left and Rodney could see the slope of the hillside as it swept out onto the flatlands, where the highway ran free in either direction. Far into the distance he could make out the tiniest dots of white light and while he wasn't entirely sure, they seemed to be moving.

34

They came up to the house and right away, Lester hollered for Rodney to come up onto the porch, wherever he was. The porch lamp breathed yellow and brought up the low, draping pine branches against the railings. Lester moved closer to its halo, his face oil-slick and his eyes dancing like he was following hummingbirds.

"Where the hell is that kid?"

"Lester," Nadine said.

He stared back at her, his mouth slack and his brow collapsed in layers. "What Nadine?" he said, rolling his hand at her impatiently, aggravated. "I don't have time to try and be a goddamned mind reader."

She didn't care now, not anymore. "What the hell was that all about?" she said. "Throwing that man down the hole. We could have taken his body into town. We didn't have anything to do with what happened to him."

Lester let a puff of air out through his teeth. "I don't want a single thread connecting me to that sonofabitch," he said. "I want this place wiped clean of him and the kid." And with that, he hollered for Rodney again.

"Oh come on," Nadine said. "He's harmless." She felt her voice losing its steadiness.

He walked up onto the porch and leaned out over the railing. "Where'd that little fucker run off to?"

She stared out into the direction of the outhouse, to the van and the trees beyond, and when there was nothing to see she melted into the warm embrace of relief. "I'm sure he's just scared out of his mind. He's a kid, for Christ's sake."

"You're too soft, Nadine," he said. "That kid's a hell of a lot tougher than you give him credit for. Look at who he showed up with. I wouldn't put it past him to have taken out poor old Otis all by himself."

Nadine laughed at that, a laugh that nearly sent Lester off the ledge.

"Keep on with that," he snapped. "See how funny you think it is doing the long walk in handcuffs and leg irons." With no response from her, he grunted and stomped away into the dark, down the path toward Otis's Bonneville. She watched as the dome light flickered on and he crawled inside.

"Lester!" she called out. "Lester, what are you doing?"

He moved from the back seat to the front, flipping the visors, popping open the glove compartment. Then he reached up behind him and fiddled with the ceiling, and the interior space fell into darkness.

"Lester!" she shouted again.

"Go to the garage and get my toolbox," he yelled.

She didn't like the sound of his voice. It was too leveled, too calm. "What's wrong?" she asked.

"Get my tools," he repeated. "Damn thing's busted."

Reluctantly, she turned and went into the house, to the mudroom in the back where she knew his toolbox sat against the wall. If there was something to be fixed, she told herself, it would take time, and attention. She could stall if she needed, give Rodney time to do whatever it was he was doing to get the hell away from there.

She had just come from the mudroom when a bank of head-lights swept over the windows.

"Oh no," she said, dropping the metal box in its place and running out onto the porch, just in time to see the taillights of Otis's Bonneville flickering down the drive toward the highway.

35

There were moments when he broke into a run, partly out of fear, partly due to gravity. The slope of the drive dipped more in some places than others, and before he realized it was happening, the cover of trees dwindled, the groves of pine and fir giving way to solitary stands, piles of salal and, like everywhere else around, the pungent scent of sage. Stripes of light blinked over the ground and Rodney knew that he was coming after him, the crackle of tires on gravel and finally the bellowing of Lester's voice.

"Rodney!"

His name, catapulted out, like the blocky, dripping letters of a comic book panel. *Oof! Plack!* In almost every issue he'd ever bought, or stolen, nobody got away.

"Come on back, kid! It's dangerous out here!"

Rodney thumbed the switch on the flashlight and gave into the moonlight. He felt his way through the sparse brush, to a cluster of salal and the skeletal trunk of a fallen tree. As the white sheet of headlamps swept over his vast world, Rodney sank down to the ground, surrendering himself completely to the landscape. Invisible.

"You better look out for snakes!" Lester yelled. "This place is riddled with 'em and they don't take kindly to being woken up!"

Rodney held himself still as that log, the rocks beneath his body seeming to melt into the wood as Lester rolled on past, the Bonneville creaking over ruts, the engine thrumming, congested, winding down that last hundred yards or so to where the highway lay. The taillights glowing like two angry red eyes as the car waited there, the cloud of smoke tumbling blue. Then the engine howled and the car lurched to the right, kicking into a sharp whine as it charged out onto the open highway, disappearing around a bend and reappearing half a minute later, the headlights almost a breath of yellow now.

Rodney lay there with the skin of the dead tree brushing his face, the scent of pine and dirt and his stale breath, listening for Lester's return, which happened in short order, the Bonneville navigating the drive with a lot less care and intention than it had on its way down, a clanging, boneless surrender as it headed past Rodney, homeward.

36

Louis moved through the kitchen as if Vinnie might be just on the other side of the wall, sound asleep in his bedroom. But the door was wide open, and the bed made, the old checkered quilt smoothed over and folded down at the head, just as he had left it. As Hattie had left it, rather. Vinnie hadn't made a bed since the days when their mother was there to stand guard over him.

He ran a mug of yesterday's coffee through the microwave, then went on into the front room to watch for Mitchell's arrival. It was just after six in the morning, and the sun was already creeping up over the east slope. Not much of anything else seemed to be awake out there. Cars waited empty in their driveways up and down the block, porch steps dotted with the morning newspapers, still rolled, banded and uncollected. At his lawn's edge, a single crow waddled along with its head scanning from one side to the other, looking like a man who'd had lost his keys the night before.

It had taken some time for Louis to readjust to Vinnie not being there, to put things right-side-up again. Beyond a thankful silence, it was the small things that snagged him: the random appearance of drinking glasses on window sills, or a pair of nail clippers, unfolded and sitting behind the television. A jar of mustard in the freezer. Whispered clues showing the remnant roadmap of what had been Vinnie's day-to-day existence.

At the end of the block Mitchell's cruiser came into view, headlights flickering as he steered into the driveway. Louis gave him a wave through the window and drank down the last of the smoky, day-old brew, a layer of grit settling in his throat on its way down.

"You sleep all right?" Mitch asked as Louis eased himself down the porch steps.

"Fine," he lied. In fact, it had been a rough night. Waking up every couple of hours, straining to make sense of the quiet. He had been riddled with nightmares the last couple of nights, though he could not remember a single detail about them once he was up and holding familiar to the space around him. It had seemed so real, though, the spiraling and screaming, the sensation of something sharp raking at his sides. And then the sudden kick into consciousness as his arm would claw at the air, desperate to catch himself before falling.

"Must be glad to have your place back," Mitch said.

"It's quieter, that's for sure."

Mitch said, "You sure you're all right? You look like you were up watching the late movie."

"Lester Fanning," Louis said, changing the subject. "We're just gonna talk to him, okay? Keep an eye out for anything obvious."

"Louis, we talked about all this already," Mitch reminded him.

The initial plan had been for Louis to make the drive to Whiskey Hill on his own, but Mitchell put his foot down hard against it. What they already knew about Lester was reason

enough for caution. What they didn't know could well end up
with a bullet in the back of both their heads. "And," Mitch added,
"if it turns out he needs his ass brought in, you'll want a second
pair of cuffs."

They walked through a half-dozen scenarios before finally
getting into their cars and driving out onto Highway 16, Louis's
cruiser in front, the breaking sun intruding through the passenger window and blinding out his periphery. He leaned over and
flipped the visor across the window and laid onto the gas. They'd
spent way too much time at the house going over everything in
too much detail just for the sake of repetition. The last thing he
wanted was to give Lester the benefit of the morning.

There were rigs passing from the north now, and movement in the distance, black spots of cattle grazing in the grass-
land against the low hills. It was like this when Louis had come
to Stevens County for the first time, the sun hovering low like a
giant dandelion flower, and an emerald sea of wheat fields that
rolled on forever. Something so simple as a blown front tire had
brought a half-dozen offers of help within twenty minutes. An
off-duty smokejumper guided him to the nearest garage while
the man's pretty young wife gave Louis a warm bottle of 7Up
from the back seat and told him she'd pray for him, though he
was not sure why. Not up until then—nor since—had he experienced such generosity in his life.

"Watch out up ahead." Mitchell's voice crackled on the
radio. Some hundred yards in front of him a figure moved on the
shoulder, loping from the pavement to the shoulder, at one point
almost disappearing in the line of fence posts.

Louis took the mic in his hand. "I see him," he said. He let
off the gas, hit the lights, and began to steer carefully toward the
shoulder. As he got closer, the figure seemed to shrink deeper

into the fence line, finally ducking down into a mound of sage at the base of a leaning post.

"I think it's a kid," Louis said. He pulled off the road and shut off the engine.

Mitchell was already out and walking up the shoulder when Louis climbed out of his car. The kid—a boy, it looked like—came up from the brush now and held to the fence post as if it were the only thing holding him up. Louis figured he was about eleven or twelve and a sad thing for sure, his bare arms scratched up, blue jeans streaked with dirt and his hair in good need of a heavy comb, or a clipper.

Louis stood against the front wheel well, looking past the boy down to the nearly endless belt of highway, to where the road finally disappeared between a set of little twin hills.

"You're out in the middle of nothing, aren't you?" Louis said.

The boy nodded. His dirty face showed patches of clean under his eyes, wiped over his cheeks to his ears.

"You hurt?"

He shrugged, and looked down at his own body, reviewing his condition, maybe, before answering. "I guess not," he said finally, his voice like baked mud.

Mitch said, "What's your name?"

The boy looked between the men, from one to the other. "Rodney," he said. "Rodney Culver." And then he pulled back just slightly, as if he half-expected they would know just who he was.

"Where'd you come from, Rodney?" Louis asked.

"Wyoming."

"You're a long way from Wyoming, son." Louis looked back to Mitch, who cocked his head in acknowledgement. "You didn't come all the way to Washington by yourself, did you?"

Rodney shook his head, then stared down at his dirty shoes. "You hurt, son?"

Again, a shake of the head.

"Where might your other half be, then?"

Rodney looked up from his shoes. His eyes were welled up now. He looked ready to break up.

As usual, Mitch was one step ahead. "I'll bring him back with me," he said, and then he went on over to his cruiser and reached in through the window for the handset.

Louis said to Rodney, "You'll head on back with my deputy," and when the boy's shoulders sunk, Louis added, "He's a nice man, has a little kid of his own. He'll drive you into town and see if he can't figure all this out for you, get you where you need to be."

Mitch came back and said, "We're all set. I'll run him to the station and get things situated there, and then come right back if I can. In the meantime, you can go on up to Tiny's, or head back to the The Blue Plate and wait for me. Have a cup of coffee."

Louis said, "I don't need any more coffee."

Mitch leaned into him. "I don't want you going up there on your own, Lou," he said. "I want you to promise you'll wait to hear from me." The boy was at Mitch's car now, standing with his hand on the passenger door.

"If he's that Wyoming kid," Louis said, changing the subject, "and that fella brought him across state lines as a fugitive, the feds are gonna have to come in to sort it all out."

Mitch stood there for a moment, looking at Louis. Waiting for an answer he wasn't going to get, Louis supposed. Finally he went on back to his car and got in, then hooked a U-turn and sped off back in the direction of Boone, the little pale face of the boy staring out at Louis through the passenger window as he circled back. As soon as Mitch disappeared around the bend, Louis climbed back into his car and fired it up. He drummed his fingers on the dashboard and considered the distance to Tiny's Roadhouse, and back to The Blue Plate, where the service was always slow and the coffee disappointing. It was already past seven o'clock. Out to the west, a tawny cloud lifted into the sky.

"To hell with this," Louis said, tossing his hat onto the passenger seat and knocking the car into gear.

It was just under a mile past the substation, marked by a big green transformer box right there at the highway. The dirt road broke left and snaked up to the northwest, through the low-lying firs and white oaks, up to where the line of pine trees began, where weekend hunters and anglers tended to wander. There were enough tributaries in there to lose a man for days, but Louis steered on in anyway, keeping himself to the right, driving past the NO TRESPASSING signs, the warnings of guard dogs and stenciled pictures of shotguns.

He kept to a crawl, giving himself a quiet trail of dust and ample opportunity to make sense of the view that spread out in front of him. At last the road leveled out and he came upon an injured-looking wooden gate, the planks cracked and warped by the weather. The drive dipped to a swale before rising up into a thicket of Ponderosas and larches. Through an opening near the top he could see the rough-hewn siding of a house, and the front end of a familiar sedan peeking out from behind the trees.

He brought his cruiser to a stop next to the Buick, and got out of the car, his thumb hooked over his belt, near his holster. There were vehicles here to rival the U-Pick, rusted-out sedans with sprays of grass reaching out of open hoods, pickup trucks on cinderblocks, a paneled van with half-drawn curtains in its windows. At the front end of the Buick sat a good-sized stack of boxes, a heap of clothes piled over the top. Men's flannel, denim and such.

Halfway between the Buick and a vine-choked Volkswagen Beetle, a slick-looking green Bonneville sat with its windows rolled down and its rear driver's side door swung wide open. Wyoming plates, in fact.

"Well I'll be damned," Louis said aloud. If the circumstances were different he might have knocked the car in reverse, and slipped back down the mountain. Waited for Mitch after all. But there was the tired sound of a weathered screen and Louis turned to the front doorway, where Lester Fanning stood gaping, his mouth slack and stupid, a cardboard box the size of a television balanced in his arms. He wore a duck-billed cap on his head, pushed back like a yokel, eyes ticking from Louis to his cruiser, to the Buick and the Bonneville.

"Lester."

"You here to check on my taillight?" Lester gave a throaty laugh and took a step forward, raising the box to his chin. "Mind if I set this down?" he said. "It's heavy as a sonofabitch."

Louis nodded.

"I would not want to spook you," Lester said, lowering the box to the porch. "End up shot on my own porch."

Louis said, "I appreciate the consideration." He unsnapped his holster, just the same. "Looks like you're headed somewhere urgent."

"Just clearing out some clutter," he said, walking toward Louis. "Getting an early start before the sun starts punishing us."

"It will do that," Louis said. He fought the urge to look back over to the Bonneville, but gave in to a quick scan over the area.

The myriad of rusted-out cars, the pine-cloaked shed in the distance, its orange, mossed roof poking above the smaller trees. *One thing at a time, Louis.*

"As long as you're loading things up," he said, "I wondered if I might take a look at that trunk of yours. Once more."

"You came all the way out here for that?" Lester laughed and shook his head. "Seems like a long drive just to get a second look but come on then."

Louis followed him to the rear of the car, standing back as Lester popped the trunk open. It was like he'd remembered. The red and green wool blanket, folded like a gift over the bottom. Jumper cables and jack, tucked against the side. The wires to the taillight were secure.

"You want me to take all this out?" Lester asked.

Louis shook his head and leaned against the fender, running his hand over the length of the open trunk door. The paint was smooth, unblemished all along the edge. "I guess I'm just curious is all."

"Curious, you say? What about exactly?"

"I'm curious why you swapped out the old one," Louis said. "The old trunk lid."

"That's it?" Lester asked with a laugh. "You want to know about the old trunk? That's easy. The old one, it got all dented up when I was in town one day. One afternoon. Some kids playing ball. Kids' stuff is all."

"In Boone?"

"Naw, I was up in Colville. Stopped off at the park to eat some takeout. Some Indian kids. They were playing is all. No real harm."

Louis thought of the old trunk lid there at the U-Pick, and all the divots that had poked up from below, from the inside. He would come back to that.

"You've got quite a collection of rigs here," he said.

"One of my vices," Lester said. "I bring 'em in but can't seem to take 'em back out." He laughed again, that sickly crackle from deep in his throat.

Louis thumbed his holster and looked back over to the Bonneville, at the door that lay open like an invitation. Lester's breathing heavy, clipped. Beyond them, the drone of Louis's radio carried on inside that car, the windows rolled up tight. He should go and see what the chatter was about, to check in with Mitch. But he could not stand in two places at once. Lester stood there smiling at him, like some little schoolboy standing for a portrait.

"Out of curiosity, what else do you bring in, Lester?"

"Excuse me?"

"What else do you bring in? You ever bring in guests here? People looking for a quick stopover on their way to somewhere else?"

"Ain't that what guests do? Stop over?" When Louis didn't answer, Lester stepped back on his heels, his lips tightening over his teeth. "I don't know what you're sniffing at," he said.

"I'm sorry," Louis finally said. "I meant family. Old friends." He gave a pause then, just enough to draw out the question.

Lester's face shifted a slight bit, a single bead of sweat rolling down his temple like rain on glass. Louis took out the little red booklet from his trouser pocket and slapped it against his leg. Lester looked down and locked onto it, and Louis was struck by his face in that moment, how he seemed to go through a half-dozen thoughts in the blink of an eye.

The creak of the screen hinges from behind snapped Louis's attention from Lester and the Buick, and the green Bonneville, and Wyoming, from the radio still crackling in his cruiser. A woman came out onto the porch, a cardboard box in her arms, the tangle of cords spilling over the edges like tendrils. She held in place, the screen door resting against her shoulder, her mouth in an *O*.

Louis told her *Good morning*, and it was when he took a single step toward her that she reached out her hands to him, the box slipping from her cradle, tipping outward, the contents of radio and clock, and glass jar—a vase, maybe—blue as a peacock, the white of the sunlight catching its rim as the thing tumbled end over end to the ground.

37

The room smelled of bleach and coffee and suspicion. The deputy named Mitch had the seat opposite Rodney, the chair turned backward between his legs. Like Rodney's father had done that night, those suitcases of his sitting at his feet, the wash of surrender all down his face.

"Do we have any food in here, Holly?" Mitch asked.

"I could scare up something," she said. She walked off to a back room and came back with a package of little donuts, laying them carefully on Rodney's knee. She grinned back at him as he devoured them, those round apple cheeks of hers, her yellow hair—too yellow, really—piled on her head like a sleeping bird.

Mitch took the papers and rolled them up in his hand, picking at the edges, staring down at it as if he could read through the layers. It was Holly who had produced these, when Mitch had told her Rodney's name.

"That's you," she'd said to Rodney. "Parents, Rose and Gilbert?" A question, testing him. The APB itself had gone missing, she explained to the deputy, lost under a handful of fresh Most Wanted bills, drug runners who were probably already halfway to Mexico by now. The kid should have stayed on top, she told him.

Mitch told her not to blame herself, that he was where he needed to be now. He unfurled the stack and began to thumb through them, his eyes clicking between Rodney and the papers. "What can you tell me about Otis Dell?"

The name was still rot, and it floated in the air as the sick stench that it was. Rodney felt himself melt into his chair, his head spinning with the downward slide. And then there came a flutter of images, of Otis walking away from him and folding over the ground, and falling from Lester down into the earth, legs tumbling like a rag doll's. And there was the smell, the rotten stench from deep below, from where Otis now lay all alone in the dark, so far from the living.

Holly said, "I'll go put a call into Wyoming."

Mitch put a hand up. "Before you do that, check in with Lou." he said. "Tell him I said Lester Fanning can wait till tomorrow."

Rodney had not expected to hear Lester's name like that, not there in that room, with these people. Not yet. And he had not expected the power it would have over him, safe as he was now, Lester on that mountain or wherever he was. His gut bobbed like a log in the water, and he leaned over his knees and gave up those donuts in one yellow heave, all over the linoleum floor.

Oh lord, Holly gasped, jumping back. She ran off down the hallway and back again, a fistful of paper towels waving in her hand like it was a fan. Taking the seat next to him, she pressed the towels to his mouth until he took them from her, and as he moved them over his face, she rested her hand on his back, moving it in little circles.

Mitch said, "Well, now. Something isn't setting right with you. And I'm willing to bet it ain't the donuts."

Rodney wiped at his mouth once more and bunched the paper into his fist.

"Rodney," the deputy said. "Tell me about Lester."

"It's okay, honey," Holly said.

Rodney flashed on the hillside and the yellow spotlights that fell through the trees, and the smell of Otis as his body swung like a sack between Lester and Nadine. The way Lester swore at him and snatched that flashlight out of his hand like he might beat him with it. How he told him to move closer to the well. The sound of his voice calling from Otis's Bonneville, the wash of light over the ground. Rodney, invisible.

"Lester," he said, "put Otis down the hole."

Mitchell looked to Holly, who swooped round the counter as if a starting gun had fired off, snatching the handset from the radio.

38

When the sheriff stepped toward her, Nadine didn't have time to think, much less do anything as Lester swung the iron over his head like it was a fly swatter, and that was when Nadine let go of everything, dumping the whole box onto the porch as she sucked in a day's worth of that wicked air.

The iron landed hard, and the sheriff's eyes squeezed shut as he reached back with his hand, a reflex no doubt, since of course there was no way he could know what had just happened to him. He grabbed hold of his head, the wash of blood seeping through his fingers and spilling down his forearm. He staggered forward, each step pulling him closer to the ground until he finally fell to his knees, the blood painting the crabgrass below his face with tiny red specks.

Nadine leaned back hard against the screen, her hands pressed to her teeth. The sickness in her pushed at her throat and she knew that any second it would be all over, over the porch, her clothes, everywhere. Lester paced the sheriff from head to foot, hovering down at him like he was a deer shot out of season. "Oh, Lester," she cried. "You've lost your mind."

"Damn it, Nadine." He drew the tire iron far behind him

and hurled it overhead, launching it into the forest in an unexpectedly long arc. "Don't you turn on me now."

For a moment she felt like she was lifting from the floorboards, like she might float right over the railings and be carried off by the breeze. She took hold of the post and then came down the porch steps to get a better look at the sheriff, to see what Lester had done to him. His eyes were open just slightly, though she had no idea if he was seeing anything out of them. His chest rose and fell in broken, random waves, the tiny blades of grass at his face quivering with each breath.

"We need to call someone," she said.

"Go get the wheelbarrow from behind the garage," Lester said. He circled around the sheriff's body and went to the passenger side of the Skylark, swinging the door open and climbing inside. "Load up as many bags of quicklime as you can get in there!" he shouted.

Nadine stumbled back and felt the porch step dig into her ankle. She would not move up those stairs again, and she would not go to him. She would not answer him, or even look at him. She just couldn't do it.

"Nadine," Lester said, standing up and slamming the car door behind him. "You hear what I'm saying to you?" Something moved at his side, the metal catching the sun just so as he drummed it against his leg. He was doing that on purpose, she knew. All for her.

"Why do you got the gun, Lester," she asked. "It's just you and me here, now."

"I don't know who's coming," he said, walking back to her. "And to be honest, baby, I don't know what kind of shit you might pull from one minute to the next."

"Oh come on, now," she said, taking hold of the porch railing and forcing a smile. "It's me."

"That's what I'm saying."

He followed behind her to the garage, where he watched as she piled the bags of quicklime into the wheelbarrow. He didn't hold the gun on her, like she was some kind of prisoner, but he didn't tuck it away, either. He held it there at his side, slapping the barrel against his thigh like it was something he had to do in order to keep from going to sleep or something.

She gritted her teeth until the ache reached up into her head. "This is crazy, Lester," she said. "I don't need to be any part of this."

He took two steps toward her. "You were there when them China people came through here, right?" he said. "You fed 'em, made up their bed. You lived off the money I made from it. You're just as much a part of this as I am."

"That's not fair."

"Push me far enough and find out how much I care about *fair*."

He took the red passport from his pocket and flung it at her, sending it ricocheting off her chest. She bent down to pick it up, thumbing to the little square photo inside. The man looked to be Lester's age or thereabouts, fat teabags under his eyes, waves of curly hair crashing from either side of his head. There was not an ounce of happiness in that face.

"It's Russian?" The print was a kind she had seen somewhere before, maybe in the movies, or one of her magazines.

Lester moved back from her, leaned against the side of the garage and gave a jittery nod, a single drop of sweat holding onto the tip of his nose. "It just happened," he said. His arms fell loose at his sides now and his body slouched, as if some imaginary plug had been pulled and drained half of Lester onto the ground.

The possibilities settled in her gut like a coil of snakes. "What just happened?" She took a step toward him, as if the conversation should be more private than it was. "What did you do to this man?"

He swiped his hand over his face, then brushed it down over his trousers, leaving a dark, damp patch against the denim. "If you'd of hustled your ass to get there when I called you, I wouldn't of been stuck in that jail all night, would I?" He held the pistol at his side now, and Nadine noticed then a rub of blood over the flannel of his shirt. The old sheriff's blood.

"By the time we got back to the car it was a fucking oven inside there," he said.

"The trunk," Nadine said.

"He should of only been in there for an hour, hour and a half, tops. It should of been fine."

"Oh, Lester." Nadine felt the sick coming on again.

Lester looked at her so coolly, so resigned. "Let's get a move on," he snapped. "Before half the police in the state show up on this drive."

Just as she could see that the plywood had already been pulled back, the miasma of decomposition enveloped her, fruity and thick. Nadine navigated the wheelbarrow as best she could, the bucket top-heavy with quicklime and rocking like a boat, all the while Lester paced beside her, the pistol now tucked into his waistband. In each hand he held a black plastic garbage bag, swinging them at his sides like he was ringing bells.

"What are we doing with all this?"

He ignored her, instead pitching one garbage bag into the well, and then the other, both in a gloriously high arc.

She set down the wheelbarrow and went to pick up a bag of lime from the top.

"Hold on," Lester said. He looked at her hard, and she knew in an instant what was working inside that head of his. His eyes twitched as they held onto her gaze, almost vibrating, and it was only when she glanced up the hill toward the house that he gave her the slightest nod of his chin.

"No," she said.

"Nadine."

"I said no, Lester. The man's not even dead."

"You don't know that. And if he's not now, he sure as hell will be soon enough." He reached out and took hold of her arm, and she snapped it back from him. "Nadine," he said.

"Don't you dare touch me," she said, glancing down at the pistol tucked there against his belly.

He paused for the shortest of moments, a snapshot, really. Eyebrows raised in surprise. Lower lip sunk like a caught fish. Shock, maybe, that she should stand her ground like that. But just as suddenly the moment was gone and he came at her—his hands out at his sides, the fingers curled like roots.

"Woman," he hissed, reaching for the gun, "I'm gonna make you wish I never picked you up that day."

It all happened so quickly, quicker than the sheriff and the tire iron, and absolutely a hell of a lot quicker than it had to have been for that poor Russian. Nadine's arms left her sides like they'd been attached to springs, launching out in front of her before she even knew what she had done. She struck him squarely in his stomach, the blow against flannel like pressing on a baby's blanket, so soft and peculiarly warm against her bare hands. It all gave way so easily. What had pulled at Lester's face only seconds earlier let go of him, his mouth dropped slack, his eyes as wide as they had ever been. He took three or four steps back to keep his balance, to regain control over what his body was doing, thanks to her. Unfortunately for him, they were only two steps from the well.

With the exception of a single, primal howl, he dropped as easily as Otis had, though there was a good deal more from Lester in the way he carried on, the windmill of arms, a futile effort to grab hold of what was not there. Within a blink, he disappeared into the blackness and it was only when the sharp cry rose up, like a dog's yelp, that Nadine finally had a sense of how deep things were down there.

"Don't tell me what to wish for," she said, spitting into the black pit. "You son of a bitch."

She took up the wheelbarrow and dumped it and all five bags of quicklime into the opening. There was the sharp, momentary echo of the metal's impact and that was it. Taking the corner of the plywood, Nadine slid it over the opening. And as she walked back up the hill to the house, she paused every few steps or so to look over her shoulder, to remind herself of how quickly that spot hid itself once you got a certain distance from it.

39

It was Hattie's laugh that woke him up, the sound of a chicken cackling, really. She cozied up by the corner window, her hand holding a leaking cigarette through the open wedge. Vinnie sat in the lounge seat next to her, his legs stretched out, almost touching the end of Louis's bed.

"Welcome back."

Louis lolled his head to the side, an iron grip over his scalp. Mitch straddled a stick chair, his arms folded over the seatback, a radiator grin stretching from sideburn to sideburn.

"I guess I got my bell rung pretty good," Louis said, reaching to touch the back of his head.

"That you did," Mitch said.

Louis pushed himself up from the mattress, the tug of a needle pinching at his forearm. Mitch leaned forward and took the little control box sitting on the bunched blankets, handing it over so Louis could fumble with it, giving himself a couple false starts before riding the drawbridge up.

"How long have I been out?"

"Better part of a couple days, give or take."

"Give or take a day?"

"Give or take *out*," Mitch laughed. "Holly's been beside herself."

Vinnie called out from his corner, "We thought you might be a goner for a while there. Son of a bitch got you a good one." He took up the TV remote and clicked at the screen, scrolling channels like dealing cards, round one end and down the other, never settling on any one station long enough to decide if it was worth watching or not.

Louis looked to Mitchell. "I'm supposing it was Fanning who did the honors."

"I kind of hoped you'd be able to shed a little light on that. But yeah, that's my guess."

"You got him in custody?"

"In a sense," he said. "It's kind of an ugly discovery. They're gonna be up there for a while, sifting through it all. Looks like Lester's been up to no good for quite some time."

"What about the girl?"

Mitch said, "Hide nor hair. We don't know anything about her, other than what little the kid could—or would—say. She called in on your radio and bandaged you up before taking off. Lester's got so many rigs up on that place, God knows what she's driving."

When Louis asked if they had a name for her, Mitch just shook his head. "For all we know she was a temporary thing for him. The kid seems to think she saved him from being right there next to Otis Dell. I'd say he's right."

Hattie hummed along with the radio and steered the Fairmont with one hand, holding her cigarette at the wing with the other. Vinnie rested with his back against the passenger door, watching over Louis as he sat in the back seat as if his little brother might fall out onto the pavement at the next turn of the wheel.

"I'm thinking this is it," Vinnie said.

"What's it?"

"This," Vinnie said, waving his fingers over his head like casting a spell. "You could have been down at the morgue, Lou."

"No."

"Yes. And then what? Who's gonna take care of me?" He side-eyed Hattie, who shot him a look. "You're good for shits and giggles," he said to her. "But I ain't counting on you to bail my ass out of jail if it comes to that."

"Good," Hattie said, "Neither am I."

"Nor me," Louis said.

"Damn it," Vinnie said. "That's no good."

They turned down Polk Street, past the cherry trees already dropping their blossoms in wide skirts of pink over the edges of the roadway. Hattie brought the car to a stop in the driveway and offered to walk him inside. Louis declined, swinging the door open and climbing out.

"I appreciate the taxi ride," he said, and then he went up his walkway without looking back.

Vinnie rolled down the window and leaned out. "You give a holler if you need anything," he said.

Louis put up his hand, giving a thumbs up. There were at least a half-dozen people he'd call first if he got in a real bind, but Vinnie's offer was worth that much.

He let himself into his house, dark, the smell of overripe bananas. The photo of him and Vinnie on the shelf as young fellows, against the scaffolding of the Grand Coulee, smiles like Boy Scouts. Had he ever been that young and happy? What he didn't know about the world that lay ahead of him.

The moment was cleaved by the hard ring of the telephone. Louis moved quickly to the kitchen, snatching the handpiece from the cradle.

"I'm alive," he said.

"I know that." It was Holly. "I wanted to make sure you got home okay."

"I got a ride."

"I know that, too. I also know who drove you, which is why I thought I'd call." She laughed then, soft and throaty. "I'll be by after my shift to check up on you."

"I don't need that," he said. He leaned against the jamb and looked out the little kitchen window, in the direction of the station.

"Says you." He could see her there at her phone, winding the spiral cord through her fingers like she always did. Probably working her crosswords as she talked.

"I appreciate the offer. I don't want you to put yourself out for me."

"I wouldn't dream of it. You're just a couple turns out of my way." She said *Just a minute,* and then there was some muffled talk, the scratch of her hand over the mouthpiece, and then she was back.

"I'll bring by some fried chicken," she said. "You just settle in that big chair of yours and watch something on the tube till I get there." And before he could say anything to that, she hung up on him.

He set the phone down and went over to the picture window in front and pulled back the drapes, letting the afternoon sun in to wash over everything, every dusty shelf and tabletop, coffee rings in places he never set his own mug. The carpet could do with a vacuuming.

He found a can of furniture polish in the laundry room and he couldn't remember the last time he'd used it, though not remembering didn't concern him. He supposed these things were good for quite a while.

Something caught his periphery, a flash of pink from out the window in the street. The little boy with the name of Luis pedaled that bicycle of his from one end of the block to the other, back and forth, pausing now and then to pick something out of the basket, to hold it up to the sky. And even though the kid was far enough away that Louis couldn't even gauge a guess as to what he had in his hand, there was no mistaking the smile. A smile so big that you could say there had to be nothing greater in the world for him at that moment than a low-bar bike with a good-sized basket, and tassels so shiny they could catch the sun on a day when nothing else could.

40

Mitch stood behind the counter and talked into the phone, taking pains to keep his voice low, eyes clicking up at Rodney now and then, mostly keeping his back to him. Whoever he was speaking to did not ask to talk to Rodney.

"Someone will be here for you soon," Mitch said, but then he added that "soon" could mean in a few hours or a day. He wasn't sure who that someone would be, either, but he hoped it would be a parent. "Your mom and dad will make the trip, don't you think?"

Rodney thought of the question with his mother and father together, the two of them side by side in the car, and that didn't seem likely. Not for him.

Mitch set Rodney up in a back room on a well-worn sofa with a stack of old scouting magazines and a twelve-inch color television, a few small bags of chips, and supermarket-fried chicken. The television played continuously as Rodney drifted in and out of sleep, sometimes dreaming of Charlotte Street and the endless warehouse floor, and his mother seated on her stool behind the counter.

Only once did he find himself on the drive leading from

Lester's, though it wasn't the drive, really. This one was riddled with cactus and snakes, and the steaming vapor of a swamp somewhere off in the distance, and he jumped from boulder to boulder as the sound of tires crackled over gravel behind him, Lester's voice bellowing into the night.

Rodney opened his eyes to see a man on the television screen standing on the ledge of a tall building, his arms spread out at his sides like Jesus. The man was shouting to someone behind him in the building, maybe, or down below. There were policemen looking up at him and it appeared as though he might jump from the ledge at any moment.

"Well, look at you."

In the doorway was a man who did not look like the person who had left his family behind months before. His arm stretched upward, hand gripping the jamb like he always did. The hair was shaggy at the ears, though, and the thick mustache he wore was not his. For a good moment it seemed to Rodney that this person who might be his father could not possibly be him. But the smile.

"We've been half crazy," he said. "Your mother and me." He came over and sat next to Rodney on the sofa, and Rodney lay down over his lap, neither of them saying anything, not about where the other had been all this time or what had happened to them. Or the mustache. It was just the feeling of his father's body against him as he breathed, his hand moving in little circles over Rodney's back.

The view was clear and free through the windshield as they made their way out of town, southeast, his father said, in the direction of Montana.

"You got it fixed," Rodney said, reaching up and running his fingers over the glass.

"It's against the law to drive with a busted windshield," his father said. He glanced over at Rodney. "I didn't need to be reminded of that day."

Rodney nodded, and traced his fingers over the glass again.

"You know what I mean?"

"Yeah."

They came down from the hills, leaving behind Boone and its tumbles of sage and errant rocks, settling into the expanse of farmland, sheets of green stretching out like one long, deep breath.

"I know about that Otis fellow," his father said. "About him and your mom."

Rodney nodded, his stomach rolling, not from hunger.

"I know about what happened to him, too, up there at that place," he said. "You shouldn't have had to see that."

Rodney looked over at his father, and his eyes were red and pooling, and he blinked at the roadway as he drove.

"Did he do anything to you?" he asked. And when he looked at Rodney a single bead had dropped from his eye, holding place just above his cheek. "Did he—"

"No," Rodney said. He thought of the slap, when he had been crying and Otis snapped. But that had been after Kruger's, and the crack on Otis's head. Rodney wondered, now, that perhaps Otis hadn't known better.

"Is Mom coming?" he asked.

"To Missoula?" His father nodded, slowly. "Eventually. That's the plan. She's tying things up in Hope, and then we'll get it taken care of."

They drove in silence for a bit, Rodney listening to the click of the patched roadway beneath them. Up ahead, a long freight train moved into view, and the crossing arm lowered slowly, red dots winking like Christmas lights. They came to a stop, Rodney's dad cutting the engine.

"Looks like a long one," he said, craning his neck and looking past Rodney.

"Yeah."

"Timing," he said.

Rodney nodded.

They sat there, his father scratching at a spot on the steering wheel with his thumbnail, as the first of the cars clicked past, flatbeds and livestock cars, mostly, cattle gazing through the slats like bored tourists.

"I know about Mr. Kruger, too," he said. "About the robbery."

Rodney wasn't surprised about this. Of course he'd know about it. He felt his throat tighten, the warmth of his blood rushing to his face. "I'm sorry about that," he said. He caught a tear with his sleeve before it could fall.

His father put a hand on his knee. "You don't need to feel guilty, Rod," he said. "You're a kid for Christ's sake. Otis Dell—" He stopped, cleared his throat. "It's going to be okay."

Rodney gave a hard shake of his head, biting down on his lip until it stung. It wasn't okay, he wanted to say. Nothing about what happened was okay.

Rail cars continued to clip by, the rust and paint of boxcars blinking past like an old film. The whole train seemed to stretch from one end of the world to the other, and for a moment Rodney imagined that they could be at that crossing forever.

A single pickup truck, its rounded hood and its old cowboy hat-wearing driver, blinked at them from the opposite side through the gaps of the rail cars.

"But he's dead," Rodney choked.

"Yeah, I know."

"Otis killed him."

His father pulled his hand away. "Who's dead?" he asked. "Who are you talking about?"

"Mr. Kruger." Rodney was crying now, his sleeve working over his face like a washrag. "Otis killed him."

"Oh Jesus, Rod. That's what you've been thinking all this time?" He ran his hand over Rodney's hair, warm and soft against his scalp. "Kruger's fine," he said. "Walking around on crutches. A good shiner, I guess. But he'll be fine. He's a tough nut to crack, that fellow."

His father fired up the engine as the last of the cars rolled by, the green caboose trailing off down the line.

"People make mistakes, Rodney," he said. "If they're lucky, they get the chance to fix them. If not, well—they do what they can to make up for them."

The road opened up ahead of them, a black slice through an endless green plane. Rodney counted the cars passing them from the opposite direction, wondering why on Earth any of them would want to go back there.

41

Nadine had unpacked a lot in the months she'd been on that side of the mountain with Lester, from occasional bouts of misery, to flashes of joy, to moments of genuine relief. But there was nothing like the wonder of watching that mountain range shrink behind her, watching her rearview as she dropped over the pass westward. As rugged as it was, Lester's old Ford sailed reassuringly over the pavement, clearly thankful for the downward slope after the steep, alpine climb.

She had fit as much as she could into the cab, and it was fine that there wasn't a great deal for her in the end. She had no need for the dozens of stereo receivers and CB radios, and boxes of silverware and miscellaneous cheap watches that littered that mysterious shed of his. After the weeks of secluded business having taken place in there, Nadine was surprisingly disappointed to see that, for the most part, it was all just a bunch of useless shit.

There had been the things he'd already placed in the Buick, though. More interesting pieces. The can of silver coins, a hat box heavy with jewelry that Nadine knew at a glance was the real thing. There was money in bundles, too, cash bills of twenties and fifties, as if Lester had been running his own bank—too much for her to take the time to count there on the hill. And the suit-case. The horse and cowboy stitched on the side. She'd thought it was a child's thing at first, something for plastic toys or wooden blocks. But there was enough in there—rings, watches, cuf-flinks—to dress a fancy man from New York to San Francisco and pay for the trip five times over.

She told herself that Rodney was okay, that he'd found his way out. Flagged down some kindly trucker on his way into Boone, maybe, or even a passing cop out on patrol for drunk drivers. He had to have done so, otherwise how would the sher-iff have known to come up there? That part stayed with her, and she was thankful for that. God knows, she needed something to smooth all the thorns still holding onto her.

But the thing with Lester wouldn't let go of her. Lester there at the well, looping back to her in a never-ending slideshow. The glance of horror on his face, the recognition that she had betrayed him. That the ground beneath him had disappeared, those arms of his stretched in impossible ways, reaching for what was not there. The soles of his shoes, white from the sunlight that poured in from above. And the sound at the end. The hideous sound.

She took a hand from the wheel and worked the radio dial, turning it slowly in search of something. So much got filtered out by the mountain that most everything she landed on was angry talking or masked with heavy static. When at last she found something, she was half-relieved and somewhat surprised to hear it was a gospel station. A woman's voice, bell-like, almost smoth-ered by the rainstorm of guitar picking around her:

Someday I'll cross the river, being inside the home gate
I may look back to earth here below
I may see a dear brother I've known along the way

Sitting down by the side of the road.

Nadine reached back to the dial then skipped over to the volume, turning it up higher.

Jesus, she thought. Was it Sunday already?

ACKNOWLEDGMENTS

There are more people to thank than can fit on this page, so I'll distill it down to the golden few.

Thanks to Robert and Elizabeth at Ig Publishing for taking me on this second time around, and to Stewart Williams, whose incredible cover design managed to capture the whole story in a single, stunning image.

Huge appreciation to my Rainier Writing Workshop mentors Scott, David, and especially Kent, whose early guidance remains ingrained in me years later. To my writing cohorts Mary, Andrea, Jessica, and Lynn: That long weekend we spent creating, reading, laughing, and staring out at the fairgrounds of Fort Worden was the genesis that brought Otis from a scatter of notes to near flesh and blood. And to my mother, for her unbiased fandom and eager copyediting skills.

Finally, heart and soul to my patient and generous husband Shayne, for giving me the time, space, and encouragement to bring this thing from a mere idea to the bookshelf.